Calling MR. KING

Calling MR. KING

a novel

RONALD DE FEO

OTHER PRESS
NEW YORK

Production Editor: *Yvonne E. Cárdenas*
Text Designer: *Simon M. Sullivan*
This book was set in 11.5 pt Galliard by
Alpha Design & Composition of Pittsfield, NH.

10 9 8 7 6 5 4 3 2 1

 Printed in the United States of America on acid-free paper. For information write to Other Press LLC, 2 Park Avenue, 24th Floor, New York, NY 10016. Or visit our Web site: www.otherpress.com

LIBRARY OF CONGRESS CATALOGING-IN-PUBLICATION DATA
De Feo, Ronald.
Calling Mr. King / by Ronald De Feo.
p. cm.
ISBN 978-1-59051-475-7 — ISBN 978-1-59051-476-4 (ebk.)
1. Assassins—Fiction. 2. Self-actualization (Psychology)—Fiction.
I. Title.
PS3604.E1226C36 2011
813'.6—dc22
2010054082

Part I

CHAPTER 1

I WAS IN LONDON when they phoned. They asked me to meet them in Regent's Park. It was a gray afternoon, but the white terraced houses by the park still glowed like small palaces. A man in Derbyshire had to be taken out. That was the gist of it. I was really more than a bit tired from my last job, but I didn't let on. He's at his country house, they said. He won't be there forever. It'd be nice if he could be hit this week. We were counting on you. Of course, I said. They gave me the details as we watched an elephant in the zoo. He takes long walks alone with his dog in the countryside, they said. There should be no problem. Fine, I said, while thinking how odd an elephant is. Whoever thought up such a weird thing? I wondered. Something wrong? they asked. You look like something's wrong. No, I said, I was just thinking how peculiar that is. What is? they asked. The elephant, I answered. Elephants in general. They stared at me, then at the elephant, then at each other, and shrugged.

I had just finished a job in Paris. It had ended well enough, clean, the way I like it. But there had been a lot of waiting on this job. An awful lot. And there had been some odd problems that had left me a bit shaken. I kept quiet about them, though. Instead I concentrated on the elephant.

Sometimes your mark falls into a pattern quickly—he walks the same streets, drives the same roads, visits the same shops and restaurants, has lunch at the same hour each day, every day, sees the same friends and associates. At other times, particularly on holiday, he may go on his own merry way and be full of surprises. I suppose that's one of the reasons for a holiday—to do whatever you want, when you want. So there he is, enjoying his freedom, being very unpredictable, and unconsciously making my life miserable—until, of course, I find an opening, the right time, the right place, and end his vacation abruptly.

I think that's the worst part of this profession, the waiting—all of the tracking, the observing, the time spent allowing things to fall into place. But it's absolutely essential if you want to do the job right and, even more important, stay alive after it's over. All the while I'm waiting, of course, I'm seeing a pattern develop. And the better you know someone and his routine, the better and safer you can do the job. You learn to anticipate his gestures and moves, even predict how quickly or slowly he'll react if he catches sight of you before you pull the trigger. You can sense if he senses you. And after a time, doing so much of what he does, you become his shadow. You form a kind of bond, although it's a one-sided affair—you get to know him, but he isn't aware of you. And before he is aware, before he even so much as gets a chance to know you, you put a bullet in his head. A very strange business when you come to think of it. Very strange.

This man in Paris was exhausting. Maybe he realized that he didn't have much time. Yet he gave none of the usual signs. He didn't appear nervous. Didn't even look back once to see if someone was following. He went about freely, without a care in the world.

It was an early spring in Paris. The weather had grown very reasonable over the past few days. The daily drizzle and damp had been replaced by soft breezes, sunshine, shadows of leaves on pavement, people filling sidewalk cafés, and all that. Perhaps it had gone to his head. Since he wasn't a young man, you had to conclude that the weather had revitalized him. Moving back and forth across the city, he acted like someone half his age. He hurried to a café near the Parc Monceau, then went to a men's shop near the Madeleine, then took a taxi to meet a friend with a cane by Notre-Dame, then it was off to an art gallery near the Beaubourg, where he chatted with a smartly dressed woman with very long legs, then he was down in the Métro, ended up at the Opéra, stopped in a pastry shop for dessert, bought a few magazines at a newsstand before heading for the Saint-Denis canal, where he talked with two men in dark suits on a very old bridge. I didn't know what to expect each hour, never mind each day. They hadn't told me that this was going to be one of those bloody holiday jobs. And this wasn't the right time for it. The season hadn't quite started. Yet he moved about like a tourist in midsummer.

They didn't tell me much. They never do. But they did say that the mark would be on a business trip. Well, what kind of business was all of this? As the time went by, I became absolutely convinced that he knew his days were numbered. And since he knew, he wanted to get a lot of living done before the end. What I was watching then, all of this peculiar energy, was very simply a pathetic attempt at a last fling.

In my line of work you can't feel sorry for anyone, and I didn't feel sorry for him. In fact, I began to resent him. He was aware of me—not me specifically, of course, but the idea of me in general, a stranger out there who was going to take his life. And he decided to toy with his killer, go out with a certain dignity and courage, throw his zest for life in my face, so to speak. What a fool. There was nothing to prove here, nothing to win at this point. He had lost the moment they had taken out a contract.

Maybe he was just plain stupid. I'd dealt with stupid marks before. I remember the three-hundred-pound ex-bodyguard I'd taken out in Lisbon. He walked about in a daze, as if being a human shield for half his life had wasted away a good part of his brain. I don't know whose idea Lisbon was. But he looked even more ridiculous there than he would have looked, say, in New York or London. He stood out against all of those white walls. He wandered the narrow streets and alleyways half-unconscious, not knowing what to do with himself. He had no one to protect anymore, no one to kill. And he had no interests, no hobbies. He didn't belong in Lisbon. He really didn't belong anywhere anymore. A huge, sloppy, useless mass of flesh, he was dead already.

But this man in Paris was something else again. He had a certain bearing. Thin, trim, with a healthy head of perfectly cut gray hair. You couldn't miss it. It gleamed in the sun like polished silver. You could see he had taste and style—finely tailored, a different outfit each day. A real Continental. A killer with the ladies. Probably a killer, period. There was a certain intelligence, an alertness about him. Yes, this man knew exactly what he was doing. And although he seemed a bit past his prime now and rather harmless, I bet he'd been one clever, nasty bastard in his heyday. After all, they don't want you dead for nothing.

So he kept moving about the city. And I kept following, looking for the right moment. What are you waiting for? I asked myself time and again. There had been several chances for a clean shot. But I had hesitated each time. Something felt wrong here, very wrong. This carefree, careless attitude of his seemed much too exaggerated. I couldn't quite buy it. In fact, I began to wonder if the whole routine was just an act, a kind of setup. While I was following him, someone might be following me. As he bounced around Paris, I had to do the same. As he left himself open, so did I. He and his people were trying to draw me out. They hoped to hit me before I hit him.

This was only a possibility, of course, and maybe it was all in my head, but I became extra cautious nonetheless. I began to look over my shoulder more, notice anyone, anything out of the ordinary. A stranger or car I'd see more than once. Any person glancing my way for no good reason.

I was down in the Métro late one afternoon, waiting on the platform for the train my man was waiting for. With his money, I couldn't understand why he was taking the subway. Anyway, I followed him, cautiously.

He stood, just several yards to my left, stood in his elegant, dignified way, reading a newspaper, as I pretended to be reading mine. One good push when the train comes, I thought crazily—because, of course, this wasn't my style at all. But the job was getting to me, no doubt about that, and I wanted to be done with it. Play all you want, I said to him in my mind, have your fun, pretend you don't care, take subways, buses, bicycles, tricycles. But you're finished. You'll never leave this city alive. He turned slightly in my direction as if he could hear my brain. I quickly glanced the other way.

That's when I noticed a man in a blue blazer standing not far behind me and a bit to my right.

Something about him seemed familiar, but I couldn't say what. I searched the pockets of my raincoat for a book of matches I'd picked up in some café. When I found it I purposely dropped it on the platform so I could bend down and at the same time sneak a quick look at this new man. The buttons of his jacket immediately caught my eye. Gold. Big and flat. Too large and showy even for a blazer. More like huge coins than anything else.

Yes, I had seen them before. In the Tuileries. Just the other day. I remembered the way they had blinded me briefly, those little yellow explosions. The buttons are wearing him, I remember thinking. The sight and the thought had lasted a few seconds. They had come and gone, had meant absolutely nothing. But now they meant a lot. I couldn't tell if this was the same man. I hadn't really seen him then. But I had seen his buttons. And the ones staring me in the face now were either the same or duplicates.

As I straightened up I reached inside my jacket for my gun, resting in its holster under my arm. I did this by instinct, just covering the gun with my hand. It felt good knowing it was definitely there and that I was ready if necessary. But the station was filling up with people and I doubted that the button man, if he was involved at all, would try anything here.

This new situation, this possibility was about the last bloody thing I needed on this job. Now I had to keep an eye not only on the man I was after but also on another man who might be after me. And I had to pretend to be looking for the train, which was long overdue. So my eyes shifted back and forth, taking in the tunnel and my man to my left, and then trying to take in the button man slightly behind me to my right. I began to feel something I hadn't felt in a very long time. It surprised me. I began to feel nervous.

A businessman with a leather briefcase anxiously stepped to the edge of the platform, stared into the empty tunnel, momentarily blocking my view of my man, looked down at his watch, and shook his head repeatedly. "*Merde!*" he cursed. "*Merde!*"

I stared into the tunnel as well. I wondered if they—my man, the button man, maybe even some other gunman—would move in on me once the train arrived, using all the confusion of the people boarding and getting off as a kind of cover. The button man would come up from behind and plant a knife in my back. What's happening to me? I wondered. I was panicking, and I am not the panicking sort. No one was after me. No one even knew I existed.

People kept coming down into the station. There was still no train in sight. Workers, shoppers soon surrounded me. By staying down here too long, I had become part of a rush-hour crowd. "*Merde*," a young woman commented behind me. This is getting contagious, I thought. I was suddenly grateful that I didn't have a normal nine-to-five job, didn't have to deal with all of this damn nonsense every day. *Merde* is right. How do people stand it? It's enough to make you want to kill somebody. Other heads kept blocking the silver head and I found myself constantly shifting my position and maneuvering my own head to keep my man in sight. I didn't know where the button man was, since his jacket and buttons were now covered by the crowd, leaving only his head exposed. And I hadn't really gotten a sufficient look at that head to recognize it again.

No one's on to you, I told myself. It was my imagination running away with itself and nothing more. I had given this job just too much time. And in doing so I had given myself too much time to think. Years ago when I was younger—though I am hardly old now—and more foolish and took more chances, I'd complete a job almost immediately. I'd see an opening and take it then and there, no matter how dangerous. I'd bring someone down right in the street, hit him in the back as he walked alone, then duck into a store or building. Or I'd casually go up to the window of his parked car and shoot him in the head. Done. Finished. And I'd move on to the next job. But as the years passed I grew more careful, realized that if I was going to make this my life's work and stay alive until retirement I had to develop a more professional attitude, rely less on luck and nerve and more on planning. I had to insure my safety. I had to become an adult. But maybe I was overdoing my maturity now. Because I had never gotten this jumpy on a job.

So there I am in a crowded Métro station—where I didn't really have to be in the first place—keeping track not only of a target but also of a possible gunman, a phantom train, and a collection of cursing Frenchmen, my poor head turning this way and that, that way and this, there I am giving myself a lecture, chewing myself out, forcing some logic into a brain that is beginning, for no good reason, to go a bit off.

A lot of jackets have big gold buttons, I reasoned. There are probably hundreds, thousands of big gold buttons in Paris. The chance that the big gold buttons in this station are the same as those in the Tuileries is so remote it isn't even worth considering. And the idea that those buttons are following me, are out to get me, is just plain crazy. Yet I couldn't shake the thought completely. I kept on the lookout for any gold in the crowd.

Suddenly the train emerged from the tunnel. The crowd moved forward all at once, terribly excited, as if some kind of god were arriving. As the cars rolled by you could see that they were already well filled with passengers. But this didn't discourage the waiting mob, which continued to advance right up to the still-moving train.

When the doors opened I glimpsed the distinguished silver head among a group of undistinguished heads moving or being forced into the car just ahead of me. Where the button man was at this point was anybody's guess. I myself was shoved by these typically rude, pushy French, but I put up resistance. In this stupid stampede one of them even stepped on my foot. I was tempted to draw my gun and blow the frog away. I stood my ground. People cut around me desperately, as if not getting on this train would mean certain death. No, I'd had enough. There was no way I was joining my man in that mess.

I backed off. Why exactly was I down here? Tracking him for the sake of tracking? After all, I wasn't planning to take him out now. I knew where he was staying, and he'd eventually end up back at his hotel. I could easily catch up with him later. As people stuffed themselves into the cars, I kept moving away. The doors finally closed, and in window after window, from the front of the train to the rear, I could see passengers solidly packed in—crushed bodies under glass. I searched the car my man had entered, but I couldn't find him. He was probably in the middle somewhere, being squeezed from all sides. Go ahead and act distinguished and carefree now, you overactive bastard.

As the train pulled away and the cars swept by me, I noticed for a split second some big gold buttons pressed against a window of one of the doors. I couldn't help but laugh. I wished the buttons well. Probably going home to a wife and children. Good-bye and good riddance. So much for my notion of a conspiracy. Ridiculous, I thought, shaking my head. Ridiculous.

I climbed the stairs to the street, and when I emerged from the station the intense sunlight hurt my eyes. A headache seemed to be coming on—again something I was not used to at all. I hadn't had a real headache in years. Since I wasn't too far from my hotel—an inconspicuous, homey little place just off the Avenue de l'Opéra—I decided that the fresh air would do me good, so I started walking back. I thought I knew Paris reasonably well;

though, like London, which I know more than reasonably well, it has enough small streets to drive you mad. Rue this and rue that, going every which way.

I expected to reach the main avenue soon, but all I came upon was still another small, narrow, unknown street. It was as if the streets were multiplying just to keep me from reaching my destination, some sort of stupid fantastic joke. My temples were beating and I felt hot and vaguely sick. What's happening to me here? I seemed to be falling apart. Although I normally have a good sense of direction, it was failing me now. Where in hell was I?

Just then I noticed a taxi stopping halfway down the street—the rue something-or-other—and I ran for it as if my life depended on it. A fashionable older woman holding several fashionable shopping bags was getting out of the cab as I leaped for the door. I almost knocked her over. *Pardon* was all I could say. My French is not good. In fact, it hardly exists. She then yelled something about God and something about me being impossible. I wanted to say, You're the rudest people in the world and you've got the nerve to lecture me. But of course I couldn't manage that in French. I couldn't manage any long reply in French. So I just told her in English to piss off. A good all-around expression I'd picked up from my years in London. I think she got the idea.

As it turned out, I was only some six or seven blocks from my hotel. I felt like a fool—a hit man who couldn't locate his own street.

I was sweating a lot, which again was unlike me, and I must have looked like an agitated mess because the chatty young desk clerk asked me if I was all right. "Too much sightseeing," I told him. "The Eiffel Tower was packed. The lines were absolutely incredible."

"Ah, the Tower," he said. "My dream one day is to see the Empire State Building."

"It's a little overrated," I told him, wiping my face with a handkerchief.

"Ah, but New York City," he said. "And King Kong. You remember King Kong?"

"Yes," I said, "they shot him to death a long time ago."

Once in my room, I closed the drapes, lay down on the bed, and tried to rest.

I had left the window open, and now a sudden evening breeze made the drapes billow as it flowed into the room and stroked my stocking feet. The coolness felt good. And I needed soothing. This had been a confusing day. I couldn't remember ever having gotten so worked up over a job. Oh, maybe on the first one years ago when I was still green and nearly broke and wanted to make a good impression. But the more I worked, the calmer I became. It was all a matter of getting used to the business. And I've kept my head ever since. Like any true professional. Until now.

As the breeze tickled my feet, I tried to understand my peculiar behavior. But I couldn't come up with anything. I hadn't been nervous before the job. I never am. Nothing unusual had been happening. Nothing to shake me. If anything, I'd been getting a little tired of the steady work, one job after another. No real chance to rest. Here I was traveling from city to city, country to country, and I never had time just to relax and maybe see a few of the sights. That's the problem with being too good at your job, too talented—you're always in demand. And it's hard to say no. It's not very professional. And it's also not very wise. You don't want to be labeled "difficult" or "unreliable" in this business. No, not in this business. It just isn't healthy.

There weren't too many challenges anymore. I had to admit it. I had gotten so good at my work that the job was becoming somewhat routine, maybe even a little stale. The targets and locations were different but the job was still the same. And things always ended the same way. They had to. I need a bit of a rest, I thought, I have to slow down. I wonder how they'd feel about a brief vacation.

A siren sounded outside, somewhere in the distance. It was faint, then grew louder, then faded. Somehow the sound jarred me, touched a nerve. I realized that I had walked off a job. Just like that. I had allowed my man to get away—temporarily, of course. But still, this was not done. This was not done at all.

I got up, wet my face with cold water, and started to put on my shoes. That's when the phone rang. "Mr. King?" the voice asked. "No," I answered as always, "you have the wrong number." But, of course, they had the right number. This was our signal for me to get to an outside phone.

I headed down to the café, just off the corner. The Café Triadot. I often ate there. Grilled shell steak and French fries. First-rate. I ordered it every time. I pretty much keep away from real frog food. A big mirror on one of the walls was decorated with painted figures of Mickey Mouse, Donald Duck, and Goofy, though I couldn't understand why.

The phone booths were in the back. When I got the number I simply said "It's me" into the mouthpiece.

"You were supposed to call in," they said. "We take it the job is done."

"Not quite," I said.

"What does that mean? Either it's done or it isn't. What are you talking about?"

"It's not."

"*It's not*. Is that what you're saying? It's not?"

"Yes. No. I mean, no, it's not. I ran into some problems, but everything will be fine."

"Problems? You never have any problems. What do you mean?"

"I didn't like the feel of it. I'll go ahead when I'm ready. I'm almost ready. I want to get this over with as much as you do."

"Almost ready?! You've been there more than a week. How much more ready can you get?"

Sometimes you have to risk being forceful with them. This was one of those times. "I'm always very professional, right?"

"What are you talking about?" they said.

"I've never let you down. Right?"

"Right."

"I've always delivered. Right?"

"Right."

"And you trust me?"

"Yes. Sure. What are you saying?"

"Then trust me when I tell you that this didn't feel right. I had to make sure it was okay to go ahead. You don't want any problems, and I certainly don't want any problems. I'm just making sure. That's all. But it's feeling better. I'm almost ready."

"Our client won't be happy. And it's costing us money. We're not financing a bloody holiday here."

"It'll be done. But it'll be done when I'm perfectly ready."

"So when will that be?"

"Possibly tomorrow."

"Make that *for sure* tomorrow."

"For sure—possibly."

"Christ. This isn't like you."

"Our friend is bouncing all over Paris. You didn't say he'd be bouncing all over Paris. It's like trying to keep up with a damn kangaroo."

"Tomorrow then?"

"I think so."

"You *know* so."

"Have it your way."

And with that I hung up.

I cursed them. I was mad. Damn mad. It just goes to show you. Get too good at your job and people will take advantage. They have these expectations, and if you deviate a bit, just a bit, they come down on you hard. Whereas with some poor run-of-the-mill slob who isn't half as good, they expect a slob-like job and they get a slob-like job. If the slob merely delivers, they're grateful.

Since I was in the café, I went over to the bar and ordered a couple of whiskeys and soda. I'm not much of a drinker and liquor affects me quickly, but that's what I wanted—to be affected quickly, to calm myself somewhat. It was unlike me to take a drink. It was unlike me to need to calm myself somewhat. All around me customers were babbling in a foreign tongue. Why don't you talk English, for Christ's sake?! I wanted to shout. It was unlike me to even care.

I returned to my room. The whiskey had done its job. I was vaguely light-headed now and the feeling lingered for a long while. It was very nice indeed. I switched off the lamp and stood in the dark, staring out the window at the elegant old house across the street.

Facing me was a large apartment that had French doors leading to a small terrace with an elaborate wrought-iron railing. The place was all lit up inside and I could see the tenants quite clearly. A man, a woman, and a young boy were sitting down to dinner at a big round wooden table with a vase of flowers in the center.

I watched them as they ate. I seemed to be in a kind of trance, because there wasn't anything very interesting about what they were doing. The boy was talking the most and gesturing a lot with his hands. A lively kid. The parents, though, were pretty subdued. The man, especially, looked rigid, sitting stiffly in his chair as if he were in military school. He still had on his office clothes (white shirt, tie), which added to his tight, formal appearance. A good, solid citizen, or else an annoying bastard. But considering his animated, cheerful-looking son, I had to assume that he was a good father. Probably just prided himself on his neatness and perfect posture. The mother had long red hair and, unless my eyes were deceiving me, appeared to be quite beautiful. I kept watching them, fascinated for some reason, as if they were creatures from another planet.

As I looked at them eating away, I was reminded that I hadn't had supper yet and that before it got too late I would have to go down again to the Triadot and order my usual. It was hard to turn away from the little scene, which was lit up in the dark like a set in a theater and seemed to be going on for my benefit alone. After all, I was their only audience.

Dull, I told myself in an effort to finally break the spell. A boring life. It was so boring and so different from my own that it had stupidly hypnotized me. Deadly, I thought, absolutely deadly. I checked the time on my luminous watch and was surprised to learn that I had been looking at these people for over twenty minutes. I really must have been drunk. I turned away from the window and went downstairs.

The next morning everything was different. Everything had changed. I had changed. I don't know why. But I felt like my old self. Maybe it was a matter of focus, of having only one thought in mind and then staying with that thought and only that thought. I knew what I had to do and I was going to do it.

When the alarm clock buzzed I immediately shut it off and got out of bed. I opened the drapes, stuck my head out the window. A cool, clear day, with a touch of dampness in the air. Good enough, I thought. Up the street the bake shop was just opening. Down the street a man wearing a tan raincoat and carrying a briefcase was on his way to work. I'm going to work too, I thought.

I did my exercises—knee bends, sit-ups, push-ups—like a master, working up a good sweat. But I had plenty of strength in reserve.

I washed quickly but well, brushed my teeth quickly but thoroughly, shaved quickly but cleanly, using a minimum of strokes. I even did my business quickly and efficiently, getting that nonsense out of the way as soon as possible. I then rang for breakfast—the usual: orange juice, croissant, jam, coffee.

While waiting, I laid out my clothes, holster, gun, and silencer on the bed. I got dressed without a wasted gesture. My clothes were arranged in the order I would put them on. So I just moved down the row, quickly putting on one item after another—from underwear to white shirt to black slacks to black socks. Then down to the floor, where I had positioned my black shoes. Then back up to the bed and the remainder of the row, checking each item in the mirror as I dressed—dark blue tie, holster and gun, black jacket. I was completely dressed in no time. I may have set a world's record. I was as efficient as a machine.

Then a quick once-over in the mirror. Combed my hair a bit. Checked my gun, the silencer.

Breakfast arrived. The usual woman, her usual greeting. "*Merci*," I said coldly. I don't remember actually tasting the food. It could have been anything. My only purpose was to get it in me.

I finished in five minutes or so. Did one last check in the mirror. A brief check of the time. And one last check of the gun and silencer.

I was ready. Nothing, no one would stop me today.

I waited by the kiosk across from his hotel. Ornate as a wedding cake, the building was big, old, and expensive, and he probably ate breakfast in its big, old, expensive dining room. Although he was unpredictable in other ways, he always left after 10:00 a.m., roughly at 10:20.

He was ten minutes late on this day. I waited patiently. Heavy, distracting traffic flowed by on the avenue, but I kept my eyes fixed on the hotel entrance.

He finally appeared, looking as well turned out and full of energy as usual. I noted the gray silk suit and wondered how many hundreds, maybe even thousands it had cost him.

All these people around us were of absolutely no importance. They didn't really exist anymore. They were part of the scenery. They were nothing. Paris now contained only him and me.

This is the last day of your life, I announced to him in my head. The final hours.

He started down the street, but then abruptly stopped as if he had forgotten something, turned, and walked back toward the hotel. What's this? I thought, afraid that he might be retreating just when I was most ready to go ahead. He stopped again, though, and went into the flower shop next to the hotel.

He came out a few minutes later wearing a big white carnation in his lapel. This was the limit. This was the last straw. This was arrogance like I'd never seen it before. With that stupid flower, he was calling even more attention to himself. He was both challenging me and laughing in my face. He was showing me how alive he was and how alive he planned to stay. He had no way of knowing it, but this little gesture sealed his fate.

When he stepped into the street and hailed a taxi, I acted fast and hailed one too, telling the driver in rotten French to follow that car—one of the few handy lines I'd learned. He was surprised by the order so I said, "Police. *Anglais*. Scotland Yard." He shrugged but seemed to enjoy the challenge of the chase.

We followed the taxi to Rambuteau and the rue Beaubourg, where it stopped and my man got out. I quickly paid my driver—probably too much, because he seemed abnormally pleased. "*Merci*, *merci*, Monsieur Sherlock," he joked, laughing at his own line. "Go choke on a snail," I mumbled back in English, not needing any humor at this point, and, without missing a beat, stepped from the cab and immediately got in pace with my man, who was now a quarter of the way down the block. My eyes never left that silver head. Some man coming from the opposite direction unconsciously cut in front of me, momentarily blocking my view. Without even looking at him I pushed his body away hard. He whined something in French, but I ignored him and remained perfectly fixed on the head.

Since my man was so close to the Pompidou, near where he had visited the art gallery and the woman with long legs, I expected him to go in that direction, but instead he entered a side street and began walking into the heart of the Marais. His silver hair was gleaming in the sun as usual. But as we walked on it began to lose its sheen. I then realized that the light had suddenly faded, and when I looked up for a split second at the sky I saw gray storm clouds moving over us. Here again Paris was like London—you could forget about predicting the weather. He looked up at the sky too and he moved faster, hoping to get to his destination before a downpour. But what was his destination? He seemed to be heading for the Vosges. Certainly knows a lot of people here, I thought. Has the gift of gab, as my father used to say. My father liked that line—the gift of gab. He thought he was being funny and clever when he said it. He wasn't. The old man had no genuine sense of humor. He was a genuine bastard though. As a bastard he had few equals. And he was a fantastic hunter, an amazing shot. You name it and he could kill it.

A few drops began to fall, only here and there at first, as a kind of warning. One hit my cheek, another my wrist. He lightly brushed his silver hair a couple of times as drops dotted his head. Neither one of us had bothered to carry an umbrella. Well, I thought, at least he'll get that bloody flower of his watered.

He hurried down a narrow street. Probably heading for someone's apartment. I wondered who my target was exactly, what he was. The head of a mob? A drug dealer? Some sort of corrupt businessman? He appeared super-polished and slick but you could tell he was dirty. He was visiting all of his dirty friends, and whether they knew it or not, these were the last dirty calls he would make. I wondered what his name was. He looked like a Joseph or an Anthony or a Carlos. He might have been Italian or Spanish or even French, since he knew so many people in Paris. Maybe he was French-Italian or French-Portuguese or some such combination. But he was Continental for sure and positively no damn good.

Strange that I was going on like this so late in the game, trying to figure him out, his life, while at the same time preparing to end that life. Was it last-minute curiosity? A kind of softening, knowing that this man had no chance, no hope? I can't say. Maybe I was trying to put together a kind of obituary, no matter if any of it was true or not. Maybe I felt that need after spending so much time—wasting so much time—on this assignment.

Rain suddenly poured down. Waves of it swept through the street. We both ran for cover and took shelter in a stone archway that led to a courtyard with old buildings from another time. I stood several feet or so behind him, watching him as he examined his rain-splattered suit. "Damnit," he said to himself, "damnit." So he spoke English. That surprised me. It was the first time I had heard his voice. It was a deep voice, coarse, hard. I wouldn't worry about your precious suit, I said to him in my mind. Your suit doesn't matter anymore. Nothing about you matters anymore.

I was taking a chance standing so close, but he seemed to ignore me completely. I was just another stranger on the street. Maybe I had been wrong all along about his sensing my presence.

The rain kept coming down hard. Water rushed along the curb like a miniature river. He wiped his wet hair with a handkerchief. He concentrated on the front at first. When he reached around to the back of his head and neck, I noticed a gold ring on one of his fingers. It was large and elaborate, with a dark red stone in the center. I wondered if some dirty relative or dirty friend would inherit it or whether the police or some morgue attendant would steal it before anyone even had a chance to claim it. I noticed the deep tan of his hand. He probably had been living a life in the sun, semiretired at a luxurious resort town, with a bay and yachts and half-naked girls at his disposal. The tan, however, couldn't hide the aging skin. In fact, it emphasized all the wrinkles and cracks. The bastard, I concluded, didn't have long to go anyway. Maybe I was doing him a favor. The rain came down heavier and was blown into the archway by a shifting wind. He stepped back. I did the same.

I continued to stare at his head, framed against the downpour and view of the street. I turned briefly to check the courtyard behind me. No one in sight. No movement except for the rain. No sound except for the rain hitting the cobblestones. I backed up a bit and slowly reached in my jacket for my gun. I didn't want to alert him by making any sudden, obvious move. I slowly attached the silencer. I raised the gun to the line of his head and extended my arm until it was almost straight out in front of me.

And then, for some mad reason, I stood frozen in that position. Odd thoughts were entering my head again. And like before I had no idea where they were coming from. Odd, crazy thoughts: another job just about done, after running stupidly about for days, all the tracking, waiting, time spent and wasted, and what do you get but another dead body, then on to the next hit, another city, another bastard to track, another doomed man, to be taken out by me or someone else, it really made no difference, dead is dead. The same story, the same routine. You pull the trigger, the man falls. But what if you didn't pull the trigger?

That would be different. That might even be exciting. That would change everything.

Just then the head seemed to turn slightly, as if it sensed something was wrong, but before it could turn more I aimed dead center and fired. The muffled shot sounded more like a harmless little puff than a fatal blast. I like that about silencers. They make a noisy, messy job seem almost quiet and clean. They make death easy. He fell back against the stone wall, collapsing like a marionette whose strings had been cut all at once. He lay still in the shadow of the archway, blood pouring from his head. Only a few seconds ago he had been the picture of elegance. Now he might be a bum, dead drunk in an alley.

I gave the courtyard behind me a quick check. Nothing but the downpour, large puddles growing larger. On the street a woman with a shiny red umbrella hurried by; cars cut through the long needles of rain. I reached down, pulled the carnation from his lapel, and dropped the soggy flower on his body as a kind of funeral decoration.

I now moved quickly through the streets, keeping close to the buildings but still getting soaked. When I was far enough away from the shooting, I huddled in a doorway and waited for the rain to let up. I'd walk to a Métro stop or take a taxi back to my hotel. In one way, I was relieved, and I felt lighter because I was relieved, as if I had lost several pounds in a matter of minutes. I even felt a bit weak.

So I stood there in Paris, watching the rain. Nothing about this job had gone right except that I had finally managed to complete it. Yes, the end had gone right. But I had taken far too long to get there. I could have finished him off the very first day. It was almost as if I had wanted something more to happen, something different, maybe even wanted a problem. I had been nervous part of the time, angry the rest. Angry at the target. Yet it's absolutely unprofessional to feel anything. And getting nervous is just as bad. Something was wrong with me. I didn't know what. Standing there in Paris in the rain, I was worried. And soon I began to worry about being worried.

I followed some of the raindrops as they struck a large puddle in the street. I stared at the puddle, at the steady small splashes. When a car drove over the puddle, it broke my concentration. Then I began considering the old building across the street, a kind of mansion gray with age. I traced the lines of the stones, the rectangular slabs, and then the windows and the individual panes of glass. My mind went blank as I shifted focus from the house back to the puddle, back to the house again, from the straight lines of the mansion to the slanting lines of the rain. And all the while I half listened to the steady, soothing beat of the raindrops. Everything came down to just seeing and hearing. I could have been anyone or no one. I was there, and yet not there.

Whatever happened, for however long, it was pleasant, peaceful, my most restful moments in Paris.

After leaving the elephant, whose true wonder or weirdness neither of the men seemed to appreciate, we sat on a bench by the park lake and they gave me a map of the area in Derbyshire showing the mark's country home. I don't know Derbyshire, I told them. I don't know it at all. They then handed me a sheet of directions and photos of the house and the surrounding land. Now you know it, they said. The house was a huge three-storied redbrick affair with a great expanse of lawn, so solidly green and so smoothly, perfectly kept that it looked fake.

"And this is him," the larger man said, handing me a group photo taken in some restaurant or club. The mark had a red circle drawn around his cheerful face and bald head. "This is our friend."

"Our *ex*-friend," the smaller man corrected.

"Our *late* friend," added the larger man. "Like I said, he takes walks alone in the country with his dog. He dresses up like a regular country gentleman. Tweeds, boots, cap. Looks quite the sport. He usually goes off the road into the fields. They're open and dead. You could probably take him out with a rifle from your car. Should be no problem for someone like you. Of course, you can do it any way you want. I'm only suggesting."

I didn't appreciate the suggestion. It was as if they had lost confidence in me because of the overlong Paris job.

"Outside the car, inside the car. Whatever. So long as it's done and done fast. He'll be out there alone, just him and that dog of his."

"If he's out there with his dog then he isn't alone," I said.

They stared at me oddly again.

"Well," I explained, "if he doesn't have his dog with him then he's alone. But if he does have his dog with him then he has company. You can't say he's alone. Not with the dog."

They continued staring, a bit dumbfounded. These men were not geniuses.

"The dog doesn't count," the smaller man finally said. "Animals don't count."

"They count with me," I said. "Particularly dogs. I don't like dogs around. They sense things. They give warning. They bark. They make noise."

"I don't believe this conversation," the larger man said to the smaller. "I don't." He turned to me angrily. "Shoot the bloody dog if the bloody dog bothers you so much."

"Maybe he won't be with his dog at all," said the smaller man, excited that this brilliant notion had popped into his brain. "Did you ever think of that? Maybe he'll be alone."

"You're contradicting yourself," I said. "You're on my side."

"What?" he said, confused.

"You're saying that he'd be alone if he didn't have his dog. That's what I'm saying. I'm glad we agree."

"What? What are you talking about?" The larger man intervened again. "Let's put an end to this bloody nonsense right now." He turned to his partner. "You—you're pathetic. And you—" he said to me, "what in hell's gotten into you? You were never this way. What are you playing at here? You used to do jobs like this in your sleep. Christ."

I wanted to answer back. I wanted to say a lot. I was the one out there, not him. I was the one with the talent. I was the one always on call. I could never rest. And what did he do? What did they do? They met people in parks and pubs. They phoned people up. And the rest of the time they hung around London, or wherever, like men of leisure. They were two well-paid bums. That's what they were. Two bums.

The weather had taken a turn for the better. We stared out at sunlight on the lake, at a family of ducks in the middle, followed a jogger in a stupid turquoise sweat suit on the opposite bank. And we calmed down a bit. I realized that this might be one of those rare good days in London and that I should try to enjoy it. Even under the circumstances. I hoped for them to finish with me at last so I'd be left alone with the lake and the grass and the trees and the fine blue sky.

"That's it," said the larger man. "So are we clear on this?"

"How soon?" I asked. "You did say sometime this week."

"How about tomorrow? Make it tomorrow. Get it over with."

"Yeah," echoed the smaller, dumber man, "get it over with. Then you don't have to think about it."

"I don't think about it."

"Tomorrow then?" the larger man said.

"Fine," I answered.

"And *only* tomorrow," he added.

"Very funny," I said.

They sat there awhile longer. They said nothing more. They could see that I was very irritated and they both backed off. I think they finally remembered who they were dealing with.

As they were about to leave, the smaller man paused a bit by the edge of the lake, as if something out in the water had caught his eye. He turned to me. "You know what's really weird?" he said. "Ducks."

CHAPTER 2

FROM MY CAR WINDOW I had a good view of the house through an opening between a cluster of trees. Even at this distance and at a bit of an angle it seemed bigger and better than it did in the photograph. Although the place probably had been built in another century, it appeared new, with clean red bricks, which stood out against the green of the trees and the blue of the sky. I used my binoculars for a better look, but I couldn't quite see inside the house. Instead the tall, shiny windows acted as mirrors of the outside, reflecting on different floors the land, branches, sun, clouds. The lawn was even more peculiar in person, looking as if the grass had been sprayed with deep green paint. I wondered what this man had done to warrant such an estate. He had to be a major crook or a major businessman—there wasn't much difference as far as I was concerned.

I sat back in the car and enjoyed the view for a while, somehow not worrying much about the fact that if I could see his house he could most likely see my car. Must be pleasant living in a house like that, I thought. Looking out through those big windows at all the greenery. Sitting there in your living room with all the greenery and light coming in. A spacious white room with a white fireplace. Clean. Neat. Open. Elegant old furniture, aristocratic.

You could pretend you were living in another age. It was the sort of house I'd be happy in. I haven't lived in a house since I was a kid. Lived in an old clapboard then. A bit of a dump. In a small town on a hill overlooking a river. The town was a bit of a dump too, at least as I remember it, though it had a lot of greenery. It looked best from a distance. Yes, from the river, the Hudson, it looked rather pretty—cozy, quaint, a postcard sort of town. It was only when you actually set foot in it that you realized it was a bit of a dump.

But this house, this place, this was what England was all about. "Georgian" they call such a house. I learned that from *Country Life* magazine. When I started earning some good money here and took a modest flat in London, I'd flip through *Country Life* looking for Georgian houses for sale. For my early retirement. All I needed was about a million pounds. Then God knows how much more for the upkeep. But I could save. And, anyway, I could dream. Nobody could stop me from doing that.

I had arrived a little early for his usual ten o'clock walk so I had some time to kill. And this was the way I killed it—taking in the Georgian house and its Georgian windows, taking in the area itself, the bushes and trees, branches and leaves, the birds and bees, nature and all that. I followed a big, puffy white cloud shaped like a man's face with a ridiculously long nose as it drifted across the sky, just above the Georgian house. Clouds are odd, I thought, maybe because I had never much considered them before. This one put me in a kind of trance, moving ever so slowly, all that puffy white silence sliding across the deep blue. You also could see it as a giant clump of cotton tinged by the sun, glowing a bit here and there at the edges. I wasn't drunk now, of course, but I felt as if I'd had one or two, felt a little off, vague and calm and relaxed, strangely at peace. Like watching the rain in Paris.

That fake-looking grass all around the estate seemed so smooth that I wanted to walk on it, feel it. I could see myself as a property owner, lord of the manor, going out for a stroll on my own land, in tweeds with a walking stick, pipe in mouth. I didn't smoke, but I'd take it up and I'd learn to enjoy it. Just puffing away as I surveyed my acres. Suddenly there I was, with my dog, leaving my Georgian house, as if my daydream had come to life. I watched me, or at least this older actor playing me, as I crossed the driveway, stepping onto the expanse of deep green grass, walking on it as if on an enormous super-soft carpet. Weirdly absorbed, I watched this man as he moved toward the road. He walked briskly, seemed sprightly, in very good spirits and health—but you would be too if you had his money and a Georgian house. The trees by the side of the road now blocked my view and I would have to drive my car a bit down the curved dirt road to catch sight of him again.

I stayed where I was. I didn't start the engine. I sat still, resting, thinking. It was as if I had finished my job, had already done more than enough. I mean, after all, I had driven out here in the early morning hours, all the way from London, down unfamiliar roads, past unfamiliar towns, had come to this far-off country place, had basked in nature in a way I hadn't done since I was a boy, had seen the Georgian house, spent time admiring it, studying it, dreaming about it, spent time considering the whole estate, and now I had found the man and his dog, had watched them carefully, had tracked them with my eyes. I'd accomplished quite a lot, all things considered. And I was tired. That seemed only natural. Didn't it?

It did. But as much as I wanted the morning to be over, as much as my job felt over, as much as my body was telling me to stop, telling me that this was the end, I knew, of course, that I had to go on. The end would come only when this man lay dead.

The road was at a slight incline so I just allowed the car to roll very slowly down and around, sort of creeping up by machine on the man and his dog. The road began to straighten and soon I had a clear view of what was ahead. The trees that lined the right side of the road continued on, but on the left they gave way to a great open field, with small hills rolling far into the distance. Houses, looking like miniatures from here, were scattered about in this ocean of grass and greenery. And close to the horizon were what looked like a collection of rooftops huddled around a church steeple. "Beautiful," I remember saying to myself aloud. The word just came out. *Beautiful*.

I kept on doing nothing except enjoying the view. Yet at the moment this seemed like something, like an event of sorts. I'm in England, I remember saying to myself. This is the real thing. The English countryside, the kind you see on a calendar or in a guidebook or in *Country Life*. Since living in London I'd seen very little of the rest of the country. I'd spent a half day in Manchester on a job, and another in Newcastle and another in Liverpool, but I hardly recall them now. I remember the heads I tracked more than the cities the heads were in. The man appeared now in the field, walking close to the road, while his dog ran off to the side in the direction of the hills, then hurried back to his master, then headed out for the hills again, as if beckoning the man to follow. It was an Irish setter and moved with a certain grace, even though it was running about nervously like an overactive child.

I had to stop the car or else I'd overtake the target. I lowered the window, shifted back in my seat a bit, raised the rifle, and picked him up in the scope. I followed the back of that happy head of his, now divided into quarters by the crosshairs. A very stylish tweed cap hid his bald dome. I'd wear a cap like that when I finally had my own Georgian house in the country. I wouldn't be hiding anything though. I had plenty of hair. I'd wear it for the effect alone. I wondered where I might buy such a hat. I didn't know much about clothes. You have to wear inconspicuous things in my profession, the duller the better. Maybe Harrods would have a hat like that. Or one of those fancy little shops in the Burlington Arcade. I had followed another rich crook there a few years back; though, of course, I finally killed him somewhere else.

While I was having these dress and style thoughts, I followed the man and his dog with my eyes, but I suppose I wasn't really conscious of them—a kind of looking but not looking. Because when I stopped thinking about my fashion plans, I was fully aware of the man and the dog again and how distant they were now. In fact, they were all the way out in the middle of the field and already heading for the top of one little hill.

"Jesus!" I said aloud, suddenly realizing that they were moving way out of range. "Jesus Christ!" I quickly started the car, pulled it over to the far right side of the road, slid out, grabbing my rifle and my coat, and hurried across the road into the field. With the coat oddly draped over the rifle, I moved steadily through the grass toward the now tiny man and dog. They disappeared from view briefly, lost in all the green, but then I saw them in the open again, advancing to another little rise. I looked around, scanning the whole countryside. Not a soul. At least I couldn't see anyone. All the privacy in the world in the middle of nowhere. I could do what I wanted.

I almost had to run to catch up, and when I was finally close enough—close enough in this empty, open, completely exposed field—I stopped short, caught my breath, dropped the coat, lifted the rifle, steadied it through all my puffing, and looked through the scope. I picked out the man, who was throwing a stick out into the grass for his dog to retrieve.

I had a perfect shot, but I wasn't sure I could hit him at this distance, particularly with him in motion. And I didn't like the entire situation—me trying to pick off a man in the open, standing there with a rifle, revealing myself to anyone who might be in the area. Half my brain was telling me to fire and get it over with, avoid tracking him on foot, which would only take me farther away from my car and a clean escape. But the other half was urging me to play it safe, slow down, act coolly, sanely, and do the job right.

I kept following. Somehow I ignored the possibility that he might turn around at any moment and see me and wonder who in hell I was. It's one thing getting lost in the crowd as you track a man through city streets. It's another trying to remain inconspicuous in a big, empty field.

I pressed on, figuring that I'd know when it was time to act, know when it felt right. I always did. Didn't I? I chose to take my time here. But maybe there was something else. Maybe I thought it was too easy to take somebody out like this, using a rifle on a man in an open field. Maybe I thought I was too good to waste on such a simple, nothing job.

I kept on tracking him all the way over to a small rise with some tightly grouped trees on top, what I think they refer to as a "copse" in *Country Life*. We cut through the trees, all of us—me, him, and the dog—weaving this way and that, playing hide-and-seek. Beyond the trees the hill took a steep drop, and below, to my complete surprise, was a road, and across that road, looking like something out of English history, was an old-fashioned inn and pub, a Tudor-looking place of white walls and dark wood beams, clinging vines, a high brick chimney, sharp angles, and windows with tiny, diamond-shape panes of glass. A wooden sign hung above the main doorway—a Ye Olde Inn sort of thing. I stood there, among the trees, looking down with some amazement at this scene from another age. You could imagine fox hunters stopping off here with their horses after a morning of tallyhoing and all that. Just then the sun must have come out of a cloud, because the whole place suddenly lit up and gleamed white. Birds started to sing more in the bright light, or so it seemed. I felt I was in a dream.

The man disappeared inside the inn, leaving his dog to wait outside. A well-behaved animal, he sat rigidly by the door, staring in at his master. I got down on one knee behind a tree and rested my elbow on the other as I raised the rifle and put my eye to the scope, using it more as a telescope than as a target guide, pointing the rifle down the hill at the inn and picking up the doorway the man had just entered. It was all black inside, though I thought I could detect a moving shadow or two. I shifted over to the main ground-floor window, decorated with a window box filled with flowers, but the little reflections of sunlight prevented me from seeing beyond the glass itself.

I realized that even when he came out I could only watch. I'd be mad to pull the trigger from here. I had stupidly put myself in the exact situation I'd wanted to avoid—I was too far from my car now to go ahead with the job. Damnit, I thought, I knew what I was doing and yet I went right on doing it. I had created my own mess.

I could have gone on cursing myself but I calmed down by remembering that I still had much of the day left to take one lousy little well-aimed shot.

I had to wait him out. There wasn't much I could do in the meantime so I lowered the rifle and went back to surveying the inn with my naked eyes. I noticed the gravel out front that made for a kind of patio, and the four picnic tables used for outdoor eating and drinking. The whole place—the tables, the vines, the historic house with its old-fashioned windows and colorful window boxes, nestled in among bushes and trees—had what they call real charm. You might very well walk about your estate a bit, then roam the countryside, and then end up here for a pint and a rest. Not a bad existence at all. Not a bad way to go out when you've reached that point in life. I had the strangest feeling that I wasn't so very far from that point, even though I had years and years ahead of me. I didn't understand the feeling. It was, as I said, strange.

I was wondering what the inside of the inn looked like when the man came out carrying a mug and a plate with something on it. The dog jumped about upon seeing both his master and the food. The man gave him something to munch, and then sat down to eat at one of the tables as the dog stood beside him waiting for more. I raised the rifle again for a closer look. The face was as happy, puffy, and rosy-cheeked as it had appeared in the photo. This man looked more like somebody's jolly uncle than like a rotten bastard. He stuffed his jolly cheeks with a roll and sipped what was probably coffee from the mug. I remembered that I had gotten up too early to manage breakfast and was really hungry now. My stomach remembered it as well and growled a bit in emptiness. Then again, I thought, getting back to the man, there's no reason a crook can't be jolly. After all, what does this man, with this kind of a life, have to be unhappy about? I should be so lucky.

A lot of people, I suppose, have a jolly uncle or at least some jolly relative, the kind of character everybody likes to be around. There wasn't one in my family. My family was hard and quiet. Except perhaps for Uncle Ed. You might have called him jolly, but most called him a drunken bum. When he and my aunt would visit us, he'd cheerfully demand steak and beer. Ed had a lot of nerve, but the nerve was always of the cheerful sort. Steak was expensive, so my mother would give him chicken and beer, or eggs and beer, or bologna and beer. He drank so much beer that soon he wouldn't know what in hell he was eating anyway. That's about as jolly as our family got: a beer-loaded drunk cheerfully chewing a bologna steak.

When the target, who was genuinely jolly, finally finished the roll and coffee, he went back inside with his empty plate and mug. Again his dog, who you might say was jolly too, waited by the doorway. I bet even his wife, if he had one, was on the jolly side, and the children as well. He didn't look like he could harm a fly. But then again, he owned a Georgian house, and you had to be some kind of villain to own a house like that. I reminded myself that when I got back to London I might want to pick up a book or something about Georgian houses. For my own enjoyment, as they say. I'm not much of a reader and I haven't been one for enjoyment, but I could use a bit of a change.

I stood up and prepared to move. He had to do one of two things now: either he'd continue his walk down the road, to God knows where, and give me a big headache, or else he'd just return home, and do me a big favor. So I waited. And I waited some more. And I leaned against the tree for support. But he remained inside. Come on, I ordered him under my breath, say your good-byes and let's get going. Come on already.

At last he appeared in the open. I was tempted to take my shot and be done with it, but I kept my head. I reminded myself that the only way back to my car was through that open field and if I fired now and made a run for it, they'd see me for sure. The police couldn't be nearby, but then again, I didn't really know where they were or how long it would take them to get here or how soon they could call for help or set up a roadblock or two. I'd be lucky if I knew how to get back to the main road, much less how to dodge country cops on country roads.

I thought about being back in my London flat and sitting in my easy chair reading about Georgian houses, and I began to feel more in control and reasonable. I then saw that he was coming my way, him and the dog. Yes, they were going back the same way they had come. God was with me.

I moved back among the trees and waited for them to descend into the field. The dog was feeling frisky again and dashed down ahead into the grass. I noticed how the wind swept across the field, bending some of the blades, making sections of grass look like hair being parted.

Now that I knew he was returning to his house, I had to get there before he did. The closer I was to my car after the hit the better it would be for me. So I decided to descend the hill, get onto the road, hug the far side of it, keeping very close to the line of trees, and circle around to my car. The field was obviously a shortcut, but I'd be taking the long way back, so I'd have to make tracks fast to beat him home.

I must have looked like a bloody madman jogging up the road with a rifle and a raincoat. As I ran I glanced over at the field to see how far he was getting and I was glad to see that I had already passed him. Jolly soul that he was, he had stalled in the middle of the field to play with his dog.

I saw my car now and it was, believe me, a sight for sore eyes, but I decided not to get into it just yet. Since

I had already made such a mess of things, I didn't want to risk missing a shot. The trees up ahead that hugged the road and led into the field would put me a bit closer to my man, so I threw my coat into the car and headed for them.

As I positioned myself among the trees, I could see him still playing with his dog; more of the throw-and-fetch business. He stood fairly fixed in the middle of the field, allowing his dog to do all the work as it ran this way, then that way to again retrieve its favorite stick. I raised my rifle, but I waited for the man to move more toward me and home.

I had him perfectly lined up. The head was now turned in my direction. I think he was ready to call it a morning. A little more, I said to him, as I held the trigger, keep moving this way, that's it. Suddenly his head turned. He was reacting to a sound coming from farther out in the field. Then I heard it. "George!" someone was shouting. "George!" Probably his name. Someone was calling out to him. Someone else was in the field.

I lowered my rifle and scanned the area. A man was waving to him in the distance. He waved back. What in hell is this?! I thought. I used the scope again as a telescope and picked up this new problem. An old man in a blue sweater and what looked like a very worn brown corduroy jacket was heading toward my man. "No," I said to myself.

"Goddamnit! Son-of-a-bitch!" It was some country bumpkin, maybe some neighbor of his.

Goddamnit!

I couldn't shoot now. This old man wasn't part of it. Damn the luck. The dog obviously knew the old man because it ran out to greet him and started jumping all over him like he was a long-lost brother. Jesus Christ, I thought, now I have one big happy family on my hands.

I sighted the two men as they joined up. They were all smiles. My man was walking in my direction, walking home at last the way I'd hoped, but, unfortunately, he had a goddamn witness with him.

I had to wait. But I couldn't. What if this old bugger followed him all the way home? I couldn't take the chance. I didn't know what to do. Nothing quite like this had happened before, in all my years. I had bungled this job but good.

I continued to track the two men, moving steadily toward me. Soon they'd be cutting away slightly to the right as they made for the road and the Georgian house. I realized that my forehead was damp. I realized that I was sweating, even though I was in the shade of the trees.

Again I thought of a scene from a calendar or travel book. Two country gentlemen and a dog walking through a lush green field on a beautiful spring day in the English countryside. It was the kind of picture I longed to enjoy in my easy chair at home.

A plane roared across the sky. It didn't seem to belong in this country setting. And somehow it sparked me into action. Because I centered the crosshairs on my man's jolly head and pulled the trigger. And as that head exploded I shifted slightly to the old man's and fired again. He dropped across his friend—the wrong friend to have.

They both lay there in the grass, with part of their heads missing and their blood now staining the lush green. The dog stepped nervously around the bodies and then began howling. I let it alone.

Speeding down the country roads, anxious to leave this place and this mess far behind, I could feel my hands shaking even as they gripped the steering wheel. I couldn't believe what I had just done. This was a screwup to top all screwups. Taking out a passerby, a stranger, a private citizen. But I had no choice, I told myself. I had to do it.

Trees flew by. The sun kept flashing through the branches, blinding me. I lowered the shade. Houses. White patches. Red patches. The dirt road turned to concrete. Highway. More trees, though more scattered now. An overpass. Brief darkness. The car seemed to be driving itself.

How was I going to explain this? You had to be there to understand. You needed to have my thoughts at the time, to be inside my brain. Otherwise, it made no sense. Absolutely no sense at all.

And yet they had instructed me so many times to avoid witnesses, if possible. Had I let the old man live, he might have caused trouble. But what trouble exactly? He'd been too far away to identify me or to get my license plate, and he'd been too far away from anywhere to call the police—I would have been long gone before he'd reached a phone. The fact is, I could have left him alone. The fact is, I had panicked.

As I drove I tried to come up with a reasonable story—other than the complete truth, of course. Since they hadn't been there, since nobody but me had been there, I could pretty much tell them anything I wanted, as long as it didn't sound too far-fetched. They'd find out that two people were dead—the mark and some poor old slob—but that's all they'd find out. The only way they could know about my stalling, my little mental drift, my drawn-out stalking, was if I told them. And I'd be a damn fool to do that. Oh, I'd tell them a story, but I needed to shorten it. I wouldn't lie so much as reduce. I couldn't change the ending, of course. The ending was that two people were dead. But how the ending had come about could be simplified.

My mind was working so hard at this point that I couldn't concentrate on the road, so I pulled into a lay-by and just sat there thinking the whole thing out. Traffic was too heavy anyway. Cars were still pouring into London.

The man left the Georgian house with his dog. I remained in my car with my rifle. I waited for him to get far enough away from the house to fire. He crossed the road. He entered the field. I was about to take my shot when some old man ran over to him and they began walking together. They were heading way out into the field. I was afraid I'd miss my opportunity. After all, who knew where they were going or how long they'd stay once they got there? I had to act. So I acted. I shot both of them in the head and drove off.

This version seemed completely convincing to me. And I came across well. I couldn't be faulted. I'd done everything by the book. They themselves had told me to shoot the dog if it was trouble. That was like saying shoot anything in sight if it interferes. Just get the job done. The old man had interfered. So I shot him and I got the job done.

Good as this version was, I could improve on it. Maybe they'd wonder why I hadn't taken him out as he was leaving his house, why, instead, I had waited for him to cross the road and enter the field. I could tell them that when I'd arrived the man was already in the field. It wasn't that I had gotten there late, but rather that he had started on his stroll early. Yes, this seemed very possible. But why, they might then ask, didn't you kill him right off—why didn't you fire before anyone even had a chance to join him? All right, how about this: when I'd arrived the man was already in the field with the old man. And already they were walking away from me, heading across the countryside. So I pulled the car up to the edge of the field, rested my rifle on the open car window, aimed, and fired, killing them both. There had been no other choice. I had acted quickly and decisively and had gotten the hell out of there fast.

I didn't know which version I'd actually use. Maybe this last one sounded a little too convenient. But any of them was a lot better than the real story. I kept reviewing them in my confused head as I got back on the road and neared London and probably big trouble.

CHAPTER 3

I WALKED ABOUT MY FLAT, trying to settle on the best story, trying to work up enough courage to report in. The city sky was overcast. It looked like we were in for some bad weather for a change. So I paced. And kept pacing. Sure enough, rain soon began beating against the windows.

There's not much room to pace in my flat. The living room is the biggest room. It's really the only room, when you come down to it. The living room doubles as a bedroom. There's a daybed in the corner. It came with the place. I covered it with a dark green plaid bedspread (to go with the dark green carpet) and put a few pillows on top, upright, resting against the wall, so that the bed might look something like a couch. When you're ready to go to sleep, you toss the pillows onto the easy chair, pull the spread back, and you have yourself a bedroom. Reverse the whole process and you have yourself a living room again. There's a tiny kitchen off to the side and a small bathroom, which has a tub but no shower (you have to use a wire hose for that—hose yourself down as if you were an animal in the zoo). I really should have moved a couple of years ago. But I didn't feel the need for anything lavish then. I wanted an inconspicuous place on an inconspicuous street with inconspicuous people, the kind you can blend in with. The place is clean and it has two big, tall windows in the living room—something like Georgian windows, a reminder of the real thing. I'm very fond of those windows. Live modestly now, I thought, save your money, and you'll have the real thing someday soon.

I stood by one of the windows and stared out at the street and at part of the long row of squat houses, attached dark gray brick buildings that looked so similar you might easily return to the wrong home if you were drunk, doped up, heavily medicated, or just plain stupid. In the sunlight the block was pleasant and quaint. But in the rain and drizzle, like now, it seemed old and sad. No doubt about it, I needed a more elegant address, either in the city or in the country. I was changing. My tastes were changing. Something. True, Bloomsbury wasn't far away, and it had some very nice squares and fine Georgian houses. And Dickens's house was nearby, and that was in all the guidebooks, though I myself never visited the place. In school they'd shoved *A Tale of Two Cities* into our young brains and tortured us with "quizzes" about it, and ever since then I haven't been able to tolerate that bearded old bird.

I watched some small children walking down the rainy street in red and yellow slickers. They were talking loud and I could make out some of their words. I always thought little kids with English accents sounded weird. I thought the same about little French kids speaking French. Somehow it didn't fit their size and age. Anyway, these English kids seemed to be enjoying themselves and yet they weren't doing much of anything except making a bit of noise and walking in the rain. I didn't have much fun as a kid, even though I lived in the semi-country. You're supposed to have a better life as a kid if you're brought up in the country rather than the city. Well, maybe I was the exception to the rule. The only fun I really had was with paper clips and rubber bands, water pistols, slingshots, dart guns, bows and arrows, BB guns, air rifles.

I realized that I was still wearing my holster and gun and here I was, standing by a window for anybody to see. I backed away. I was about to continue my pacing, but decided enough was enough and that it was time to make my call, get the damn thing over with. As I put on my raincoat, took my umbrella, and headed downstairs to the phone booth up the street, I tried to be positive about the whole business. After all, I had done the job and done it in one day and nobody had seen a thing.

I told them the second version—about me arriving and our man already walking in the field. I was taking a chance using this story, because they could accuse me of arriving too late. But it was a lot better than reporting the truth. I assumed my story was going over well, because they made no comment, and so I babbled on. They suddenly stopped me. "Why are you telling us all of this?" they asked. "You did the job and that's that. Where you were, where he was, what the bloody weather was like—who gives a shit. He's gone. That's all. The End." That's when I sneaked in the bit about shooting the stranger. "Jesus Christ," they said and kept saying as I went into detail. "Jesus H. Christ." "I couldn't leave a witness," I explained. "I had to kill him." They then switched over to "Fuck."

When I finished going through this part of the story—and it had sounded pretty logical to me—there was a long silence on the other end. I could hear a radio playing in the background, some woman singing "Our Love Is Here to Stay." "A stranger," they finally said. "A bystander. A private citizen. Nobody'll be happy about this, believe me. Nobody. This is a royal cock-up—a royal cock-up with a capital *C*."

I wasn't sure what I was supposed to do now. Lay low, they said, until they could assess the damage. Stay close to home. "So I guess I can rest for a while?" I said, sort of asking their permission. "Are you sure you can do that right?" they said with anger. I didn't bother to answer.

Luck was with me for the next several days. The weather turned good again. In fact, spring finally looked like it might stay around for a while. Sunshine lit the city. It blinded you at first. There was so much of it that it was hard to get used to. It seemed to be lighting streets that had remained in shadow for years. It was so bright, I thought, laughing to myself, that it might reveal bodies dumped in various dark alleys long ago. You felt suspicious of it, like it was teasing you to be cheerful and then might suddenly disappear and leave you in gloom again. In the squares, birds chirped madly, trees were fat with leaves, and people walked about, sat on benches, chatted with one another. The cool, sometimes chilly, breezes of past days were replaced by milder ones that sort of brushed your face and made you feel a bit warm and encouraged your mind to stray. I began to notice women again, after having put them on hold for the winter. It's hard to think about all of that when you're occupied with my kind of work. But now I took notice of the freer, lighter clothing that nicely displayed legs and breasts. So many women and girls looked seminude. It was as if they had undressed just for me. It was amazing.

Yes, I was in luck. Because if I had to linger in London, hanging around when the weather was good was a lot better than hanging around when it was rotten.

After a couple of days, the worry over the bungled job began to fade. These things happen, I thought. They happen and they pass. Besides, it could have been worse. I could have killed no one at all.

I figured the worst was over because they didn't bother to call me. Maybe they wouldn't call again for a long time. Maybe they realized now that I needed some peace and quiet. So I decided to enjoy myself. I purposely didn't read the papers. The hit probably would make the news, but I didn't want to find out. It was over, that's all I knew.

I regretted the business with the old man, but I really wasn't sure who he was—he might have been part of it after all. He might have been a colleague or the man's father or uncle, or maybe a one-time crook who had retired to the country, another no-good bastard nobody would miss. I might have done two jobs in one. I might have given them a bargain.

I roamed about London in a relaxed way, casually dressed—dark suit, plaid shirt, no tie, sunglasses. I probably looked something like a tourist, and, in fact, I felt something like a tourist. I knew that I confused people any way I was. I mean, I wasn't English, but I wasn't really American anymore either. I think this dawned upon me one day about a year or so ago when I was buying a Tube ticket. In telling the man in the booth my destination, I suddenly realized I was speaking with an English accent. I began noticing too that when I talked to other people—talked to Them, I should say, to the Firm, because they were mostly the people I talked to, these poor excuses for mates—I began noticing that I was phrasing things in an English sort of way, even tossing in words like "indeed" and "chap" every now and then. I think I was even beginning to look English. One afternoon not so long ago when I was walking in my area, a man with a young boy stopped me. "Pardon me, gov," he said, "would you happen to know where Dickens's house is? I'm taking the boy here." An Englishman, probably a Londoner, asking me directions! That was rich. I was weirdly impressed and more than willing to play the part. Because even when I'd lived in New York I hadn't been a true New Yorker. That's someone who lives in New York City and not in a dumpy town upstate. I was technically from New York, but I was really from nowhere.

I hadn't taken a leisurely walk in the city for some time so this stroll was a bit of a treat. Once I started strolling, I couldn't stop strolling. It seems I couldn't get enough of strolling. The movement, the air, the nothing-to-do, no-target, new-man sense of it all, did me good. Yes, I felt uneasy at first to be just walking, to be following no one. Usually your target takes you somewhere. You don't take yourself. He sees the sights, if he's so inclined, and you see him. He's the sight. He's the only sight for you. But now I could look at all the people on the streets and at the streets themselves and at the buildings and shops. Not one of them mattered. I mean, none of them were part of a scheme, a job. They were all just there, for me to take in, enjoy or not enjoy. This take-it-or-leave-it attitude was quite refreshing. I could walk without tension, roam to my heart's content. I felt something like a prisoner who had just been released from jail. Yes, being outside this way definitely felt odd. Nice and odd.

I crossed Gray's Inn Road into Theobald's Road, went from Bloomsbury Way into New Oxford Street, and then strolled along Charing Cross Road. As someone who had grown up in a hick town and been expected to remain and finally croak in a hick town, I'd surprised myself by getting along so well in foreign places, in London especially, which was now something like a home. I never expected to stay. I was originally sent over on a job. They needed an outsider, someone who wasn't known here, who couldn't be traced. Since I'd done good work for them in New York, I was recommended. Apparently it was a big job, a major hit. I got it done without a problem. Maybe we oughta call you back here once the heat is off, they said. We could use a deadly bloke like you. So I returned home, and some months later they sent for me again. This time I stayed. I never planned on it. But then again, I never planned on following this profession either. It all began back home in a seedy bar in a neighboring town, which, if anything, was even dumpier than my town. A vague friend of mine got to talking about my skill with guns. He had a friend, he said, who was retired now, but once was paid good money for that skill, damn good money. What did he do? I asked. Well, you might say he was a kind of exterminator, only he used a gun instead of a spray can. You think your friend might know of an opening for me? I asked. As it turned out, he did.

I was something of a nervous wreck on that first job. I didn't know how I'd feel about killing a person. After all, it's not something you normally do. But I had reached the end of the line. If I didn't get some money fast I'd end up back home. And considering my mentally disturbed family, I'd be better off dead. I also needed a profession, and this seemed to be it. They had given me a break, taking me on like this. I had to do well, prove myself. So to make this business a little easier to accept I pretended that I was tracking down a wild animal. I thought of one that looked like a man. I thought of a bear. Except I knew of no bear that lived in a house in the suburbs.

It was a cold late afternoon in winter and I watched his house, a gray ranch-style number, from my car parked out front. He was supposed to arrive home by four o'clock and I was supposed to drive up, shoot him a few times from my car, and drive off. It all seemed easy enough. But four o'clock came and went and the mark was nowhere to be seen. It began to get dark and I noticed that this quiet, tree-lined street wasn't particularly well lit. Suddenly a light went on in the picture window of the house. I was startled because I didn't think anybody was home. A minute or so later the light went out and the front door opened. Two people emerged, one tall, the other short. As they moved toward me down the walkway I could see that it was a young woman and a little girl. They were carrying what looked like ice skates. Jesus, I thought, he's got a family. I'm going to make that woman a widow and leave the kid without a father. They reached the sidewalk, walked down the empty street hand in hand, and disappeared around the corner. I could hear the kid talking and giggling. No way, I thought, I can't do this. The bear not only had a house in the suburbs but also a wife and daughter.

It was getting really dark now and the house and front lawn were turning black. I hadn't counted on this. I hadn't counted on trying to hit someone in the dark. I was beginning to freeze. I couldn't get warm. I was soon shaking like a leaf. It wasn't just because I had the engine and heater turned off. It was also because of the whole rotten situation I found myself in. He's probably leading a double life, I then thought; his family doesn't know what a rat he is. I convinced myself that in the long run they'd be better off without him. His wife was probably young enough to find somebody else, somebody legitimate. The kid would be a lot better off too.

He drove up about twenty after five. I was a bloody ice cube by then. I was so frozen that I couldn't even tremble properly anymore. But I managed to roll down my window and take aim at the black blotch that had just left its car in the driveway. My fingers hurt as I gripped my gun. Christ, I thought, I can't tell what I'm shooting at. The lawn was black, the house was black, the mark was black. I was afraid to get out of the car and approach him. After all, he might be carrying a gun himself. Or he might hear me and make a run for it and blow the whole job. Moreover, to be frank, I just didn't want to shoot him up close. I wasn't sure I had the stomach for that kind of thing. I really had the urge to get the hell away, but I needed that money and that profession. I squinted as he moved to his front door, trying to make out his outline. Suddenly my luck changed. It was as if God or whoever had come to my rescue. Because just then the mark switched on a little lamp by the side of the door. I could see his head perfectly. It became just another target, like the kind I used to set up in the woods. A bottle, a tin can. I steadied my gun hand with my other hand. I aimed for the head and fired. He went down immediately. I'd killed him with one shot.

I sped away down the block, anxious, cold, hot, somewhat disgusted, somewhat proud. I'd arrived at that house as a shaky amateur. I now drove away as a very promising professional. The rest, as they say, is history.

It's Saturday, I remembered as I walked along Charing Cross. The large number of people on the street reminded me of that. Saturday in the early afternoon. When you have time off from my kind of work you tend to lose track of the day and date. You're hanging around mainly, waiting for the phone to ring or expecting that message on your machine, the signal for the next job. You can't really get settled in your place or in your mind because you don't really know where you'll be tomorrow. You're always on call, something like a doctor or cop. One of those vital professions. But now I was fairly certain that I was free for a time. Strangely enough, my screwup had freed me, given me a bit of a vacation. The thought amused me.

A young couple was walking my way, arm in arm, snuggling while walking. He was a less-than-average bloke, verging on the noticeably homely, but she—rusty blond and very leggy, with an incredibly cute, perky face and bangs, or what they call a fringe over here—was something of a sweet knockout. I wasn't one for public displays of affection, but somehow this display reminded me that I needed to find a girlfriend, and it also gave me enormous hope—if a creep like that could land a beauty, I, who was better looking, should have absolutely no trouble if I put my mind to it. But putting my mind to it was the problem. I had to force it in that direction. Get a bit away from my usual concerns. And, of course, I needed the opportunity. To meet someone normal, that is. I had to mingle more with average people. I certainly wasn't going to find my woman among mobsters and murderers.

While on Charing Cross I thought I might look for a book or two on Georgian houses, since the street is something of a book lover's paradise. So I stopped in at Foyles, Books Etc., Waterstone's, Zwemmer, whatever. You name it and I was there. I felt peculiar asking clerks for architectural stuff—or, for that matter, asking them for anything at all. I couldn't remember when I'd last bought a book. I mostly read magazines on planes that carried me to hits. Or I read train schedules or road and city maps, always related to a job. But after I got over the business of now being a book buyer, I felt sort of good asking the question, as if I were a man of wealth and education, a dignified chap, pursuing things intellectual, hunting down a book instead of a crook. Yes, my question—"Do you have anything on Georgian houses?"—was respected. In fact, a few of the clerks were unusually pleased by it, as if I'd hit on a pet subject or one that didn't interest your average, run-of-the-mill customer. One clerk, a skinny wound-up character with four pens in his ink-stained shirt pocket, was particularly impressed and was crazily eager to show off his knowledge. He rattled off names of books, authors, publishers, publication dates. He evaluated the "volumes," talked about their "historical accuracy and scope," their "intellectual breadth" and "prose style," "the quality" of their illustrations, indicated his "own personal favorites," adding as a warning that he did, "of course," have "very quirky, eclectic taste." Christ, I said to myself as his mouth kept moving. This is more than I bargained for. I've unleashed an architectural mental case. "What I want to know," I finally said, interrupting his lecture, "is if you carry any of those books. That's what I want to know. If you have any of them here, now, in this store, today." "Right, yes, of course," he said, sounding somewhat hurt. "Well, let's take a look, sir, shall we?" And we pranced over to the art and architecture section.

I came away from the various bookshops with a nice selection—*Georgian Houses for All* by John Woodforde; *Georgian London* by John Summerson, which the ink-stained clerk had assured me was a "classic" and "even more handsome and useful in this revised, enlarged, and profusely illustrated edition"; and an old, though pretty ordinary, thing from 1952 called *Looking for Georgian England* by Raymond Francis, which another clerk had described as "a real find," but hadn't gone on to explain why. In the street I removed the books from their bag and carried them along exposed. I bet people walking by took me for a professor or some sort of scholar on his way from the British Museum after a morning of important study.

I eventually wandered into Piccadilly Circus and then walked along Piccadilly. I thought that while I was in this unusual shopping mood I might stroll along Bond Street and take a look at what the fashionable man might buy in the way of a suit. But then I noticed that I was just across the street from Fortnum & Mason and I decided to treat myself to a little snack at the fountain restaurant they have there.

I'd been in the place a long time ago on a job, tracking some rich out-of-town crook as he and his flashy girlfriend made the rounds of the city. I finally took him out in a quiet loo at the National Theatre one dead afternoon, while his tart waited for him forever in the lobby. So this visit to the restaurant was a lot more pleasant. I could actually concentrate on what I was eating—scones with jam and cream.

I stay away from junk food. It fills the stomach and satisfies the taste buds, but it weakens the mind and it turns the body into flab. And I have to keep in condition. You might say I'm health conscious, though I wouldn't be caught dead in a jogging outfit or in a health club with brainless workout freaks. Muscle-bound poofs is what I call them. Stick a gun in their faces and watch those muscles melt. Maybe that's why I enjoyed the scones so much—I rarely give in to sweet cravings. Giving in now, I sipped coffee and ate my scones as I surveyed the restaurant crowd—a majority of chit-chatting lady shoppers, a few men with their wives, a few tourists. Just another Saturday afternoon out. Hard to believe, I thought, but I was out for the day too. At least for now, I resembled them. This was what it was like to spend a normal, ordinary, slightly boring day. I sort of liked the feeling. I sort of liked the boredom. I sort of liked everyone remaining alive. With just a little effort, I could have fallen asleep at the counter. That's how relaxed I was.

All sweetened and junked up, I left the store and wandered into a nearby men's shop. I gave the suits a once-over, even felt some of the material. Nice fabric, I thought. It put what I was wearing to shame. I began to feel somewhat like a slob. I caught a glimpse of myself in one of the full-length mirrors and I could see how cheap I looked. Any one of those fancy suits on a rack seemed more alive and fresh than I was. It also looked a lot more healthy.

"Can I help you, sir?" a salesman asked as I sneaked over to a mirror in the corner, put my books on the floor, and held a black suede jacket up against my chest. I couldn't very well try it on because then I'd first have to get rid of my holster and gun.

"Very becoming, very handsome," he commented upon seeing the garment of my choice.

"You think so?" I said.

"Definitely. Why don't you try it on?"

"Now that I think of it, it isn't very practical for my kind of work. I mean, it would only get dirty and worn."

"What sort of work do you do?"

"It's a hands-on kind of job. Somewhat messy."

"I see. But how about for the evening?"

"The evening?"

"Evening wear. You know, the theater, a dinner party, a date with that certain someone."

I stared at him for a while, saying nothing. He stared back, smiling nervously.

"Maybe the house should come first," I finally said.

"Excuse me, sir? Did you say 'house'?"

"Yes, house. The Georgian house. My house." I handed him the jacket. "One thing at a time. You know?"

He didn't. He stood there, with the overpriced suede in his hands, completely puzzled.

As I put on my sunglasses and was about to head up Bond Street and consider more clothes just for the hell of it, I noticed a poster in front of the Royal Academy advertising the art show they were having. "A House in the Country," it said. I got closer to read more. "Three centuries of art and the English country house." This was just my kind of thing. This was my area, my cup of tea. It was following my recent line of thought.

So for the first time since I was small I walked into a kind of art museum and looked at pictures on a wall. As a kid my mother would take me along with her on trips to the city to visit her older sister. Aunt Peggy, a retired teacher married to a dull but rich dentist, couldn't stop educating people, and she would drag us off to some museum not long after we'd entered her apartment. The museums with only pictures bored the life out of me. I liked the ones that had armor and weapons. Yet here I was now, standing before paintings of mansions and estates—just a lot of houses, grass, and trees, when you really came down to it—and I was having something resembling a good time. I found that if I stood close to a painting and stared at it for a while, I'd feel that I was part of it in a way. Maybe I was going a bit mental, but that was the effect. I'd take in a Georgian house—and they were all over the place in this exhibition—and I'd imagine myself on the grass there in the countryside, viewing the house from a distance.

One house particularly appealed to me. It was all white and had very big and very tall windows. Inside the house you probably felt that you were outside. The rooms were probably huge. You could pace and pace and not bump into a daybed or an easy chair. You could pace *around* the daybed or easy chair. You had space to roam. Enough space to circle things, sort of take little trips around them. I moved even closer to the picture, my nose getting very near to the surface. It was as if I wanted to enter the picture. God knows what I was thinking.

"Excuse me," someone said to me in a vaguely nasty tone, "but other people would like to look too."

I turned to see a red-faced, distinguished, obviously wealthy old gent, with a white mustache and a mane of white hair. His face was almost in my face. You're supposed to respect your elders. That's what they'd always drummed into me at home. Forget it. I'd already killed one old man this week. So I gave him an ice-cold stare and told him to bugger off.

"What did you say, sir?" he responded in disbelief.

"I said to bugger off. You've got about a hundred pictures to look at in this place. Go look at the other ninety-nine."

"How dare you? I'll call for a guard."

"Call Scotland Yard for all I care."

He huffed and puffed a bit more, but then he suddenly got quiet as he glanced down at my jacket. It had come unbuttoned in some way and he must have spotted my holster and gun. The man not only moved away from me and the picture—he left the room completely.

"Nice suit," I called to him as he nervously cut through the crowd.

I tried to get back to my favorite house, but the annoying old coot had broken the mood. I looked around a bit more and then left the building. I wondered, as I reached the street, if they had anything like hit men back in the eighteenth century.

I found myself by the Burlington Arcade so I walked through, stopping every now and then at a shop window that caught my fancy. There was one shop that specialized in knitted wools from Scotland—thick scarves, sweaters, caps with pom-poms on top, real Highlands stuff—and I was tempted to go in and look around, but nobody was inside except a salesman and I didn't feel like being attacked again, so I walked on. It wasn't the season for that kind of thing anyway, but I thought that I just might return in the winter and make a few purchases. After all, I had saved quite a lot of money now and didn't need to be so frugal. I had accounts in a number of banks so nobody would get suspicious about all the cash I was taking in while apparently doing nothing for a living. I hadn't added up these scattered funds in a long time. I'll do that tonight, I thought, heading up into New Bond Street, see exactly where I stand. Maybe I should consider some sound investments. Maybe I should consider the possibility that I've already peaked in my profession and that everything will go downhill from here on in. Yes, I had to think seriously about my future. The time had come.

But the sun was out in London and I still had the day to myself and so I shoved these troubling thoughts far back in my brain. I came to Herbert Johnson, a hat store and a pretty famous one at that, from what I could gather. This time I had the courage to enter and browse around.

They had a nice selection of caps, perfect for the country. This time when a pesky salesman came over, I cooperated and told him exactly what I wanted—the shade, the style, the material. I really sounded like I knew what I was talking about. I couldn't tell him the truth, of course—that I was looking for the kind of cap worn by the man I had just killed. Anyway, he was impressed by my authority. A little lesson in life: with just a bit of effort and nerve you can come across as an expert in anything. I realized that I could be as much of a phony as anyone else.

I tried on quite a few caps before I found the one that suited me, that fit my face. A brownish-tweed country affair, very much like the one the jolly man had been wearing before I'd blown his head apart. I shook off the memory and gave myself over to the image in the mirror—I was the very picture of a country squire.

"What do you think?" I actually asked the salesman.

"Quite becoming, sir. Yes, that seems to be the one. Most definitely."

"Do you think I might wear this in the city every now and then? Or is it simply too suburban?"

"Well, of course, it's meant as a country hat, but I don't see why you couldn't wear it for a stroll in the park on weekends."

"No, you're right. It's more suited to the country." And then I added, out of the blue: "I'll use it when I'm in Derbyshire. I have a house there."

"Ah, how nice. Lovely county, Derbyshire, just lovely. Yes, this would perfect for Derbyshire."

I was amazed by how easily I had lied and how easily the lie had been accepted. This middle-aged salesman, beautifully tailored and obviously trying to appear well-to-do even though he'd probably been a lousy little clerk much of his life, was particularly impressed by the Derbyshire bit. He tried to be casual about it all, but envy was written all over his face. I was tempted to go further and mention my Georgian home, but I figured I'd gotten away with enough already.

As I left the store with my country cap and my wealthy airs, I realized a sort of interesting fact: since so few people knew me, I could play with others just as I'd done with the salesman. I could tell them anything within reason about myself and they'd believe me. Because they had no immediate way of checking. For those people I could be anyone I wanted. And outside of the Firm, "those people" amounted to pretty much everybody in the world.

I walked over to Regent Street and then up into Oxford. Shoppers crowded the sidewalks, their heads bobbing up and down. Traffic filled the streets—chrome and windshields gleaming, buses glowing red. Half of London seemed to be out today. It was like a holiday, as if people were celebrating the sun. I was getting a bit tired and thought I might return home so I took the Tube at Oxford Circus. But as the train rolled on, I thought of my flat and an evening spent flipping the telly and decided I wasn't quite ready to end the day like this. So I got off at Holborn and roamed about Bloomsbury and beyond, moving from square to square—from Bloomsbury to Bedford to Russell. I ended up on a bench in Tavistock Square, a good spot, as it turned out, to have a look at books on Georgian houses, since some of those houses were just across the way, beyond the trees.

The big paperback book on Georgian London was good for all its pictures, but it was just too wordy for my taste. This Summerson guy went on and on, with history and dates, facts about this person and that, and I wondered when in hell he was going to get to the point. *Georgian Houses for All* was more my kind of thing. Simple, direct, no-nonsense, and you learned a lot right away. The author pointed out that if you were to ask a kid to draw a picture of a house, he'd probably draw a Georgian house—that is, a square with big windows and a door. I smiled. The man was right. As a kid I'd made pictures just like that. Who knew then that I was drawing the house of my dreams. I also learned that there were five types of Georgian houses and that those big windows I liked so much were called "sash windows." I even learned something from the back cover of the book, where there was a quote from *The Guardian* about there being over a million Georgian houses still standing in England today. Well, in that case, I thought, I should be able to find at least one somewhere that I can afford.

The sky was growing dim and I now noticed a few windows lit up in the houses facing the park. The darker it grew, the brighter those windows became. I decided to start for home. My street wasn't all that far away so I thought I might as well walk the distance. I could have hopped a cab, but I suppose deep down I wanted my time out to last as long as possible.

It was night when I got back to my flat. The answering machine had four or five messages, though they were all the same, all purposely wrong numbers, all for "Mr. King." Damnit, I said, damnit. The one time I decide to go out and they have to call me half the day. I hurried back downstairs and nearly ran up the block to the phone booth.

Some damn punk kid was standing inside, with the door partially open, jawing away like an idiot. "Fuck 'em, that's what I say. Bloody bullshit is what it is . . . Yeah, right. Real cunts. Tell 'em to piss off. I ain't afraid to tell 'em neither. I ain't afraid of any of 'em. And they know it. They fuckin' know it."

A real genius, I thought. With a real command of the language.

"Other people wanna use the phone," I shouted to him.

"Hey, man, like I'm talkin' here," he replied, and was about to pull the door completely shut when I grabbed it and pulled it completely open and stuck my gun in his face.

"Go mug somebody, you little prick," I said.

"Shitttt!" he cried and beat it fast, dashing across the street like a spastic.

I was surprised I'd blown up like this. I suppose I was more nervous about my situation than I thought. Anyway, I called in.

"It's about bloody time," they said, and went on to tell me that they needed to talk to me, now, in person, to get over to Farringdon Road and wait by the post office for a big black car.

"To take me where?" I said, though knowing full well you don't ask such a question. But their request was more than a little unusual. I didn't like the sound of it. Not at all.

"Just be there," they said.

CHAPTER 4

IT WAS A BLACK LIMO and the two men in black inside were unknown to me. I sat between them. They said nothing. I said nothing, at least for a while. Then I thought I'd break the ice, try to get on their side.

"Nice clear night for a change," I said.

They thought about that for a bit and then one of them replied, "Yeah."

I pressed on. I don't know why. Maybe deep down I was remembering those gangster movies I'd seen as a kid and especially the parts where people were taken for rides. "I'm originally from the States," I babbled, "New York. Don't get me wrong. We have bad weather in New York. The winters are lousy and the summers are miserable. But here, here it's pretty much always bad. I've been here for a few years and I'm still not completely used to it. The other day I was thinking—you know how you do sometimes—I was thinking what if I could enjoy rain and lousy weather, and hate sun and good weather. I mean, just like I was taught to love the sun, I can unteach myself and learn to hate it. Then I'd actually look forward to crummy weather. I'd look at all the rain and say, 'What a beautiful day.' London would become a kind of wet paradise. You know what I mean?"

The big man to my right nodded his head, and then said: "Yeah. You got some kind of point there."

The big man to my left said nothing. I glanced out the window trying to figure out where we were. It looked like we were heading deep into the East End. I thought I'd take a chance now that we were so chummy and all. "You fellas mind my asking where we're going?"

"To the ballet," my talkative pal answered.

The other man laughed loudly. "Hey, I like that one," he said. "Very good, very good. 'The ballet.'" And he laughed some more. "I gotta remember that."

Yeah, I wanted to say, your partner here is ready for a comedy club.

As we traveled down dim streets lined with what looked like old warehouses or factories, I began to tense up. There wasn't a soul in sight. You could knock off someone down here, leave his body lying in the gutter, drive off, and be done with it. Yes, this was the perfect place to commit any sort of mayhem you wanted.

Anxious though I was, some anger was beginning to slip through. All the damn jobs I'd done for them and this was the way they were going to thank me. Because of one little slip! I used to think these people were on my side, were semi-friends, you might say. But now I knew that no one was on my side. I had no friends. I'd been a pro, the very best there was, but that wasn't good enough for these bastards. Christ, I wanted to say, I haven't even lived a full life yet. I haven't even been able to enjoy the fruits of my labor. I wondered, stupidly, if there were any Georgian houses in Hell.

I started to feel a bit relieved when it looked like we were leaving this area behind and heading into more regular streets. I also remembered something that gave me even more comfort: I was still wearing my gun. If they were planning to get rid of me, they would have already taken it.

Sure enough, I was still in one piece when we pulled up to a pub in Whitechapel. The two men escorted me into the place, past a collection of noisy, disreputable types, to a staircase leading to the floor above. We walked through a big room with a long table, probably booked for private parties, to an office in the rear. There was nothing much to it, except cheap wood paneling, a big oak desk, and a small bamboo bar in the corner. Two men were in the room. I'd never seen them before. One, a somewhat overweight character with a fat head, was sitting behind the desk. He had on dark-tinted glasses for no particular reason—the room wasn't that bright. He was smoking a thin cigar and he looked like he was supposed to be important. But I doubted that he was the big boss. The big boss wouldn't use a dump like this for his office. The other man, a first-class creep—thin, with flaking skin, thick glasses, bug eyes, stringy dyed brown hair, and the look of a practicing pervert—was sitting in a fake leather chair by the side of the desk. Another fake chair was facing the desk. That one was for me.

"Sit down, relax," the important man said. His voice was soft, soothing, friendly, almost close to intelligent. It didn't match his looks at all. "Something to drink. Scotch, bourbon, gin?"

"No, thanks," I said. "I'm not much of a drinker."

"Club soda, seltzer?"

I declined. He smiled.

"Yeah, I heard that about you. That you don't have many vices. A pretty straight sort from what I gather.

You gotta respect that. It's rare in our business. You can't imagine the sick freaks we come across. You have to be a goddamn shrink to figure them out. And you can't trust men you can't figure out. That's a fact. But you, you're devoted to your job, from what I hear. And you're damn good at it, right? Nothing screwed up about you. No, sir." He turned to the other man—talk about freaks. "Yeah, Harold, this boy is a regular marksman. Did you know that? He never misses. He aims, fires, and down they go. Doesn't waste one bloody bullet. That's how good he is. One day this boy took out four men from a rooftop. Fired right into their hotel window across the street and took them all out—two of our ex-friends and two of their blokes. They didn't know what hit 'em. Four head shots. Our boy here didn't even have to worry about someone catching up with him because no one was left alive to catch up with him. Is that impressive? I ask you?"

"Impressive," answered the freak.

"Where was that hit? Madrid, wasn't it?"

"Barcelona," I corrected.

"Oh, yeah, right. Good old goddamn Barcelona. I was sick to hell there once. I thought my guts were coming out. That bloody spic food. Oil or some shit. Yeah, I should remember good old Barcelona. I'll bet the food didn't bother you, though. Right?"

"I don't eat much," I said.

"You don't do anything much, do you? Now, look, I'm not complaining. Everybody's made different. You're what you Yanks call 'a cool customer.' Yeah, a cool customer. But I tell ya, maybe it's not so good to be too cool. You might be all tight inside, all knotted, a bloody mess, and then one day, without warning, all those tight springs come loose and you find yourself falling apart. You get my drift? I mean to say maybe even the coolest of us has to relax a little every now and then. I assume you've used our escort girls on occasion?"

"On occasion."

"How'd you find them? Good? So-so?"

"Fine," I said, lying. They'd been too made-up, cheap and cold, not to mention possibly diseased. Women you settle for when you get the urge. In short, trash.

"What do you prefer? I'm curious? Boobs or bums? Or maybe you're a leg man? You have the look of a leg man to me."

I wondered what a leg man was supposed to look like, but, then again, all this bastard was doing was jerking me around. "I like everything," I answered. "The whole package. The whole woman."

"I'm glad to hear it. Because women can relax you. You show me a mental case and I'll show you a man without women. Maybe what you need is more of them. You see, I feel—and correct me if I'm wrong—I feel that you need to relax more, get those springs to unwind in private instead of on the job. You get my drift?" Suddenly his soft voice got loud and nasty, as if his own springs were unwinding. "Because we do not, we most definitely do not want a colossal cock-up like this Derbyshire job. Now maybe I'm being a little harsh here, maybe I'm not understanding completely, but would you mind telling me, would you mind explaining what the fuck went wrong?!"

"Take it easy, boss," the creep advised. "You remember what the doctor said. You know, about you being at risk."

"Screw the doctor. I'm at risk just being in this goddamn business. Never mind my bloody heart. I could walk outta here tonight and some sharpshooter, like our boy here, could blow my head off. What's the goddamn doctor gonna do for me then—give me a head transplant?"

The two men from the limo had been standing behind me guarding the door. I'd forgotten all about them. I was reminded when the comedy fan burst out laughing at the boss's line. "Hey," he said, "I like that. 'A head transplant.' I gotta remember that one. A head transplant."

"Shut the fuck up," the boss said.

He took a few puffs on his cigar, which stank like something dead. The puffs, though, seemed to do him good, because he soon got all soft again. "Excuse me," he said, returning to me. "I've had a lousy day. The wife is sick. My daughter is screwing around with some turd. Family life, you know?" I nodded, but didn't know. "Now, you were going to explain . . ."

I gave him the same story I'd given over the phone, except this time I didn't need to be discreet about the ending, because he knew all the gruesome facts already. "Believe me," I concluded, "I had no other choice. It was unavoidable. Anybody else would've done the same thing. If you'd been in my shoes—you yourself—I think you would have done the same thing."

"I'll never be in your shoes, my friend," he said firmly.

I'd gone a bit too far here. "Just a figure of speech," I explained. "I'm just trying to stress—"

"Okay, okay. Enough." He picked up the stink weed again. Puffed again. He leaned back in his chair and grew thoughtful. "Look," he said, "I personally don't care who you kill. If you have to kill somebody, well, then, kill him. So long as it's not me you're killing or my family, I don't much care. Maybe that's being heartless, but it's honest. There're too many damn people in this bloody country as it is, and this city in particular is getting too overcrowded, what with all the foreigners, blacks, towel-heads, homeless vermin. It's enough to make you sick. I'm speaking personally here. Life isn't all that precious to me. I can take it or leave it. But my own opinion is one thing. The Firm's opinion is something else again. And I work for the Firm. Like it or not, I have to do things their way, and I have to worry when they get worried."

He paused a bit for a few more puffs. Funny, I thought, I never finished college, never had a really wise professor. Maybe this is the closest I'll ever get—listening to a lecture by this puffed-up bag of garbage. The business depressed me. To think that this was the continuation of my "higher education."

"Your little Derbyshire fiasco has caused us some embarrassment and some trouble. At this point, we don't know how much trouble. The press is crying for blood. All the usual crap about cracking down on crime, mob violence, demanding the villains be brought to justice, blah blah blah. They get people worked up with all their self-righteous crap. And that's all it is—crap. They don't give a flying fuck about justice. All they care about is selling newspapers. Believe me, I know the press. They give bullshit a bad name. But the unfortunate thing is that too many people believe them.

"You see, if you had fucked up this way in the city, I don't think it would have caused such a stink. After all, city life has its hazards. You wanna live here, you gotta take your chances. Sometimes people get caught in cross fire. Sometimes they're hit by stray bullets. It doesn't happen here like in New York, which is the fuckin' Wild West, but it happens. And, of course, we had all those crazy mick bastards running loose blowing off heads, legs, and dicks any time they felt like it. But it's all part of living in good old London. You understand.

"Like I said, if this old man had been shot here, I don't think it would've been noticed so much. Nobody would've been happy, of course, and there would've been some bad press, but the fact is it wouldn't have been unusual enough to make a really good story. He was a very old bugger too, so it wasn't as if he had years ahead of him. 'Old Man Killed in Street Shoot-out.' That would have been it. But what happens instead? The old bugger gets his head blown off in some fuckin' field in Derbyshire. You see the drama here? The oddness? When was the last time you heard of a pensioner being gunned down in a field in Derbyshire, or, for that matter, in any bloody country place? You get my drift? Nothing much ever happens in places like Derbyshire. Mostly what they get in the counties are serial lunatics. And that's because of boredom more than anything else. You stay in the country long enough and either you grow brain-dead or else you turn into a fuckin' madman. You begin to hate your wife or girlfriend or maybe even your very own mum. And before you know it, you're roaming the countryside chopping up women. Very sick, but there it is. And yet when you look at it, these lunatics are pretty rare. Maybe one turns up every two years, three years. Maybe that's because most people get so brain-dead in the country they don't even have enough energy to go crazy."

He paused again and this time motioned to the men at the door. "I'm dry. Pour me a Scotch. One ice cube." He was soon sipping his drink. Again he offered me one. Again I declined.

"Where was I?" he asked.

"Serial killers," the creep answered.

"Right." He turned to me again. "Well, you've seen the papers. They all ran a picture of the two bodies in the field. I must admit, those bodies did look strange lying there in the middle of nowhere. Damn strange. One paper I saw had two pictures—a close-up of the bodies with their blasted heads and a big, wide picture of the field, taken from far away, with what looked like these two black specks in the center. They drew a circle around them in white so you knew for certain that these were the stiffs. Did you see that photo? You could make out the whole countryside and all this grass, and then these bloody black specks. It looked damn weird, if I have to say so myself."

"I saw that one too!" announced the comedy fan. "It stayed in my head. I sort of got a kick out of it. It looked—"

"Shut up, for Christ's sake," the boss told him. "You see what I'm saddled with here?" he said to me. "You see why I can appreciate someone like you?" He then paused as he tried to calm down. "Yeah, this field business was very unfortunate for all concerned. I'd bet, I'd almost bet that if only Parker had been found in that field nobody would've cared all that much. Everybody knew he was a no-good, crooked bastard, especially the cops. And they don't care if we kill our own. As long as we keep the slaughter contained, keep it in the family, they couldn't care less. A good thug is a dead thug. Then again, if only Parker had been shot they might not have figured it for a hit at all. They might've taken it for an accident. After all, people go hunting in the country. There's not much else to do. Hunting is a little like going crazy, when you think of it. I mean, even killing people makes more sense—they've crossed you, gotten in your way, challenged you. But shooting up a bunch of rabbits or birds that have nothing to do with you or your business and aren't even much good to eat—that's perverted, if you ask me. Anyway, people might have thought that Parker had been shot by some stupid cockeyed hunter—the fool fires at a bird or rabbit, but he drops Parker instead. It's possible."

So is life after death, I thought wearily.

"But while an accident like that might happen to one bloke, having it happen to two blokes is a little too much of a coincidence. Particularly when they were both shot in the head. You gotta figure then that somebody was aiming at them. You see what I mean?"

I nodded. This man was brilliant.

He paused awhile to sip his Scotch and to give that overactive brain of his a rest. "To make matters worse," he continued, now that he was refreshed in body and mind, "the old bugger was one of those beloved sorts. Everybody in the area knew him. He was like some bloody mascot. Everybody's friend, the milk of human kindness, all that. What in hell he was doing with a thieving, betraying shit like Parker is beyond me."

"This man Parker," I chimed in, feeling that I should participate more, "he looked fairly jolly to me. But then, I never knew him."

"Jolly? You're right, he *was* jolly. The jolliest son of a bitch you'd ever want to meet. That was his whole thing. He'd act like your best mate, smile, laugh, put his fat arms around you, while all the time he was robbing you blind. He'd kill you with warmth, fuckin' kill you. Believe me, you did the world a favor when you took out that piece of shit. It's just too damn bad you had to take out that lovable old fart with him."

As far as I could see, we were right back at square one.

"You see, we consider ourselves a business organization. We have branches all over the world, just like any giant corporation. That's the way we like to be seen. We're not all that different, when you think about it. Like them, we make legitimate deals and not-so-legitimate deals. Like them, we have good businessmen and not-so-good. Nice guys as well as vicious bastards. True, our methods might sometimes seem a bit on the extreme side, but, I ask you, when some company tells a man that he's finished after him putting in some twenty bleeding years of his life, isn't that just like killing the poor, pathetic old sod? It's worse, if you ask me, because he was a good man, a company man, he never harmed a friggin' soul. At least we permanently retire pricks. You get my drift?"

I nodded. The professor had some kind of point here.

"So blowing off the head of a harmless old bugger isn't exactly good for what you might call our corporate image. You understand?" He finished his drink. "I could do with a refill," he told his men.

The comedy fan immediately sprang into action. "More ice?" he asked.

"You hear this man? You see what I'm saying?" the boss commented to me, as if we were old friends, and then returned to his thick-headed dog: "There's more than half a cube left. So why would I need more ice? If I wanted a glass of bloody water, I'd ask for a glass of bloody water." He shook his head at me. "Unbelievable, isn't it?"

I shrugged a bit. I didn't know what else to do.

"You're a super-intellectual compared to this bloody lot," he said.

He was breathing very heavily, as if he had been running a race, so he took a brief rest. Perhaps he remembered that his fat heart was at risk.

We all listened to him breathing. Minutes passed. I thought I could detect, dimly, the mass chatter in the pub below.

"So," he finally said, looking directly at me, "the question is: What do we do with you now? You have any suggestions? I'd appreciate any thoughts you might have on the subject."

I said nothing. I assumed he was yanking my chain again.

"No, huh? Well, that's understandable. This is the second time in a row a job hasn't gone down quite right."

"Second?" I said without thinking.

"You remember Paris? Nothing on the scale of this latest cock-up, of course. But I'd say you had a bit of a problem there, wouldn't you?"

"I got the job done. It was completely clean."

"Oh, yeah, you got it done and it was clean—when you finally got around to it. But what in hell were you doing in the meantime—applying for French citizenship?"

I started to explain but he cut me short. "Forget it," he said, "I know the whole story. The thing is, my friend, you're beginning to slip, you're beginning to lose your touch. Maybe you're even beginning to crack a bit. That's the way it looks to us. And we can't take any chances. So what do we do? We come back to that. We're certainly not going to be unpleasant with you. After all, you've been one of our best men. You've done some fabulous work, simply fabulous. And we can't very well let you go. You know a lot of our business. You've been in on some big hits. We wouldn't want you opening up to the wrong people."

"I'd never—"

"Of course you wouldn't. Of course not. But others might try to get to you if you were a free agent, so to speak. And we have to protect ourselves. We have to avoid that. You understand. So what do we do? We don't think it's time for you to retire. You're still a young man, and you're still the damnedest shot we've ever seen. In other words, we still feel you've got a lot of good work in you. No question about it. The best is yet to come, as they say."

I smiled. I was relieved. But the thought of those future jobs distressed me no end.

"So what do we do? Well, we talked it over—the powers that be, you might say. We considered the options. We debated this and that. And what we decided is that you should go away for a while, leave the country, have a rest, take a long, long trip. In other words, we want to send you on an extended holiday. How does that strike you?"

"What?" I said. I couldn't believe what I was hearing.

"We'd like to rule out Europe, by the way."

"Let me understand this," I said. "You're giving me a vacation? You brought me here to give me a vacation?"

"Yeah. A warning and a vacation. They sort of go hand in hand. Why, were you expecting something else?"

"No," I said, lying. "I wasn't expecting anything. I wasn't thinking about it one way or the other."

"Okay, then. We figured you might like to go to the States for a while. Return to New York. You see, we think it's best if you left the U.K. and stayed away from the Continent completely. Out of sight, out of mind, as they say."

I was still dazed. They were actually giving me a vacation. I was getting time off. It was as if they had sensed my feelings, read my tired mind. Unbelievable. I suddenly almost liked this fat slob.

"How long are we talking about?" I asked coolly, trying not to let on that I was thrilled about abandoning work.

"A month, two months, the whole bloody summer if you like."

Months, I thought. To do whatever I wanted, when I wanted. Christ, this was a miracle. I would have screwed up sooner, intentionally screwed up, had I known this would be the payoff. The States, though. That bothered me. That hardly would have been my first choice. I'd been done with all that.

"New York, huh?" I said.

"Yeah," said the boss. "New York. Your old home. With that tough prick mayor—Giuliani. Good old New York City. The Big Onion."

"What?" I said, and was about to correct him.

"Just joking. Just a little levity. I know—the Big Apple. The Big Bloody Apple."

"Boss?" said the comedy dog.

"Yeah."

"If you don't mind my saying—that was very clever. The Big Onion."

"You know what'd be really clever? You taking a flying leap off Blackfriars Bridge." The boss sipped some more. The comedy dog retreated to a corner. There was obviously nothing he could say right or do right. "So here's the plan," the boss said to me. "We'll put you up at a nice little posh hotel in New York. If you want to travel outside the city, just let us know where you're going and where you'll be staying. But New York's your home, isn't it? You'll probably want to get reacquainted."

"I was brought up outside the city. In a small town."

"In the bloody country?"

"It wasn't exactly the country. It was more the suburbs."

"That'd do it. No wonder you are like you are. But don't look so glum. You can visit your old town, say hello to your mum and dad, give them a bit of a cuddle. They'll be eternally grateful."

"My father dropped dead years ago. Not soon enough for me. I lost touch with my mother. For all I know she's still alive."

"A real warm-hearted sort, aren't you?"

"I'm just being honest," I said.

He smiled. "You're a cool lad. No question about that. Very cool. Then I suppose you have to be, doing your sort of work. I made a few hits in the early days, so I know how it is. I wasn't in your league, but I got the job done."

"Really?" I said with surprise, mainly because he expected me to be impressed.

"Oh, yeah. You might say I'm a self-made man. I started with nothing and worked myself up. Hard to believe, isn't it? Hard to believe considering where I am now."

Where in hell is that? I was tempted to ask. A fat, uneducated, babbling slob who had any number of even more stupid men under him. What am I doing with him, with these people? The question crossed my mind briefly. Because I knew exactly what I was doing with them—I was using my talent, maybe the only talent I had; I was earning a living, taking care of myself; I was working for them to get my Georgian house.

"We'd like you to leave quickly. Today is what? Saturday. We'll put you on a Monday flight. Yeah, Monday should be fine. Right?"

No, in fact. It was too soon. Because here I was enjoying myself for the first time in years, roaming about London at leisure, buying books, looking at pictures, reading, sitting in squares, investigating Georgian houses, and here they were pulling me away from all of this. It wasn't fair. It wasn't right. I wasn't ready. Not yet. As far as I was concerned, I could spend my entire vacation right here.

"If I have to get out of town," I said, "I wouldn't mind spending some time in Bath. I wonder if you might consider that. Nobody knows me in Bath. And nobody is expecting me to go there. Bath isn't one of our places."

"Bath?!" he said. "Bath? What in Christ are you talking about? Why in hell would you wanna go to Bath?"

"They have about the best examples of Georgian architecture and planning in the entire country, probably the entire world. It's a Georgian city. I just read that. And I'm very fond of Georgian houses."

"Georgian houses?! What the fuck— You're joking. That's it. Isn't it? You're fucking pulling my leg." He looked over at his men. "Hey, boys. This lad is tugging a bit on the old cigar. Isn't he?"

"Yeah," said the comedy dog, chuckling carefully.

"A real Oxford wit," said the creep, coming to life for a second. He'd been sunk down in his chair, lost in his own creepy world.

"I'm serious," I said. "Completely serious."

My somber tone must have convinced them. The room went dead.

"I want to buy a Georgian house someday," I explained. "Either here or in the country. So I've been reading up on them. Sort of a hobby. I've learned quite a lot already."

"Have you now? Been reading up? Doing a little study?"

"Yes. Just today, as a matter of fact, I was on Charing Cross Road and picked up a few books on the subject. There's one, *Georgian Houses for All*, that's first-rate."

"Isn't that bloody marvelous? A regular scholar. A regular don."

"I wouldn't go that far." I went on to explain more about my reading and interests and such, but it seemed to make matters worse rather than better. They all kept looking at one another and at me, as if they had discovered a closet lunatic in their midst. "Did you know," I concluded, "that when a little kid makes a picture of a house it's usually a Georgian house?"

"Really?" said the boss, as he glanced over at the creep. "Did you know that, Harold?"

"Can't say I did," the creep answered, staring back weirdly.

"It's true," I said. "The kid draws a square with windows and a front door. That's pretty much Georgian design."

There was silence again. I could hear some shouting and laughter coming up faintly from the pub.

"All I can say, my friend," the boss finally remarked, "is that I'm the one who's drinking here and you're the one who's high. Bath. Georgian houses. Bloody books. Jesus Christ. Maybe we should put you on that plane tonight."

He suddenly stopped being so chatty and chummy. My request and little report had put what you might call a damper on the proceedings. Responding to the boss, the creep took a slip of paper from his pocket and read out the itinerary. I realized that the trip had been completely planned already. I hadn't been expected to disagree with anything.

"Since you're booked on a regular flight," the boss added, "of course you'll have to leave any weapons at home. You won't be needing them anyway. You're on holiday. That's the whole point."

I protested. They couldn't leave me defenseless. I was always on call. You never knew.

"All right, all right," the boss said. "I suppose they're like condoms with you people. You don't know if you'll use them but it's best to have one or two just in case." That wasn't exactly the way I thought of it, but I agreed with the general idea. "A gun will be waiting for you in your hotel room. I suggest you keep it in your holster—and let the goddamn thing stay there."

They gave me the name of a contact in New York in case I wanted anything or had any problems. "Check in with him every now and then no matter what," the boss said. "Just so we know you're still alive." I didn't like the sound of that.

Soon after, I was back in the limo being driven home. The night was cool and clear. The back windows were open very slightly and the wind struck my hair and chilled my skull. Lights and shadows streamed by outside. I sat between the two men again. I suppose this was customary. No one said a word.

Once in my flat I sank down in my easy chair. I was still recovering from the meeting, still troubled by it. It lingered in my head. So I left the light off in the living room and kept a bulb on in the kitchen that reached across the living room carpet, a sort of yellow path in the darkness. I just sat there.

I hadn't expected a boss in the organization to be so common. All he was was a bloated thug. No, he couldn't be a big boss, but rather a sub-boss. I pictured the real bosses, the main bosses, as resembling distinguished business executives, men who lived on country estates or in penthouse flats overlooking Mayfair or Belgravia or in terraces in Regent's Park or in Georgian town houses with views of leafy squares. I pictured them as men of some intelligence and taste, men of some depth and mystery. I think I had to picture them this way. I couldn't accept the idea that I might be working for simple, everyday lowlifes. Because that would make me, as a hired hand, something less than nothing.

I was grateful for the vacation, happy, relieved, any number of things, but I wished they had allowed me to decide on my own destination. Even on holiday, I couldn't really get away from them. They had picked the city, the hotel, the airline. And I was still expected to report in, to keep in touch. They couldn't seem to let me go. I wondered if it would always be like this, even in retirement.

The more I thought about returning to New York, the more I accepted it. I had no choice, anyway. I tried to convince myself that the trip might do me some good. I'd be going back to where I started, to the beginning of my story. I might be able to remember the way it was, the way I was before I'd embarked on my career. No work, no marks, no nothing; I'd be able to contrast the old me with the new. Yes. This might be just what I needed. A good shock to the system.

Sunday was another beautiful day. I took the Tube up to Hampstead, maybe my favorite section of the city, even though I'd been there only a few times. I liked the village feel to the place, the hilly streets, the quaint old houses, the little shops. You could rest there, be lost in charm. You were safe. Since I was going off for a while, I thought I'd pay my respects. So I said good-bye to those old houses and hilly streets and little shops. And when I reached the pond and the Heath I said good-bye to them as well and to London spread out in the valley below. I began to feel sorry for myself. I was about to leave my home for some odd foreign country that meant nothing to me, that had absolutely no charm. A kind of sadness welled up in me there on Hampstead Heath. It was unlike me to weaken this way. Sadness was not part of my makeup.

I noticed a small boy flying a kite with his father. They seemed to be enjoying themselves. I wondered how I would have turned out had my old man taken me kite flying instead of animal hunting. I wondered if I would have grown up to be a kite flier instead of a professional killer. Yes, I wondered what I would be like today had my father been a kite-flying dad instead of a gun-happy son of a bitch. Then again, I hadn't followed in his footsteps completely. I knew my guns, of course, but I really wasn't a mean bastard at heart. Yes, I thought, except for my somewhat destructive occupation, I was really a pretty decent sort.

Good-bye, I said to Hampstead, like a child, as I descended Heath Street to the Tube station.

Part II

CHAPTER 5

THE HOTEL WAS A SMALL, ELEGANT PLACE tucked neatly away on Fifty-eighth Street between Fifth and Sixth Avenues. It was the kind of place you'd hardly notice unless you were right by the entrance, looked inside, and saw the gleaming white marble lobby with its gleaming white front desk—as if guests were checking into Heaven—and its giant mirrors framed in gold and its elaborate chandelier made up of what looked like several hundred fat, glistening diamonds. Seeing all of this you'd then say to yourself, Class, real class, and walk on down the street feeling poor.

The entire hotel—from the lobby to the bathrooms—was decorated with giant china vases overstuffed with flowers of various shapes, sizes, and colors. Living in my posh little suite among all the flowers, scattered petals, and sweet stink, and even doing my business among them in my posh little john, I was reminded of the English gardens I'd seen in *Country Life*, and also of funeral parlors I'd been dragged to as a kid when relatives croaked. I never understood why you bought flowers for a dead person—you could just as well buy the stiff a bottle of beer or a hamburger or a pair of shorts, for all the good it'd do him. I never understood any of it. At my father's wake, flowers were everywhere. In this case, though, I could make sense of it. Because, except for my mother, everybody was so glad to see the old bastard gone that they celebrated by loading the room with floral arrangements. They would have brought in a cake if possible—decorated with his name. I would have blown out the candles. Happy Death, Dad.

Years before he croaked, when croaking wasn't likely to happen in the near future, he told my mother that he wanted to be buried with his favorite rifle. That's not very religious, commented my mother, who rarely disagreed with him. But he insisted, and although I didn't witness it, she placed the weapon in his coffin before it was permanently closed. Over the years he had wiped out half a forest with that goddamn rifle, killing deer, squirrels, snakes, skunks, raccoons, possums, chipmunks, birds. Once, I remember, when we were by a lake, he even tried to shoot a catfish that he'd spotted swimming in shallow water. He missed and I was glad, but as we drove back home he was so angry about his failure I thought he might begin shooting up Main Street as soon as we hit town. You know the way some people need drugs or liquor or cigarettes each day? Well, he needed to slaughter something on a daily basis or else he wasn't happy. I think the old bastard hoped to die by the gun, in some sort of duel. But upstate New York wasn't exactly the Wild West, and as it turned out he dropped dead of a heart attack in his garage, like any other ordinary slob. According to a neighbor, he collapsed while kicking his broken-down old Ford in a fit of anger. You might say he'd fought a duel with a car and the car had won.

The Firm had reserved the room for me under the name Peter Chilton. I liked the name. It was very English, with a certain elegant, aristocratic ring to it. Whenever I'd talk to the man at the front desk or to the rest of the staff I'd exaggerate my English accent so I'd really sound the part. I imagined that I was a man of wealth and property, a descendant of a once-great family, who had nothing much to do now but dip into what was left of the family fortune, laze around the family mansion in Derbyshire or wherever, and go on holiday whenever the leisure at home became too exhausting and the need to flop elsewhere overcame me.

Yes, I had seen such types in the pages of *Country Life*, posing in front of their country houses—Sir Chilton, Lord Chilton, the Duke of Chilton. To continue their lavish, lazy ways, living the life of privileged bums, some of them had to give themselves over to the National Trust and open part of their homes to the public. At least, that's what I understood from *Country Life*. It must be a bit weird having strangers taking guided tours of your house. I thought of tourists viewing my old home and getting a lecture on its history. Here's the kitchen, where the woman of the house got down on her hands and knees each day to scrub the floors. She loved to clean her floors, and she loved to clean her walls and tiles and carpets, her cabinets, her tables and chairs, her bedsteads, her sinks, anything that became dusty, smudgy, dirty. But the funny thing was that no matter how hard she went at it, the place still looked old and grim. And here in this clean but grim kitchen was where her husband, Wild Bill Hickok, ate all his meals and boasted about the latest thing he'd killed or planned to kill. Two strange people, one sicker than the other—a woman who wanted everything clean, and a man who wanted everything dead.

This line of thinking was getting me depressed so I cut it short by taking a little exploratory walk about the neighborhood. I suppose I was having all of these family thoughts because I was back home, so to speak, back in all the sickness. I left for my walk as Peter Chilton. That is, I assumed a quietly dignified Chilton manner as the doorman held open the thick glass door. I acted like people had been holding doors open for me for much of my wealthy, carefree life. I gently strolled up the street, an Englishman out for the day, a classy foreigner in a crowded, noisy, dirty city. I smiled as I remembered the sub-boss's "Big Onion."

A Peter Chilton, I had to admit, would be wearing a far better, a far more stylish suit than the somewhat drab black one I now had on. Maybe a charcoal gray, pinstriped, double-breasted affair, with a red silk tie. I considered doing some serious shopping but realized as I strolled in the warm, somewhat stagnant air that one of those lousy New York summers was on the way and this was hardly the time to be walking around in a confining aristocratic suit. I'd have to look instead for loose, casual clothes, tastefully, richly casual, the kind Peter Chilton might wear on the Riviera or the Greek Isles.

Of course, I also realized that one thing Chilton most definitely would not be wearing was a holster and a .45. But I wasn't about to get rid of them. I didn't have to be that much in character. They'd been left in the bottom drawer of the night table, as promised. I was glad to have a gun at last, because all through the trip over I'd felt naked without one. Although I used a .45 myself, I didn't like the feel of this model—a bit too clumsy, the balance was off slightly, and the trigger seemed too tight. I figured I'd get used to it in time, but, then again, the only way that would happen would be if I knocked off a few people, and here I was, target-free for months. But I couldn't complain. I couldn't complain at all.

Sixth Avenue hadn't changed much. I'd been away from the city for three or four years and from this area even longer. Looking downtown from Fifty-eighth Street, I saw the same big, blank glass buildings I remembered from years ago. Yes, Sixth Avenue still had nothing to recommend it. The fact comforted me a bit. It would have been a shock if the place had turned beautiful in my absence. I didn't want to return to a beautiful city. I wanted it to be as ugly as ever, so I wouldn't feel I'd missed anything by abandoning it.

A blond, muscle-bound guy in T-shirt and shorts—all physique and no brains—rolled past me on Rollerblades. His girlfriend followed. She wore even shorter shorts. They revealed part of her perfectly proportioned bum and all of her incredibly rounded thighs and long, smooth legs, which cried out to be stroked. She had on a Walkman and was jerking her body about to the music being pumped into her brain. The perfect couple, I thought as they rolled like mad to Central Park, two perfect puppet-heads. Aren't you a little old for this kiddie crap? I wanted to shout, and I was really tempted to fire a few shots their way to throw them off balance. I hated people who had it too easy. Why in hell weren't they at work like everybody else?

I remembered when I was out of work. I certainly didn't put on any damn roller skates and take to the streets. I was living in a town a few lousy towns away from home, in a crummy one-room flat in a crummy old boarding house. Me and another guy had just been laid off as clerks at an insurance company. They needed to economize, they said. You were economizing, I reminded them. You were paying me next to nothing and I was working like a damn dog. I paced my room. I didn't Rollerblade. I didn't listen to a Walkman. I spent all my time wondering what was going to happen to me. I thought of having to return home to the cleaning fanatic and the mass murderer and I began to feel very sick. I finally thought of turning a gun on myself. Two days later that vague friend called about the "exterminating" job I'd asked about. He called just in time. No telling what I would have done. I was stupid and weak back then. I didn't realize how valuable I was. I didn't know my worth. I hadn't killed anybody yet.

I noticed a woman standing by the corner drugstore across the street. It was just after noon, but she was dressed up for the evening in a kind of cheap black silk outfit. A tart, I figured, on the early shift. Hoping to lure a horny businessman on his lunch hour or some jerky tourist who needed an oil change. Jesus, I thought, the things people do with themselves. Peter Chilton was above all this. He was here in the city and yet his mind was elsewhere—in the English countryside, in a quaint old library. Yes, Peter was something of an amateur scholar. An art lover. An architectural specialist with a passion for Georgian houses.

I passed some new joint called the Jekyll & Hyde Club, which was a few stories high and looked like a fake dungeon from the outside, decorated with creepy giant faces. Customers—mostly young, mostly tourists—lined the sidewalk, waiting to get into the dumb place, a kind of horror restaurant. I wondered where Jekyll & Hyde came in. Maybe your hamburger turned ugly while you were eating it. Who in hell knew? Some people loved gruesome stuff like this. Violence, death, psychopaths. As long as it was fake. Give them the real thing and they'd be sick to their stomachs.

You might say the Chilton mood was fading fast, so I thought immediately of England again and pleasant places—leafy squares, country lanes and country houses, big white rooms with big fireplaces and easy chairs. These little pictures soothed me, and as I reached Fifty-seventh Street and walked east the tension was almost completely gone. Talk about Jekyll and Hyde. I'd been a native New Yorker on Fifty-eighth Street and here I was now, a block or so away, feeling like a born and bred Englishman. Some young, loud businessmen, cursing like teen punks—"fuck" this and "fuck" that—passed me by, probably on their way to get tanked for lunch. How crude, I thought, Chilton-like, how terribly crude.

I stopped in at the Rizzoli Bookstore, which was wood-paneled and had a kind of English feel to it. Chilton seemed to fit in here. Wealthy snobs roamed about with their wealthy little shopping bags—Tiffany, Gucci, Bergdorf Goodman, Bally. Fashionable foreigners jabbered to one another. I noticed a couple of well-dressed wops jawing away over some wop fashion magazines—they always sounded so damn dramatic, like ham actors. Calm down, I felt like telling them. How in hell can you get so worked up over a few dumb magazines? Chilton suddenly stepped in here. They're always amusing, these Italians, he thought, remembering his various trips to Rome and Venice. Spirited. Fun-loving. Yes, good old jolly Italians. You can always count on them when you're feeling a little down.

I'd never really been in this shop before—years ago it'd always seemed intimidating, or else I was just too easily intimidated back then—so I thought I'd take a tour. I rode the elevator to the top floor and worked my way down. On the first floor the art and architecture books caught my eye. After all, this was Chilton's hobby. I flipped through a fat book on Constable. I remembered this painter from my Introduction to Art class—in my first and only year of community college—but I never understood why he was such a big deal. I mean, he painted fields and hills and trees over and over again. I came across the name again in London and in *Country Life*, where he was a super big deal. Now that I was English and had gotten to know the countryside a bit, these pictures made a lot more sense. They took me away now. They put me in the land. As I concentrated on these paintings, as I sank into them, I had to admit that this Constable character was pretty damn good.

"Wonderful, aren't they?" someone said in my ear. It was another one of those knowledgeable clerks I seemed to be attracting lately. Now that I was growing vaguely intellectual, I was becoming a kind of nerd magnet. Christ. Then again, I tried to sympathize. The world had grown so stupid that people with brains were desperate for brainy company.

"Yes, indeed," I answered in my best English accent, "quite remarkable. One of my favorites."

"One of mine too," he said, bubbling over. Wasn't this all delightfully chummy? "Might I ask," he said, "what part of England you're from?"

"London. That is, I live there now. I was born and raised in West Sussex."

"I'm afraid I don't know West Sussex."

"Wouldn't expect you to," I said jokingly—a regular British wit.

"But I do know London," he said, "at least, some of it. I've been there three times. I'm very fond of the city. It's become a sort of second home."

"Isn't that terrific."

"Where do you live in London?"

"Belgravia. Belgrave Square to be precise. Own the house, actually. It's been in the family for years. Quite lovely, really."

"How wonderful for you."

"Yes, yes, it is." I then thought I'd give him the full treatment. "Of course, I don't stay there the year round. I have some property in Derbyshire. You might say that's my second home. Do you know Derbyshire?"

"Only from books. It's supposed to be very beautiful."

"It *is* very beautiful. Quite breathtaking, really. You would think you were in another world."

He was nearly drooling now. "Have you seen the show at the Frick?" he asked.

"Show?" I wasn't sure what the Frick was exactly or where it was, but I vaguely remembered it as being some kind of museum.

"They had a small Constable show. Of the drawings, and some of the oil studies. You know, I think it might still be on."

"Really. Well, I'll certainly look it up. The Frick is where again?"

"On Fifth Avenue. In the seventies. I can never remember the exact street."

I thanked him for his graciousness. He was thrilled, as if he had just mingled with royalty. He went on some more about returning to London. I had definitely made his day, probably his entire boring week. After all, how often are you paid a visit by Sir Peter Chilton?

I continued to walk east on Fifty-seventh Street. Fifth Avenue was jammed with workers, shoppers, tourists, enough people to make you dizzy. I couldn't remember it ever being so crowded this time of year. It was like Christmas in June. I crossed the avenue and saw that since my last visit they'd made this big new store on the corner, a Warner Brothers shop—selling junk items devoted to Bugs Bunny, Daffy Duck, that sort of nonsense. Good Lord, thought Chilton, how horribly tasteless. This country is definitely deteriorating. Now they're worshipping cartoon creatures. Next thing you know they'll be selling a crucifix with Porky Pig.

I could have gone down Fifth or up, but I decided I'd be better off on upper Madison Avenue, where elegance never seemed to fade. And there were all those town houses in the side blocks—maybe the closest I'd get here to the feel of London. The crowds weren't so intense on Madison and they began to thin out even more as I reached the mid-sixties. I noticed a lot of very clean, tanned, and well-tailored people on the street—I had reached the land of the rich. The men, particularly, looked pampered, as if they had never done anything strenuous in their lives. I wondered how they could get such close shaves. Their faces were so smooth and clear they could have been embalmed. Maybe the rich didn't get beards.

I remembered how when the Firm had first set me up in the city I would travel from my apartment on the West Side to explore the East Side. I didn't like staying on the West Side during my free days. I felt more at home across town. It was a lot more quiet. It was a lot more clean. It was free of common everyday types. It was where I wanted to end up. Maybe in one of those town houses between Fifth and Madison. Yes, even back then I was dreaming of a fabulous home, dreaming of the best.

I walked by a men's shop on Madison, one of those small, beautifully kept stores where everything inside looks like it's never been touched and where if you have the nerve to pick out something and disturb the general order, you'd better damn well buy the merchandise. I used to be intimidated by stores like this as well. Now I didn't give a damn. "You know what?" I could imagine myself telling the classy clerk after he had pulled out all sorts of items for me. "I'm not going to buy anything. What do you think of that? Not one bloody thing."

Anyway, a short-sleeve shirt in the window appealed to me. It was a deep blue with thin white lines that criss-crossed to create little boxes. Some Italian name was on the label. Those good old Italians again.

I told the clerk my size and he removed the shirt from the shelf behind him—very carefully, as if the garment were made of glass. It was, I had to admit, a real beauty and it was definitely for that summer cruise on your yacht or for lounging about your villa in Nice or the Caribbean. I asked the price.

"Two fifteen, sir. And well worth it, I must say. Beautiful material, beautifully made. It's absolutely classic. Absolutely."

I didn't absolutely know what that meant, but I smiled in agreement. Now, if anyone in the old days had told me they were charging two hundred and fifteen bucks for a lousy shirt, I would have told them to piss off in no uncertain terms. But I had come a long way since the old days, and it looked as if I still had a long way to go in terms of treating myself to the good life. I needed a bit of style. And I realized that now nothing much was preventing me from achieving my goal. I never knew it before, but I actually had very good taste. Maybe I had unconsciously picked up little pointers from some of my more stylish marks and the stylish places I had followed them to. Whatever the reason, I had developed an eye for the best. I now had some money to support that eye.

"Heading for Nice soon," Peter Chilton reported to the clerk, "for the summer. Have a little place there. This is perfect for Nice."

"I don't think you could ask for more. That shade of blue, in fact, reminds me of the sea."

"Indeed."

"Perhaps you'd like to see some lightweight slacks?"

I and my two-hundred-and-fifteen-dollar shirt stopped into a coffee shop for a quick lunch. I felt like having a real American cheeseburger and a real American Coke, two of the very few things I'd missed about this country. Then again, I was a lot better off not being tempted by them abroad. Because as tasty as they could be, they also were total junk—pure poison to your system.

The place was crowded so I took a seat at the very end of the counter. It wasn't the best of seats, because I was close to the little open kitchen and smoke from the greasy grill drifted right over to me. But at least, thought Chilton, who was slumming, at least I'm not sandwiched in between two loud, gross Americans. I ordered my junk food, and I must admit that I enjoyed it, munching and gulping away like a pig. I wondered why a simple, crummy burger tasted so good over here and so lousy in London. Partly it was the meat, I thought. Cows here were a lot healthier. They got a lot more sun. But I bet that much of the taste had to do with the grease. Leave it to the Yanks. They had perfected delicious grease and had passed on the recipe to every Greek who owned a coffee shop.

I was amused by one of the Greeks behind the counter. He was huffing and puffing and looked ready to explode at the chef, who seemed to be falling behind on the orders. "Western omelet!" he shouted. "Western omelet!" "It's working!" the chef shouted back. "Where it's working? I don't see it! Where?!" The chef angrily cracked and poured two eggs. "There. Working. There it is." "There it is now. Now there it is. Who are you fooling? Not me, my friend. Not me." The chef muttered something nasty. He was twice as tall and twice as wide as this little Greek worm, who was probably a part owner of the joint. I cheered the chef on in my head. Crush the bastard, I said. No matter who he is, crush him! But just then Chilton, the voice of reason and dignified behavior, stepped in. These people are so ridiculously violent, he thought, shaking his head.

There I am watching this little show and eating my greasy all-American burger when I notice a man sitting at the other end of the counter, the section that sort of curves round the register and then straightens out and runs parallel to the front window. He's stocky, bordering on chubby. He has on a gray business suit and is wearing thick sunglasses. The sunglasses bother me because the shop, what with its big protective awning outside, isn't exactly filled with sunlight, and even if it were, the man is sitting with his back to the window. Nobody else in the place is wearing shades. Not a soul. Yes, the man stands out. No question about it. He makes no sense.

I was almost certain that he was looking at me, but I couldn't be completely sure because, of course, I couldn't see his eyes. All I could see were two big black ovals that were roughly directed at me. I had to know for sure. I had to challenge him. So I turned his way and gave him a good, long stare. I wasn't smiling. Not in the least. It was the old if-looks-could-kill routine. I'd stare down this son of a bitch, whoever he was.

Just then the oddest thing happened. He gave me a nod. And when I didn't respond, he gave me a kind of half wave. Certainly a nervy bastard, I thought. Needless to say, I didn't wave back. Who in hell was this character? I couldn't place him. And I didn't like the looks of him at all. He wasn't so much smiling at me as smirking. At least that's the way I interpreted his big mouth.

"Do I pay you?" I asked the little Greek worm as he passed by with a small bowl of rice pudding. "Pay up front," he said. But I wasn't about to do that, because the smirking son of a bitch was sitting right by the register. I demanded my check as the Greek hurried by again. "Hey," I said, dropping the English accent and sounding like my tough old self, "I'm in a hurry." "So what else is new?" the worm said, not bothering to stop for me. I got the attention of a mild-mannered Hispanic kid who was also working the counter. "I'm very late," I told him. "I had a burger and a Coke so I'm leaving this." I pulled out a twenty-dollar bill and put it on the counter. "That'll cover it," I said. "Hey, that's too much," said the kid. "Don't you want your change?" I told him to keep it as I quickly got up and hurried from the place, not even giving the smirker a glance, but keeping my hand inside my jacket and on my gun.

I moved fast up the street, found a shop window I could pretend to be looking into, and waited him out. Like I said, I had to know. Was he tailing me? I had only just gotten into the city, for Christ's sake. Was he really one of theirs? Could he be one of ours? But why would he be one of ours? Why would he be following me if we were on the same side? Was he some rat I'd crossed paths with when I used to live and work here? Or worse, was he some cop? Or was it just my imagination playing stupid tricks again?

I kept shifting my eyes from left to right, to all the overdone antiques in the window—china birds, urns filled with peacock feathers, little chests and tables decorated with elaborate gold designs—to the coffee shop, roughly half a block away. My eyes traveled over to a big china bowl that contained, for some reason, things that looked like jade eggs, and then they traveled back to the coffee shop, just in time to see the bastard exit. He was heading my way. It wasn't my imagination. I gripped my gun. I stood still, as if posing. He kept coming closer and as he approached he waved to get my attention. I pretended not to notice, but all the while I watched out of the corner of my eye to see if he'd reach inside his jacket. Ridiculous fear, I thought. This is Madison Avenue, after all, not the South Bronx. When people die on Madison Avenue they do it quietly, privately, behind closed doors.

I turned to face him, my hand still on my gun. I wanted to make my position completely clear. I wasn't fooling around. If one of us had to die, it wasn't going to be me. No, sir. But his cheerfulness threw me. If he was an assassin, then he was a hell of a happy one. He opened up his hands to me, spreading his arms somewhat, as if he expected a hug. His smile, I noticed, was really more friendly and dopey than smirky.

"Hey," he said in a booming voice, "how the hell are you? Bob, isn't it? Don't tell me? MacTaggart? MacLeary? No, that's not it? Mac-Something, though. McTeer?

No, wait. . . McAleer! That's it, isn't it? McAleer. Bill McAleer!"

Christ, I thought, I went through all this crap for a case of mistaken identity. I oughta shoot this clown just because of the grief he caused me. I stared at him with hate, saying nothing. Not a word.

"Jerry Miller," he announced, "come on—you remember me. We were at BBD and O together. You were in the Creative Department. I was in Graphics. We always used to run into each other in the john. Both our wives, it turned out, were in therapy since birth. And they both were seeing herbalists. Crazy shit like that. You remember."

I just stared at him.

He began to look a little annoyed. He took off his sunglasses to fully reveal his fat, ingratiating face. "That better? Now do you remember? Jerry Miller. BBD and O. About five years ago."

"I'm going to say this once," I finally responded, "so listen very carefully. I don't know you. I don't know what this BBO is. I'm not married. I don't have a woman, much less a wacky one. And I never ran into you in any bloody john."

"You're kiddin'?" he said. "Come on, you're pulling my leg, right? You gotta be him. You're a dead ringer for him. Maybe you're a little thinner now and a little taller, but you're him."

"Are you saying that I grew?" I asked, smiling sarcastically. I swear I was ready to take out this ingratiating pain and do the world a favor.

"Maybe I just don't remember you being so tall."

"I don't know you, goddamnit," I said emphatically, "and more to the point, I'm glad I don't know you. I'm not him. I'm me. And if you don't get the fuck out of my way, I'm going to do something rash."

"Now wait a minute," he said, sounding both offended and angry. "I was only trying to be friendly."

"Go play with somebody else," I said, and then did something foolish and very unlike me—I unbuttoned my jacket and indicated my holster. "We're not in the same profession. Get it? And you're ruining my day. You've broken the whole bloody mood."

He backed off fast, apologizing repeatedly. The fool couldn't wait to get away. And as he headed down the block, he turned around a few times to make sure I wasn't about to do something rash, like kill him.

It's hard to break old habits. Over the years I had trained myself to be suspicious, to trust no one, to always watch my back. I took this business in stride, though—or so I thought. I rarely got carried away with it. Paris was the exception rather than the rule. I was just naturally cautious. I had developed an instinct for possible trouble. I could go about casually and yet also be on my guard. But I now began to wonder how casual was casual. When I was off the job and seemed relaxed, was I ever truly relaxed? For that matter, was I ever truly off the job? Or was I, in the back of my brain, always prepared for a job-related problem?

These thoughts plagued me as I strolled various streets in the sixties, touring the quiet blocks between Madison and Fifth. When I'd reach Fifth and Central Park, I'd walk up the avenue to the next street, turn the corner, explore that street as I headed for Madison, then go up Madison to the next street, turn that corner, and walk over to Fifth still again. So I weaved in and out, like a snake, trying to enjoy the expensive town houses that lined these side streets, trying to recall London and the London houses I'd come to admire. Chilton, I thought, where in hell are you?

He returned, slowly but surely, as I moved on and the coffee shop encounter began to fade from my mind. I was determined, I vowed in fact, never to allow anyone or anything to break my mood again.

Look at these poor excuses for town houses, he thought, I thought, we both thought. What a mishmash of styles. One house fighting another. No real uniformity, except here and there where a few attached houses had the same facade. I'd learned that word—"facade," and "uniformity" too, come to think of it—from my architectural books. Yes, I was becoming quite the authority.

I moved up and around, up and around, block after block, traveling now into the low seventies. On the corner of Seventieth Street and Fifth Avenue I came to a sort of squat, fenced-off mansion, the kind of thing they did better in Italy or in Paris or in Regent's Park. The trouble with being a world traveler like myself—if you can call it trouble at all—was that you got so accustomed to seeing the best places that when you came across lesser sights they looked like lousy imitations. Anyway, this building was, for New York at least, impressive enough for me to cross the street and investigate.

It was, I discovered, the Frick—yes, the good old Frick that the Rizzoli nerd had gone on about. How's that for a coincidence? Small world, and all that rot. Ah, what the hell, I said to myself, and I climbed the few steps and went inside. In the dim lobby I asked the guard, in my classy English accent, about the Constable exhibition and I learned that, yes, it was still on and would continue for the next three weeks. I could have gone in to see it right then, but I decided to save it for another time, maybe the next day, or the one after that.

You see, I began thinking about how today had gone and about all the days left to my vacation—something like two and a half months. I'd wanted this vacation so much, had even thought about how nice a permanent one might be, but now I wondered what exactly I was going to do with all this time on my hands, all this time with no assignments. I suddenly felt like a retired old bugger with nothing to do, nowhere to go, no one to see. Peter Chilton would never feel like this. No bloody way.

Over the next several days I continued to wander the city. I went downtown to the World Trade Center, which I had last visited years ago, and I saw all the new buildings that had gone up and the riverfront park, where kids and fully grown idiots were skating around on Rollerblades. It wasn't exactly the sort of park you'd see in London—made up, as it was, of concrete instead of grass. I looked at the yachts tied up in the boat basin, from medium-sized models to the big show-off filthy-rich productions. One was so big that it had room for a helicopter on deck. I wondered why in hell anyone would need that on board. I mean, the reason you bought a monster yacht like this was to travel in comfort and luxury on water. Maybe the owner was such a big shot that he had to copter off at a moment's notice to attend some super-urgent meeting on land. Or maybe he was afraid of sinking and figured that this was one way to guarantee escape—certainly a hell of a lot better than counting on a life jacket. Then again, maybe he didn't particularly need the copter at all but kept it around to impress those friends who didn't have helicopters on their boats—which pretty much included everyone he knew.

Another day I strolled about Greenwich Village, which had been invaded by fast-food joints and chain stores. The streets were even crummier than I remembered them, having a kind of dirty, shabby look. They were filled with wandering kids and a collection of tourists, both foreign and domestic—fatheads in shorts. I think I even prefer Carnaby Street to this, thought Chilton. I walked east to Washington Square Park and thought how poorly the park, the square, compared to those in London. No charm, no quaintness, just some grass, trees, and concrete, and a lot of people bumming about. Now really, could you imagine food vendors and ice-cream trucks in, say, Belgrave Square? Good Lord, no. And if that arch was supposed to recall the Arc de Triomphe, it came across as only a cheap and shrunken imitation. Pathetic, Chilton said to himself.

I left the park and headed downtown into SoHo, which, except for all its shops, looked little like Soho in London. Here you had block after narrow block of big, dirty old loft buildings. They cast some shade, at least, and I was glad to get out of the sun, which had been growing pretty intense in the park. I suppose now that I'd become a citizen of London I just wasn't accustomed anymore to this kind of steady sunshine and heat.

I started running into crowds again, particularly on Broadway, Spring Street, and West Broadway. More out-of-towners and foreigners. Traveling from clothing shop to clothing shop. Checking out the jewelry, sunglasses, scarves, leather goods, T-shirts, socks, and other junk being hawked by sidewalk peddlers. You couldn't get away from these visitors. You couldn't get away from people here, period. "Check it out!" Summer in New York, I thought, without a doubt the worst time to be in the city. "Hey," an aggressive peddler called out to me, displaying an attaché case filled with classy junk watches, "check it out, my man. You can't go wrong. All the best brands. Check it out." "I'm not your man," I told him in my best Chilton manner. "And if that's a Rolex, I'm Prince Charles."

This whole area had become a kind of check-it-out neighborhood. Check out the shops. Check out the peddled goods. Check out the food. Check out the people. Check out the art. Then again, the whole bloody city was devoted to checking it out. Since my last visit the city had added many more things to check out. That's what you did here. Day and night. Night and day. You checked things out.

I'd been drawn to SoHo, which had never been one of my favorite spots, by a little guidebook given to me by the desk clerk back at the hotel "to add to my enjoyment of the city." The book reminded me that SoHo was an art center. This had never meant much to me before, but now that I was beginning to appreciate architecture and a bit of art it was suddenly of some interest. I'd only actually been inside a gallery once or twice before, probably in Paris or Rome, and it wasn't to look at art but rather to look at someone who was looking at art.

Unfortunately, now that I was finally down here in "the heart of the New York art world," as the guidebook put it, I felt tired and didn't fancy the idea of waiting for an elevator or walking up several flights of stairs to visit some gallery in some loft. But luck—if you could call it that considering the payoff—luck was with me as I headed down a long, quiet block somewhere between the mess that was Spring Street and the mess that was Canal. I happened to pass a gallery that was on street level, with huge glass windows and one lone visitor inside. This was definitely my kind of place.

I had expected to see a bunch of paintings, but there were only two, plus some other stuff on the walls and floor. I stared at a dozen or so rubber bands tied together to make a kind of chain. They were hanging from a spike that had been nailed into the wall at about eye level. Not far away from this bloody nonsense were a dozen or so glass vials linked together by string and hanging down like a drug addict's necklace. The string was tied to another spike. I moved on to a dark, disgusting thing lying on the floor in the corner. It looked like a beehive that had collapsed or some sort of rotting giant cocoon. Whatever it was supposed to be, it got more nauseating the more you looked at it. Christ, I said under my breath. I quickly glanced at the other bits of crap displayed here and there and went over to the paintings on the back wall. Now understand this—the walls of the gallery were white, pure white. So what was hanging on those walls? Two big white paintings. They had words on them, though. I'll grant them that. Words done in blue block letters and positioned in the center of each canvas. One read HOVERING. The other THE WORLD AS IDEA.

I stood there for a while looking at these masterpieces and wondered what Constable would have said about them. I glanced back at the other stuff I had taken in and suddenly felt that there was something familiar about it all. It reminded me of something, something from the past. And then it hit me. What it reminded me of was the dayroom of the mental hospital where Uncle Warren had ended up. My father had dragged me there for a visit when I was a teenager, assuring me that it would be "better than a Broadway show," a rare chance to see the inside of a genuine nuthouse and be entertained by a collection of first-rate lunatics. As it turned out, there were only a lot of depressed, mumbling people, like Uncle Warren, who had never recovered from the death of his nagging wife, and I tried not to look at them, even though good old Dad nudged me to take in a number of the poor souls who broke him up: "Hey, look at that crazy bastard in the corner talking to the chair." I looked instead at the walls and side tables, where patients displayed their artwork—sick clay figures and shapes, weird cutouts, senseless watercolored words on paper. Yes, that's what I was viewing in this gallery—the products of bloody occupational therapy.

I went up to the desk, where a young, precious, redheaded guy in a tan summer suit was looking at slides in a viewer. "Excuse me, young man," I said, in my most aristocratic manner, "but I wanted to inquire about the paintings over there."

You could see that he was impressed by the accent, because he immediately put down his work and stood up, as if he were about to salute. "Yes, sir, how can I help you?"

"Could you tell me the price of the two paintings?"

"Oh, yes, you mean Andrew's pieces. Really striking, aren't they? Everyone is just sort of drawn right to them. Are you familiar with the artist?"

"No, not really. I'm not here very often. Just a visitor."

"Oh, I'm sorry. Of course you are. Well, Andrew—Andrew Lipps is the artist—Andrew had his first solo show with us in December and it was extremely well received. Paul Godfrey—*the* Paul Godfrey—reviewed it for *Art Today*."

"Indeed," I said, though I'd never heard of either this Godfrey character or *Art Today*.

"Yes, it was one of the few times Paul ever came in here. As you know, he's very choosy and usually hates absolutely everything." I'm not surprised, I wanted to say. "Well, he gave the show a very positive review. Maybe he didn't love it completely, but he loved it enough. And for him to love anything, even a little, is very rare. Someone once said that he even gives his wife a negative review." He laughed. So I played along and chuckled halfheartedly. "Paul did say that Andrew was definitely an artist to watch."

Oh, yeah, I thought, I can't wait to see what other words this clown is going to put on canvas—"Bullshit" would be appropriate.

"I have copies of the review if you'd like to have one?"

"No, that's fine. I was just curious to know what the paintings are selling for."

"Oh, they're very reasonable now, even a bargain if you consider what's available by new, young artists in other galleries. They're twelve thousand each. And they're still available. It's a great opportunity to be there at the beginning."

The beginning of what? I wanted to ask him. Selling crap to suckers for twelve grand? I was very tempted to tell him what I thought, to call a spade a spade, a con a con. I was surprised that I could get so worked up over such petty business. I mean, here I was, getting angry over art. But I did have the urge to tell this gallery boy that Constable, with all his fields and trees and clouds, was a hundred times more interesting than his prize piss artist. Constable didn't paint signs, for God's sake, he painted pictures. He'd probably worked like hell to paint all of that grass, to make a field look like a field, and here's this Andrew character getting away with slapping down a few stupid words on white nothing.

I managed, however, to control myself, to thank the pretentious kid, and to leave this baloney behind me. After all, I reasoned, a few months ago I couldn't have cared less about Georgian houses, but here I was, sort of studying their history like a student and actually getting some pleasure out of it. Except for admiring a town house here and there, I'd never much cared about houses in general. At least, I'd never focused on them like I was focusing now. They'd always been in the background, like traffic, like the clouds, the sky. And as for Constable, who would have thought a few months back that I'd be lingering on paintings of a countryside, or, for that matter, on any paintings period?

Yes, you never knew. Maybe there'd even come a time when I'd appreciate the crap in that gallery, see it as something I'd like to own and live with. I doubted it, but who could tell? All I knew now was that I had to—as they say on chat shows—keep myself "open to new experiences." This, according to these TV experts, was the way you "grew as a person." And I wasn't sure that I'd done much growing in my line of work. Of course, I'd grown into a better shot than I'd ever been. I'd grown into a first-rate professional. That was the only growth I knew.

One of those stifling New York summers was now right around the corner and at this point that corner was, you might say, about half a block away. The temperature and humidity were building, the air was smelling more and more like burning rubber, and breathing was getting harder each day. In a few weeks, you'd walk a block and pass out. In a few weeks, you might just as well be in Cairo. I had to be glad that I wasn't here on business. I remember that when I'd moved to the city from upstate they'd given me a few lousy summer jobs. Back then I could have just stuck my gun under my waistband and left my shirt—one of those bright summer sports numbers—hanging outside my pants and in that way conceal my weapon. Or I could have worn an ankle holster and hidden a smaller gun all the way down near my feet. But I didn't want to take any chances reaching for a gun that was not immediately accessible. I had already gotten used to carrying a regular gun in a regular holster worn in a regular place. So there I'd been, some years ago, in New York City in ninety-five-degree weather wearing a jacket—buttoned, no less—as I tailed a mark who was probably dressed in something like Bermuda shorts. My profession has its drawbacks and this is one of them.

Even now, jobless as I was and far from my adopted city and vengeful blokes, even now on holiday I felt the need to carry a gun and wear a jacket to cover it. One morning, though, I'd actually left it behind in the hotel—the whole package, in fact, both gun and holster. But as I walked toward Fifth I spotted a black van parked across the street. It was the third time I'd seen that van on the block and it looked just as out of place now as before. The windows were coated black so you couldn't see inside, couldn't tell whether it was manned or empty. It obviously wasn't a delivery van. And it wasn't the kind of vehicle people in this area would use as a private car. So what in hell was it, and what was it doing here? I paused and pretended—in case I was being watched—to look for something, first in my jacket and then in my pants. I patted the pockets as if checking on a wallet or a set of keys, said "Damnit," as if the search had been in vain, turned, and hurried back to the hotel. A nice performance, I thought. I immediately went up to my room and put on my holster and gun. The next day the van was gone, but I kept wearing my gun.

Since I wasn't ready to abandon my weapon, I thought I'd make things easier on myself by buying a really lightweight garment to wear over it. I strolled over to Bloomingdale's to see what they had to offer. This store used to make me nervous, dizzy. Too many distractions in the place—too many mirrors and fancy, over-decorated counters, too much glass and too many gleaming things, too many customers rushing about like giant ants. If you were unlucky enough to have to track someone in there, you'd go bloody nuts. Back in those days as a mere customer I couldn't afford Bloomingdale's prices and usually ended up right across the street in what used to be Alexander's, which was dull and cheap. Good old Alexander's. I was a bit sad to see that it'd closed. The store, after all, had been a part of my late youth.

Bloomingdale's was still where it had always been and it hadn't changed in the least. The joint was the same instant headache I remembered. Glass, lights, reflections, people by the truckload. You wondered what the store was giving away to attract this crowd. I cut around the counters and the heavily made-up girls hawking cosmetics in the aisles and sought out, like an explorer in some weird department store jungle, casual menswear. I finally found the area in the basement and started going through lightweight designer jackets, removing from their hangers those that appealed to me and telling a pain of a salesman repeatedly to leave me in peace. He seemed annoyed that I had a few jackets draped over my arm and that I was still looking for more. "Are you absolutely sure I can't help you, sir?" "Good Lord, young man," I finally said in my best Chilton manner, "am I speaking in a foreign tongue?"

Unfortunately, I eventually had to ask him where the fitting room was. He seemed puzzled.

"But there's a mirror right here, sir," he said.

Yeah, I wanted to tell the pest, but I'm wearing a big

gun and if you want me to scare the hell out of all your yuppie customers, I'll gladly take off my jacket. "I'm used to a bit more privacy in London," I explained instead, Chilton-like, "in somewhat more exclusive shops."

"Oh, well, of course, it's just that I thought . . ." He trailed off at this point, clearly intimidated.

I realized that I had a gift for intimidation. "This mass of humanity is rather distracting," I continued. "You understand, my good chap."

Well, I ended up in a private room with a bench and a full-length mirror. I knew that you were watched by security people in places like this, and I wondered how my .45 was going over. They probably figured I was a cop and would let it go at that. Besides, you don't mess with a man with a gun if you're working for peanuts as a fitting-room peeper.

I tried on the five jackets. The problem with all of them, except one, was that they were so thin and light that my gun and holster created a very noticeable bulge. It looked very peculiar, like some sort of horror-movie growth. And for anyone in the know, I might just as well walk around with a name tag reading HIT MAN. So I had to settle on the heaviest light jacket—a kind of tan burlap-like number, with an Italian label, but made in Colombia. Or else I could just forget the whole thing and continue to wear my dark blue blazer, which was almost as light in weight, and which had an English label and was actually made in England.

I decided to forget the whole thing. I was glad to leave Bloomingdale's and get back outside, even with the heat and rotten air. I walked over to Madison, but instead of continuing west and returning to my hotel I headed up the avenue. I felt restless, like I didn't want to stay in a room alone. I never used to mind this all that much. I couldn't figure what had come over me now. I just knew I had to be outside, had to move about, do things, whatever they might be. Don't get me wrong, I wasn't missing work. I didn't want all that again. I was a bit tired of all that. Yet I couldn't help but wonder if I wanted all this—I mean, the leisure, the roaming, the strolling, the drifting. When you were on a job there was a beginning and an end. It was like you were living a little story. And when the story was over and a body was lying dead somewhere, you felt relieved, satisfied. You had gone through something. On the job I knew what I was doing. Now, here in this city, on holiday, on Madison Avenue, I wasn't sure what I was doing or why.

It seemed that no matter where I traveled in Manhattan, I always ended up back on the Upper East Side. Maybe because the area, the town houses, reminded me vaguely of home. That's the way I thought of London now. As a home. At least, it was more of a home than this city had ever been. I never thought I'd miss London. I had never missed any place. In fact, I'd trained myself not to miss any place, person, thing. If such a feeling had ever existed in me, it hadn't been part of me for a long time. Besides, it couldn't be. My kind of work wouldn't permit it. The more sentimental you got, the more easily you'd soften, stray, slip up, and get yourself killed. I was on Madison in the seventies again when I passed a small, narrow shop I hadn't noticed before. Even now I only glanced at it, was about to leave it behind, but then did a double take.

Some books in the window caught my eye. All of them had pictures of buildings on the front. Which, as it turned out, was only natural since the store specialized in books on architecture and interior design.

I walked in, and right by the front door, as if put there just to lure me farther inside, were bookshelves labeled GREAT BRITAIN. They held books on Georgian houses and Tudor houses and Queen Anne houses, on British architects like Wren, Hawksmoor, Nash, Vanbrugh, Soane—all these names, I thought, all this to learn—and books on country houses in places like Kent and Surrey and on country churches and Gothic cathedrals and market towns and Cotswold villages and the building of Victorian London. There was so much here that I didn't know what to look at first. But, of course, I finally settled on the Georgian stuff, flipping through several books and looking at the photos and drawings. I must have appeared quite worked up, like a drunk who had found several cases of his favorite liquor.

And then, suddenly, unexpectedly, my eyes came upon a title that stood out on a lower shelf like a special prize waiting to be discovered by me and me alone. "Hey!" I said to myself in amazement and in a voice loud enough to be heard by the two glum young women behind the counter. The spine of the book read *Bedford Square*. Yes, it was a large picture book—but with plenty of words as well—completely devoted to the houses of Bedford Square. Of all places. A mere hop, skip, and a jump from where I lived.

The book had been published in London and was by a Brit named Andrew Byrne and it looked very scholarly.

There was no price on the jacket, but scrawled in pencil on the top of the inside page was: "Out of print, $70." A while back if someone had told me they were charging seventy bucks for a book that was less than one hundred and fifty pages, I would have told them in no uncertain terms to bugger off. But I was in a weirdly excited mood, ridiculously glad to have this book in my hands, and I didn't want to let it go. If they had been asking two hundred dollars for the damn thing, I think I would have paid the price. I had to have this book and I had to have it now. I saw it as perfect for my research and study, and very practical too, because I could read about Bedford Square and then visit it in person, see firsthand the buildings that were pictured and discussed. Deep down, I think the idea that I would have something to do when I returned to London, that I would have a real pastime, a real hobby, appealed to me in a big way.

Maybe I had gone a little crazy. Because I bought the book and another one as well, called *Life in the Georgian City*, by Dan Cruickshank and Neil Burton. The second book also featured houses in London—in Bloomsbury, on Great Jones Street, and a few others around town, all easy enough to get to. More places to visit, I thought. I have my work cut out for myself. Yes, I was happy with my selections, so much so that when I took them to one of the glum women at the counter I held up the Bedford Square book and said, "I live in London, not far from Bedford Square. I come all the way over here and find this—quite amazing, isn't it?" To which she said nothing and barely cracked a smile. You snotty, damp bitch, I wanted to tell her, don't you realize that Sir Peter Chilton is lowering himself to make small talk with you, a mere clerk? And if that didn't impress her—because she probably got a lot of aristocratic types on Madison Avenue—I could simply pull out my gun, shove it in her glum face, and strongly suggest that she smile back.

But my mood was so good that it couldn't be shaken by a little deadhead clerk. The anger passed in a few seconds. Funny the effect a couple of books could have on me. When I reached Fifth I crossed the street and walked until I came to an entrance to Central Park. The sun was bearing down hard. I searched around until I found a spot shaded by trees and also fairly free of pigeon shit. The bench was one of those extended types that wrapped around the concrete path. Several old geezers were wasting away here and there along the length of it. Although I felt funny about joining this near-expired group, I badly wanted to study my books and enjoy some leisure while doing so.

Anyway, I sat down and I read, occasionally glancing down at the shadows of the leaves on the concrete. With a little imagination I could pretend I was sitting in a square back home. Nice afternoon, I thought at one point, thoroughly relaxed.

I found it dull to stay in my hotel room and read, so I took my books out with me each day. I took them with me the way I took along my gun. You might say the gun and the books were traveling companions. I tried to move about when reading—that is, to be doing something other than merely sitting around and losing myself. So I read on the Staten Island Ferry while taking little breaks to watch the wavelets and the boats in the harbor, to notice as we moved across the water how Manhattan was getting smaller and Staten Island larger. I read and looked about on the Circle Line boat, which took tourists around Manhattan Island—and I now considered myself a tourist, a foreigner. I also read on buses and in cabs. I read on the subway, the few times I took it—I'd forgotten how stifling hot a New York subway station could get in the summer.

If I had to sit still and read, I'd pick interesting places to sit by or in, places I could explore when I'd grow tired of sitting still and reading. I sat and read, for instance, in various spots in the Metropolitan Museum of Art. When I felt the need for a break and some exercise, I just got up and roamed the museum.

I looked at paintings mostly, although I did visit the old, historic, fake rooms they had put together. Most of them were done up with fancy wallpaper, fancy moldings, fancy furniture, and fancy chandeliers. It was all a bit much for me, like I was being stuffed with birthday cake. The French, particularly, never knew when to stop. Louis XIV and all that ornate crap. Leave it to the frogs—they were poofs then, and they're poofs now. Anyway, give me fairly big, fairly simple rooms, with really big windows, and I'm happy.

The paintings were more my cup of tea. Some of them, anyway. They certainly had enough, so you were bound to find at least a few things you liked. I wasn't big on the Italian stuff, the religious pictures in general, with all these saints and angels flying about. They were usually flying about Jesus Christ, who was usually dying, dead, or coming back from the dead. Who in hell ever dreamed up this hammy character? Christ, give me a break. All I know is if you kill somebody he stays killed. I'd like to see old Jesus survive a few shots from a .45. And I didn't appreciate all the religious light beams coming down from the sky and all the saintly halos. My mother, though, loved this nonsense. She was a real churchgoer. And in her handbag she kept a whole collection of cards that had pictures of Jesus and Mary, something like baseball trading cards for the devout. Some of them she had gotten in church, others at wakes she'd attended. Yes, she couldn't wait to get to Heaven and see all the angels, saints, and dead relatives. She was half here and half up there. Too bad the half down here hadn't been able to stop her gun-happy husband from torturing me.

I moved into a gallery where they had quite a lot of landscapes. By Dutchmen. I liked these a lot. None of the heavenly crap that filled the wop paintings. The Dutch were definitely more down-to-earth. Trees, dirt roads, streams, cottages, water mills, windmills, a horse and cow here and there. They were peaceful pictures, showing country areas you wouldn't mind living in. Of course, I preferred a somewhat more elegant country life, and the trees were too big and the shrubbery too wild for my taste, but if you were Dutch and weren't loaded with cash, this kind of existence wasn't half bad. It looked pretty unhurried to me. There weren't all that many people around. You might have a road or hill or field all to yourself. It'd be just you and a huge sky. You didn't need anybody else. You were important enough, there alone under a huge sky.

I took out my pad and copied the name of the dead old Dutch artist I liked the most here—Jacob van Ruisdael, from the seventeenth century. I had picked up this pad along with a ballpoint pen at a stationery store on Madison. What with all my reading lately, I had the urge to jot down facts to remember, especially the location of those houses I wanted to visit when I returned to London. And every now and then, when I had nothing of any real importance to do—which amounted to most of the time on this holiday—I could flip through the little pages and refresh my memory. For some reason I liked the whole routine, as if I suddenly had another sort of job to keep me occupied. I even enjoyed the writing itself, the pad, the pen on paper, making the letters, the words. And I liked the idea of exercising my mind a bit rather than just tracking, watching brainlessly all day, all night.

Anyway, I wandered about the museum, taking in the paintings and writing down the names of the artists I liked and even the names and dates of their pictures. I took down, for example, Monet, a frog, and Turner, a Brit, who I didn't like as much as Constable. I thought I just might come back to this museum again because it was too big and too overstuffed to cover in a few hours. And to think that I used to pretty much hate this place when my aunt dragged me here as a kid. She'd be proud of me now. We lost touch after I left home. I don't remember exactly where she and my uncle ended up. Florida or Maine or California. One of those places where you go to die.

I got into the habit of ending each day in Central Park, relaxing on a bench—free of old buggers, if possible, or even better, free of people completely—in some quiet, leafy spot with my books and pad. I was jotting down a lot of notes, like a student or scholar or just some fanatic, and the pad was getting filled with names and facts and dates. I was learning all sorts of new terms—"block cornice" and "flat window arches" and "string courses"—something like learning a whole new language, except, of course, the language was still English. I learned that Bedford Square, which so many of the Brits in the area just walked by or around and took for granted, was, in fact, something special: the most completely perfect square in London, having four perfectly uniform sides and comparing favorably with the Place des Vosges in Paris. Hey, I thought when I read the Vosges reference, I just killed someone not far from there. Anyway, I noted that Bedford Square was built from 1775 to 1783, and the architect most closely associated with the project was somebody named Thomas Leverton.

I planned, when I returned home, to study Bedford Square much more carefully than ever before. Appreciating is one thing, but knowing exactly what you're appreciating is something else again. I apparently had an eye. Now I could combine it with some knowledge—get both eye and brain working. I certainly had to examine No. 1 Bedford Square, which, according to the Byrne book, was one of the great terraced houses of London, with a great, unusually elegant facade. I must have passed the damn thing God knows how many times, but I really didn't much remember this house despite its fancy ironwork and the cross-arrow decoration at both sides of the front door. At best, it was all sort of vaguely familiar. The inside of this place, I noted, was worth looking at too—the elaborate ceiling, the panel with a painting of Venus, the winding staircase.

Following the highlights of the *Georgian City* book, I also had to check out a whole row of houses—a festival of windows and terrific doorways—in Queen Anne's Gate. And another absolute must was a house on Fournier Street in Spitalfields. Built between 1726 and 1731, it was right next to Hawksmoor's Christ Church and served as the minister's residence. I'd been struck by a photo of the rear of the house, which had been taken from what looked like a little garden area. It showed a very appealing array of angles and large windows, including a "pair of full-height canted bays." That's what I want for the back of my house, I thought, a full-height canted bay that overlooks greenery. And I also thought how nice it was to know the exact names—technical though they were—of the things you liked. Here again with this house, the interior had some interesting artistic touches, particularly a fancy "open-well" staircase with "alternating twisted and plain balusters." I wondered if visitors who just wanted to have a look around were allowed inside these private houses. I figured that my Chilton routine wouldn't hurt in this regard. I mean, who could say no to Sir Peter?

Yes, I was becoming quite the architectural intellectual. It's as if my brain had suddenly realized that it was fairly empty and now longed to be filled with facts—the more, the merrier. I couldn't quite control it so I went along with it, tried to give it what it wanted. The books I read mentioned other books, and I suppose my brain's curiosity and need to be stuffed got the better of me, because I decided to seek them out. Some of these titles were really old—including two or three travel journals kept by foreign visitors to Georgian London—and I tried to find them in shops specializing in used or rare books. When I had no luck, I decided to try the New York Public Library, the big one, with the stone lions, on Forty-second Street. I figured that if I couldn't buy the books, I might at least be able to read them in the library.

After learning from an information assistant how to check on a title and then how to request it (filling out the call slips as Peter Chilton), I began spending some time in the Main Reading Room. Yes, I had actually located a few of the books on my list. And I'd felt stupidly happy at my success. The Main Reading Room, which looked like a huge old banquet hall for book lovers, had a kind of English feel to it, what with its wood paneling and long thick tables, though it seemed a little run-down and attracted more than its share of bums and mental cases. I had to move once or twice when some nutter got out of hand, like the half-shaven character in the stained business suit who was having a heated argument with an atlas and started telling the enemy maps to go fuck themselves. Another time, when I was dipping into a book written during the Georgian period—*A Picturesque Tour Through the Cities of London and Westminster*—and enjoying this little trip into the past tremendously, I had to tell a tattered bum who sat down across from me to either stop flipping his pages so hard or risk getting his bum head kicked in. He cursed me under his breath, but when I started to get up from my chair in a threatening manner he grabbed his stuff and beat it over to another table. What a filthy derelict like him was doing reading books on real-estate investment was beyond me.

The reading room, though, wasn't at all bad, and the thick, heavy wooden chairs were maybe the most comfortable such chairs I'd ever sat in. But instead of air-conditioning there were open windows, up high, on both sides of the room, and big floor fans blowing warm air across your head. Sometimes even with all the attempts to keep in motion the stinking hot New York air—so that readers could at least pretend they were experiencing something almost resembling a refreshing breeze—the whole place got very sticky and I'd begin to get a little drowsy. A few times I had to leave my books and Georgian London to visit the men's room, where I'd douse my face with cold water.

The men's room had bums too. White marble and bums. Chilton was appalled. I doubt the British Museum Library would allow this sort of thing, he thought. One of the bums, who had his shirt off and was giving himself a kind of sponge bath by the sink, actually hit on Sir Peter for money. "Can you spare a few dollars?" the bum asked with a smile. "I'm trying to buy a condo."

I, not Chilton, responded. "Is that supposed to be funny? Is that supposed to make you charming—a bum with a sense of humor?" He seemed surprised. But bums got no sympathy from me. "Why don't you look for work," I continued, "instead of walking around like garbage? I was out of work for months one time, was at my bloody wit's end. I didn't cry to my parents for a bloody handout. I wasn't about to bow down to that crazy pair. Or to anybody else, for that matter. And I didn't start taking baths in a public sink. I pulled myself together and I got myself a job. A damn good job."

"Yeah," said the bum, "so what do you do, big shot?"

I looked him dead in the eyes and said, cold and hard, "I kill people."

With that he started to laugh. He couldn't stop laughing. It was a hellish sight. A half-naked, half-soaped-up, fifty-year-old wreck with a load of gray and white chest hair laughing his head off by a sink nearly overflowing with his dirt. He laughed so hard that he started to cough his guts out. I didn't get the joke. But, then again, there wasn't any joke to get. His screwed-up brain was the joke.

I'm never going to end up like that, I said to myself as I walked down the hall. No matter what happens. No, sir. I'd rather be dead.

CHAPTER 6

IT WAS AROUND THREE O'CLOCK one afternoon, I had just returned to my hotel and was deciding which books to take along with me to the Upper East Side and Central Park when the phone rang. I was startled for a moment because the phone—a white and gold French-poof antique affair—had been silent since I'd gotten here. It sounded loud, louder than any normal phone, and it seemed to shake the dead-quiet, overflowered suite, rattle all the big fat vases. "Mr. King," the voice said. I gritted my teeth. I hadn't missed this routine. Not in the least. "You have the wrong number," I said angrily, slammed down the receiver, and went down to the street.

I had to walk all the way up to Seventh Avenue before I found a lousy public phone that worked. I took the slip of paper with the Firm's New York number from my wallet and reluctantly dialed it. The nerve of them to bother me like this, I thought. I hadn't even settled on my books for the evening. And why force me to use a public phone? I assumed they owned a piece of this hotel, maybe owned it outright. It should have been a safe place. Damnit.

"We've been waiting for you to check in," said the voice on the other end, "so what happened?"

I didn't recognize this man, but he sounded like an assistant, the American version of a flunky for that fat slob in London.

"I've been busy. I've been all wrapped up in relaxing. To tell you the truth, you people just slipped my mind. Like you weren't there at all."

"Jeez, I'm a little hurt."

"What do you want anyway?"

"Hey, my friend, we're like doing you a favor, remember?"

"What is it you want? I was just about to go out for the evening."

"Getting an early start, huh? Big night."

"Yeah, nonstop hilarity."

"Can't say I'm surprised. That's what we heard about you. A regular night owl, a real all-out friggin' swinger. Yeah, they say there's no controlling you."

"All right," I said, "cut the shtick. They never told me that I had to check in as soon as I got here. They said when I got the chance. Well, I didn't get the chance. So I'm here. But you knew that. After all, it's your hotel. What else do you want to know?"

"Hey, take it easy, pal. All this is is a kind of courtesy call, just to see how you're doing, if you plan to do any traveling, if you need anything, you know, that kind of thing. Courtesy."

I explained in an annoyed, nasty tone that I might go upstate to visit my hometown so I could tell it to drop dead, but that I'd only be gone a day or two at most.

The pest sounded like he wanted to be chatty so I asked him to call me back or else we'd be cut off by the operator.

"I brought one quarter with me," I explained, "and I just used it. I don't have any more change. It's all back at the hotel."

He said to hang up and he'd call me right back. I suggested that there wasn't anything more to discuss and we could end the call now. "Jeez, you really know how to hurt a guy," he said, and added that he'd call me right back.

"So what have you been up to?" he asked as soon as I picked up the damn phone. Suddenly someone tapped me on the shoulder. I turned to face a somewhat dumpy middle-aged woman wearing a baggy I LOVE NEW YORK T-shirt.

"Excuse me, but are you going to be long?"

"I don' t know," I said, gritting my teeth again, "maybe another hour, hour and a half." She turned beet red, huffed and puffed, and stormed off.

"Hey, Pete, you still there?" asked the pest on the phone.

"Yeah," I answered, "I'm on a public phone, you know. On goddamn Seventh Avenue."

He told me to calm down and again asked what I'd been doing with myself.

"Reading," I said.

"Reading?"

"Yeah, reading."

"Reading what?" He sounded shocked, as if I had confessed to being a pervert.

"Books."

"Books?"

"Yeah, they have these white pages with words printed on them, and then they take these pages and stick them between two covers."

"I know what a book is," he said, a bit offended.

"Well, considering your tone I wasn't so sure."

"I mean to say, this is what you're doing on your vacation—reading books? They sent you all the way over here and that's what you're doing? You gotta admit, Pete, this is a little weird."

"It's 'Peter,' not 'Pete.'"

"Hey, excuse me. You're something else, Peter. Do you know that?"

"Are we through? I'm not exactly in the comfort of my home here, unless you think I live on the sidewalk."

"Look, I'm supposed to find out what you're doing, how you're doing. That's the little job they gave me. So I'm trying to find out, that's all. Don't blame me, man. Blame them."

Fit to be tied, I asked him again what in bloody hell he wanted to know. My attitude surprised even me. I'd never acted so openly hostile to these people. What had come over me? What in Christ was I doing?

"So," he continued, determined to complete his stupid job, "what have you been reading?"

I was about to tell him or else curse the son of a bitch when the cars on the avenue started honking their horns in response to momentary gridlock. "Jesus," I shouted, "you'd think they all just pulled a bank job. Doesn't anybody have any patience in this bloody city?"

"What was that, Pete?" the pest asked. "What's that fuckin' racket?!"

"Traffic!" I yelled into the mouthpiece, loud enough to bust his eardrum. "Goddamn Seventh Avenue traffic!"

The noise finally stopped. Cars moved freely again. Everyone felt better for letting out their anger, which was really what this was all about. An anger break.

"So what have you been reading?"

Again! This creep was like a parrot imitating itself.

"Does it really matter?" I asked him. I was still angry but trying to sound a bit more civil.

"Look, Pete, like I—"

"Peter."

"What?"

"The name is Peter."

"But that's a phony name anyway. Pete, Peter, Irving—what the fuck's the difference?"

"The difference is that I was given the name Peter. And I like the name Peter. I don't like Pete, and I wasn't given the name Pete. Besides, Peter sounds more distinguished. And I'm supposed to be distinguished."

"Brother. Maybe I shouldn't call you anything at all."

"That would suit me fine."

"So like could you tell me what you're reading?"

"You planning to go to the library?"

"Look, don't give me a hard time, huh? I have to tell them something. So this is something. Just give me like a few names or whatever you call them."

"Titles."

"Yeah, a few titles. Maybe that'll keep them happy."

The guy obviously wanted to make me feel sorry for him. But I resented his phone call, these questions, their trying to keep tabs on me when I was supposed to be basking in my freedom. I suddenly sensed a presence behind me. I'm good at this. It's a talent you develop on the job. I turned to find a yuppie with a business suit and briefcase just standing there, waiting for the phone. I gave him my meanest look coupled with my nastiest tone.

"I didn't know this was a bus stop," I said. He had to think about that one for a little while, even began to look for a sign, but then he got my meaning and he backed off.

"Hey, did I lose you?" my phone mate asked. I decided to finally make this man happy and get this stupid business over with, before I said something I'd really regret. So I told him I'd been reading books on architecture, particularly on Georgian houses.

"What kind of houses?" he asked.

"Georgian," I said, "it's sort of an English style. The Georgian period."

"Could you spell that?" he asked.

I spelled it for him and even gave him the titles of some of the books. This is completely ridiculous, I thought. When I mentioned the book on Bedford Square, he asked me to spell "Bedford," at which point I wanted to tell him in no uncertain terms that he was a first-class moron, but I managed to keep my cool. That I had to lower myself to report to an illiterate, uneducated jerk like this troubled me both at the time and later. Maybe I was becoming a bit of a snob, but I began to feel that I was too good for these people, all of them. Yes, you couldn't deny that I was at a higher level. And still climbing.

"Okay? You satisfied?" I said, after running down my reading list. "Are we through? I'm getting sick of this corner, and it's damn hot out here. My ear is all wet, for Christ's sake."

But, no, he wasn't finished yet. He asked when I planned to go upstate.

"Probably when I can't stand this city anymore. If it gets any hotter it might be nice to be in a town by the river—even that dump of a town."

"You could maybe give us a call just before you go."

"For just a visit?"

"It wouldn't be a bad idea. They'd appreciate it."

The hell with them, I thought.

"And if you want to do a little target practice, let us know. There's a range downtown. Private-like."

"Why would I want to do that?"

"I don't know. It's just a suggestion. Maybe you don't want to get rusty."

"The only way I'll ever get rusty is if I'm dead."

"Well, it's there if you need it. This is all courtesy, you understand. Courtesy."

"To tell you the truth, I wouldn't mind if you people were *dis*courteous and left me the hell alone."

I was amazed that I'd made that comment. But after we mutually hung up, at long last, and I walked back to the hotel, I was still steaming. Who in hell do they think they're talking to? I said to myself. Their days of pushing me around were coming to an end. They didn't know what they were dealing with here. Even I didn't know what I was dealing with anymore.

Because of that stupid phone call and the need to recover from it a bit, I got a late start on my usual late afternoon–early evening stroll. I ended up in Central Park as usual, somewhere east as usual, but I got there way after my usual time. People were already returning home from work and as a result the park was more populated than I was used to. Ballplayers, company teams, picnickers, lovers, joggers, Rollerbladers, bicyclists, dog walkers, jerky kids, and, of course, an assortment of nature-loving bums. I moved deeper into the park, where there might be more trees and bushes, fewer paths and fewer people, and possibly a little untamed, isolated patch.

I actually managed to find one and it was near perfect, as if it had been designed especially for someone like me. On a small hill, just below a great chunk of rock, were a bench and a lamppost. I saw this as a place where I could read peacefully and, if I wanted, could even read into the night, provided that the lamp was working.

I couldn't much pretend that I was in Regent's Park or Hyde Park or St. James's, because this place lacked their polish, was a lot scruffier and wilder. But it was pleasant enough and a nice break from the hot, smelly, tourist-stuffed city that lay beyond the trees. I had taken that Summerson book with me—*Georgian London*—and thought I'd give it another try. I looked at it as a kind of challenge now, and saw no reason why I should not be up to that challenge. After all, I had done well with the other books, even though they had gotten fairly clogged every now and then.

I had my trusty pad and pen with me and jotted down a fact or two as I read along. I found that this jotting business helped focus my brain a bit, forced it to pause and consider at least a little something of what it had read. I found, though, that there was still too much in this book to take in, and I kept drifting over to the pictures. I finally just flipped ahead to a chapter on John Nash, a name I kept coming across in all these books. He was, of course, one of the great architects of Georgian London and perhaps the greatest city planner of the time, dreaming up all sorts of plans for Regent Street and Regent's Park. I plunged into this chapter and pretty much stayed with it. There was a terrific color photo of Park Village West and another of Cumberland Terrace, two sites I'd probably passed at least a couple of times and had probably admired. I'd never known then, of course, that they had come from one guy's Georgian brain.

I read on, and evening began to creep into the park, and the sky began to change, first turning a fiery pink and then cooling down and dimming to a kind of grayish blue. The lamppost suddenly came to life and actually cast enough light for me to continue reading and for a few moths, toying with suicide, to flutter around it. I'd look up from a page on occasion and see in the far dark distance the tiny lights of cars flickering through the trees and shrubs. They looked more like fireflies than night traffic flowing through the park.

I was noting down Regent's Park spots to visit—York Terrace, St. Andrews Terrace, St. Andrews Place—was absolutely lost to Georgian London when shadows out of nowhere appeared on me, my books, my bench.

"Hey, man, you got any money?"

Standing in front of me were two giant black guys in their late teens who looked like refugees from some very mean basketball team. I noticed that their clothes—T-shirts and black pants—were about two or three sizes too big for them. What do you know, I thought, street-gang clowns. I also noticed that each of them was holding a knife—one a stiletto, the other a standard switchblade.

"Hey, man, you look like you're rolling in the shit—you wanna give us something or else we fuckin' cut you up."

I realized that to a mugger I must have looked like a dream mark, a goddamn jackpot. To these pathetic losers from the ghetto, I was dressed like a million. And, in fact, I was wearing my two-hundred-and-fifteen-dollar sports shirt.

"Hey, we're talking to you, you mother."

The problem here—for them mostly, as I saw it—was that they were looking at Sir Peter Chilton yet they were actually dealing with me. But the big problem for me, the real me, was that I couldn't be sure that if I gave them my money they would let it go at that. These guys seemed angry. They might take a few good pokes at me just for the hell of it. You couldn't blame them really. Blacks still live like shit and are treated like shit. But I had to put my social conscience on a back burner, as they say, and consider my own situation. If they hurt me and I was found before I bled to death, I'd end up in a hospital, with the cops—maybe even the press—asking all sorts of questions, like who I was and where I was from. I couldn't afford this. Peter Chilton would never survive such scrutiny. And, besides, I wasn't particularly in the mood to get stabbed, fatally or otherwise. Then again, I didn't want to take these guys out, because that would mean a murder investigation and that might lead to really big trouble.

All these thoughts flashed through my brain in a matter of seconds. I'd learned to think fast on my job. But I also kept asking: Can't these guys just go away and leave me alone? Can't everybody just leave me alone?!

"Hey," said the punk who was doing the talking, "are you fuckin' deaf or what?"

His silent sidekick, who was a little shorter—like maybe only seven feet instead of eight—was smiling from ear to ear and bouncing about nervously.

Jesus, I thought, that's all I need in this mix, an oversize hophead.

"I don't think I have much money on me," I explained meekly.

"Just give me your goddamn wallet."

That's pretty much what I was waiting for: permission to make a move. You just made a big mistake, I said to the punk in my brain, even bigger than picking on me in the first place. I reached inside my blazer but pulled out my gun instead of my wallet, and before they knew what was happening I fired down at their size-sixteen sneakers, moving from the right foot of one guy to the left foot of the other. I aimed for the big toes and blasted them apart. One bullet for each was enough. I just don't miss. Blood exploded from the dirty white sneakers as both punks fell to the ground, yelling in pain and grabbing for their suddenly destroyed feet. Shit! Fuck! Shit! they cried in panic, and then simply cried.

"You fuckin' son of a bitch!" the talker screamed out to me as I picked up my book, gently rose, and slowly moved away, making sure that neither of the victims was capable of getting up or hurling a knife.

When I reached the path, I glanced back up at the little hill. What a weird scene. The lamppost served as a kind of spotlight in the night, revealing two figures writhing on the ground, looking something like giant bugs that had just been sprayed.

My heart was beating faster than necessary, but as I moved along at a brisk but fairly restrained pace, and the incident already started to become a memory, I tried to settle into a more Chilton-like mood and rhythm. All I wanted, damnit, was a little peace and quiet. Was that too much to ask? Was it?

I was quite far now from the scene of the crime, but I could still hear the cries. They seemed to echo through the park. I came upon a young couple standing by a bench and looking anxiously in the direction of the noise. "Doesn't that sound like people screaming?" the girl asked me. "I'm telling you," the boyfriend said, "it's probably just some guys goofing around." The girl looked at me for an opinion. "I wouldn't know," I said with my English accent, "I'm just a tourist." "What is that supposed to mean?" the girl responded. "Leave the man alone," the boyfriend said to her. "But he just came from up there." "Can't you see the man doesn't want to get involved?" "Well, I think we should get the police," she said. "But where the hell are the police around here?"

I decided to stroll on. "Good meeting you," I told them, "and the best of luck." "Screw you, you British creep!" the girl called back, obviously disturbed by my total lack of concern.

I was damn annoyed by the distraction, by people once again ruining my mood, and I cursed my ill luck. But the anger didn't last long. By the time I had returned to my hotel, I already was a calm, harmless amateur scholar again. The only thing that could possibly agitate this man would be the problem of settling on the book or books to curl up with for the night. I decided on continuing with the Summerson, but breaking it up a bit with the Bedford Square. I took the books with me to a French restaurant in the fifties that the man at the desk had recommended. I felt like shell steak and French fries—my favorite meal at the good old Triadot in Paris—and as it turned out this New York place did a reasonably good version of the dish. "To go with that, sir, might I recommend a very lovely Beaujolais?" the waiter asked. "Recommend away, my good man," I said, smiling up from my Summerson.

So, without really missing a beat, I got back into my "studies." Over the next few days I spent my mornings at the library and my afternoons reading in and roaming about the Metropolitan Museum or visiting those art galleries along Madison Avenue that hadn't shut down for the summer. At the library I was happy to discover the art library, which was down the hall from the Main Reading Room, was quite pleasant, incredibly well stocked, and—big surprise!—fully air-conditioned. What more could I ask for?

One miserably humid afternoon I decided to finally take in that Constable show at the Frick. Mercifully, the air-conditioning was on full blast so the place was terrifically cool and much more fit for human life than the streets outside. The show was stuck down in some posh rooms in the basement, which was fine with me, since the tourists were hitting the main floor in a big way. There were a lot of drawings, which were okay. I particularly liked the ones of Malvern Hall and East Bergholt House—though maybe what I really liked about them was the houses themselves and their Georgian look. But what impressed me the most, just in terms of art—Christ, I'm sounding more like a snotty intellectual each day—what knocked me out, as they say, were some of the small oil paintings hanging here and there along the way. Although I had never seen Hampstead Heath under such a pink sky or looking so smudgy, and although I'd never seen a field—the East Bergholt Common, in this case—with so many intense greens and yellows or looking so smudgy, the pictures reminded me of places that were real. They were sort of painted memories of particular areas at certain times of day, with the kind of color and light and general feeling you remembered. Maybe the scenes weren't very accurate, but that didn't matter because this was the way your brain saw them now.

I looked at the Constable stuff for a long time and then decided to go upstairs, try to ignore all the visitors, and see the rest of the museum. I must say—and so would Sir Peter—that it was a very tasteful mansion, with a lot of wood paneling in the quietly fancy rooms and an elegant center court with just the right amount of plants and a fountain with just the right amount of drip and splash. And while I may know next to nothing about paintings, even I could tell that the stuff in this place was first-rate. I found more Constables—really big pictures this time—and a country lane scene by my old friend van Ruisdael.

And then I saw it. I saw the Turner. It was just one of those things, one of those unexpected moments, a sight that amazes you, that forces you to react, that gives you a bit of a chill. A good chill. I stopped dead in my tracks and stared. When I managed to shake off at least some of the shock, I moved slowly closer. Because there on the wall, above some low bookcases filled with expensive leather-bound books, was this painting by Turner called *Mortlake Terrace: Early Summer Morning*. It was unbelievable. Absolutely unbelievable. Maybe the most beautiful picture I'd ever seen. And maybe the most peaceful. The picture seemed to glow with a soft yellow light, the sun making its way through the morning haze. There was a small mansion on the right—which seemed quite Georgian to me—and it overlooked a river, stood, in fact, next to a stone embankment and terrace that were shaded by very tall, thin trees and that curved round with the curve of the river, probably the Thames. There were two men leaning against the short stone wall, either looking out at the river or talking, or both. And on the wide lawn at the side of the house were two gardeners tending the grounds.

This is where I want to be, I thought. This is where I want to live. The calm. The beauty. The river. The golden light. This was it. I have never wanted to be inside a picture more. I wondered just where Mortlake Terrace was, if it still existed, if that house was still standing. This would be my mission when I returned to London. This would go to the top of my list. Find this place. Or at least find a place like it. Imagine waking up in your Georgian house, going to your window, and looking out at the Thames. And if, by chance, you weren't in your river mood, all you had to do was go to the back of the house and you could then look out on trees and shrubs.

I felt at peace just staring at the painting. No anger, no murderous thoughts, no Firm. They were all gone. But, of course, they couldn't stay gone permanently, because I couldn't very well stand in front of this painting for the rest of my life. I did the next best thing—I bought a picture of it to carry around with me, to look at whenever I felt the need. Yes, what I did was buy a postcard—a few, in fact, in case I lost one or two. I asked the woman in the sales shop if she had any larger reproductions of the painting, something that I might frame and put up on my wall, but unfortunately they had run out and the crummy little postcard was all they had. I did find a bigger picture in a book on the Frick Collection, but the colors were even more off than those in the postcard. Jesus, I thought, what a lousy tribute to a bloody great painting. But I did discover from the book that Mortlake Terrace was east of London and that the river was, indeed, the Thames. Probably all gone, I thought. Then again, one of the nice things about the English was that they held on to a lot of their old houses, maybe because they wanted, in this rotten world, to have a little of that old peace themselves.

I stopped in at a coffee shop, probably Greek, on Madison Avenue. I was planning to go completely to hell and get another American hamburger, but I began to feel guilty about eating like a slob and actually paying to poison myself. I ordered a plain omelet instead, which was only partial poison. I substituted rice for the home fries, figuring I'd avoid at least some of that American-Greek grease. Now that I had become a reader I usually ordered food I could eat with just a fork, leaving my other hand free to hold a book or turn the pages.

I sat in a small booth in the rear. It was mid-afternoon and there were, I was happy to see, only a few customers scattered about. I had been carrying the Bedford Square book around with me for half the day and this was the first chance I'd gotten to actually read it. A cheap crystal vase with plastic roses stood at the center of the Formica tabletop. I moved it out of the way so I had room to hold up my rather sizable book and to accommodate my plate.

I was happily reading and chewing when I looked up some time later and noticed a pair of solid, shapely legs just one booth up and across from me. The legs were exposed all the way up to the thighs, where blue denim shorts suddenly covered the flesh. I tried not to be obvious but I kept straying from the top of a page to the bottom of this woman.

I finally got courageous and lifted my head completely. The legs, I discovered, belonged to a young woman with a somewhat long, narrow, but very pretty face. She had big, alert eyes and long lashes, and short reddish brown hair that was a bit spiky but fell quite a bit short of punk. Probably a student, I thought. A very appealing student. Yes, there was definitely something appealingly fresh and open about this girl. And she had terrific legs.

"Excuse me." It was her. And she was talking to me. From her table. At first, I thought she had caught me taking in her legs a little too often. But, no, that wasn't it at all. "I couldn't help but noticing. I was just there."

"Where?" I asked, completely puzzled.

"Bedford Square. Your book. Bedford Square."

"Oh," I said, and then remembered that I was distinguished. "Oh, yes, I see. This book. I'm terribly sorry, I didn't understand."

"You're British," she announced.

"Yes. Here on a visit. A bit of a holiday."

"I was in London just two weeks ago. I was staying in Bloomsbury, a bed-and-breakfast right by Russell Square. I got to know that whole area. I just loved walking around those squares. So when I saw you with Bedford Square—well, I thought that was pretty amazing."

"Yes, quite a coincidence."

"I'd love to live in London. Do you live there—in the city, I mean?"

"I have a place in Belgravia, actually."

"Lucky you. That's a pretty exclusive area, isn't it?"

"Oh, I don't know. I suppose so. If you consider the terraces in Regent's Park, the Nash houses, all that, it isn't so terribly special."

"I guess it's all relative. I mean, if you consider Buckingham Palace then no place in London is terribly special." She smiled brightly. She was making fun of Sir Peter. He didn't mind in the least.

"I see your point."

"It's nice that you're reading about an area in your own city. I don't think most people do. At least, it's not something I would do. I mean, I live here, and I wouldn't want to read a book about a New York square. I generally like to read about places I can't immediately see. Exotic, foreign places."

This girl was sharp. I decided to change my story a little. "I don't actually live in London all the time. I have a house in Derbyshire. Or rather the family does. We've had it for over one hundred and fifty years. My place in London is—"

"Say," she interrupted, "do you mind if I join you? I mean, it's a little awkward talking like this."

"Be my guest," I said graciously. Christ, but I could be debonair. It surprised me.

She immediately hung her big black bag over her shoulder, gathered up her plate, utensils, and glass of iced tea, and came over. Her legs, I noticed, were just as fine standing up as they had been sitting down. She was taller than I'd sensed and her breasts, somewhat hidden by her baggy white blouse, appeared much fuller now. She was, indeed, quite a package.

Her legs touched mine briefly as she sat down across from me. My body, my privates, tingled for a few very enjoyable seconds. Enjoyable but pathetic. Even though I was maybe only nine or ten years older than this girl, I suddenly felt like a dirty old man. My damn job, I thought, has aged me before my time.

"So you were saying," she said.

"Oh, yes. I really spend a lot of time in the country. I suppose because I was born there. So London is, you see, somewhat like a foreign place to me. Hence the Bedford Square book." I thought the "hence" was a very nice touch. Amazing what you can pick up from the telly and Brit movies. "I have a quite pleasant maisonette in Belgrave Square. But I'm only there part of the year." I liked the "maisonette" touch as well. I had to thank the real estate ads in *Country Life* and *The London Magazine* for that.

"Could I see your book?" she asked.

"Oh, of course," I said, continuing in my gentlemanly mode.

She flipped through the pages, stopping every so often at a picture. "I remember this," she said. "And this." She then went through the book for a second time, turning the pages more slowly. And she chatted on as she did so.

"I suppose you're an architect or something," she said.

"No. It's just an interest of mine. I like to look at houses. Particularly Georgian houses."

"Well, they certainly have enough of them in England."

"Yes," I chuckled, "yes, indeed they do."

"So what do you do for a living—if you don't mind my asking?" She laughed. "You have to excuse me. I'm not normally so inquisitive. It's just that I don't meet that many English people over here."

"Quite all right, no need to apologize," I said. "People are always wondering about my profession. But the fact of the matter is that I don't actually have one. You see, I have what you might call independent means."

"What you're saying is that you're rich." She closed the book and returned it with a soft "Thanks—lovely."

"I wouldn't go that far. Let's say that I'm comfortably well off."

"God, that must be wonderful. To do whatever you want, go wherever you want. No wonder you're dressed like that."

"Like what?"

"Like that. So stylishly. In this heat."

"One gets used to it."

"The summer outfit of your class, I suppose."

"Oh, no. It's not like that at all. Class has nothing to do with it. It's more a habit than anything else—what you feel most comfortable in."

"Sorry. That was rude of me. I suppose I'm just a little envious."

"No, but really. This sort of weather doesn't bother me. I'm simply one of those people."

"Well, anyway, it's nice to see that you're not a snob."

"Come again?"

"You're eating in here, for one thing. You could be lunching at the Plaza or the Pierre."

"I may be well off, but I'm not extravagant. Besides, I rather enjoy coffee-shop omelets."

"Well, there you go. And, of course, you're talking to me."

I'd lost her for a moment and shook my head.

"I mean, if you were really a snob you wouldn't be talking so freely to me."

"Please. I'm not royalty, after all."

"Oh, I'm not complaining. I think it's very sweet. You seem like a very nice man."

I kill people, I wanted to confess, but I'm nice just the same. Odd as it may seem, you can kill people and still be a good person. But I said instead: "And what do you do? I take it you're a student."

"A perennial student is more like it. I sometimes feel that I'll be in school for the rest of my life. I'm a graduate student now and I'm working on my dissertation. That's partly why I was in London, to do research. I was at the BM, then went to Oxford for a few days. Oxford knocked me out, by the way. An amazing place."

"And you're studying what?"

"British Lit. My dissertation is on Beddoes."

"I'm sorry. I don't know that name. I'm not that much of a literary person."

"Oh, look, don't apologize. Even literary persons don't know this man. He's hardly read anymore, except by specialists."

"What's the name again?"

"Beddoes." She spelled it out. "Thomas Lovell Beddoes. He was born in England in 1803, lived in Germany most of his life, in a kind of self-exile. He was a doctor, but never really practiced. Wrote these rather crazy verse plays that sound like they're from a much earlier time. His most famous work was *Death's Jest-Book*. Great title, isn't it? Anyway, he was really quite nuts, absolutely obsessed with death and decay. He eventually tried to commit suicide by opening an artery in his leg. The German doctors saved him, but the next time he took poison and that did the job for good. He died at forty-six."

"A bit morbid, isn't it? You don't seem like the kind of person who'd be studying that sort of thing."

"Oh, I think I have a dark side." She laughed. "Well, maybe not that dark. But seriously, I think all of us secretly want to be something we're not."

"Really?"

"I think so. And if we don't want that, then we want to be somewhere else. Take me, for example. I come from a small town in Wisconsin, but I always dreamed of living in New York. Now that I live in New York, I dream of living somewhere else."

"Where?"

"Maybe London. Maybe Paris. The point is, I think that most people, at least the people I know, are restless, dissatisfied. They always want to change themselves, change their lives. Give them one thing and they want something else. Do you see what I mean? Do you agree?"

"I can't really say. To be honest, I don't know that many people. I would guess, though, that all these people who want to change have a hard time doing it. It's not always so easy to change your situation. It could be very risky."

"Well, I'm sure someone like you doesn't worry about these things. If I had your life, I wouldn't want to change it."

"Believe me, I have my share of problems. Never judge a book by its cover, as they say."

We kept talking for something like half an hour. She told me about her life and I made up facts about mine. Once or twice her knees touched mine as she shifted in her seat and I felt that nice little tingle again. I showed her one of the postcards of the Turner painting and she was impressed by it and by my appreciation of art in general. She just didn't have much time to go to museums or galleries, she said, what with her research and all. But she was meeting a friend at the Met at five o'clock to chat and wander about. That's why she was in this neighborhood to begin with. The museum was open late, she reported, and there was a café set up on the balcony where a string quartet performed live. "You should go sometime," she said, "it's sort of charming, in an Old World sort of way." She told me more about Beddoes, who sounded like a really sick bastard, and I took out my pad and pen and jotted down some notes. She thought this "very sweet" but warned that old Beddoes was virtually impossible to find in bookshops over here, if that was my intention. I took down some of her favorite Beddoes lines: "He lusts after the mummy country," "Death is his boon companion," and a particular favorite: "If there were dreams to sell, what would you buy?" She said that she lived in Chelsea with a roommate and asked where I was staying. Park Avenue, I answered, in the twelve-room apartment of American friends who had gone away to their villa in Italy for the summer.

I realized, as we were talking, as I watched her lovely lips move and looked into her large, lovely brown eyes, I realized that I hadn't talked with someone in this way, casual and friendly and all, for years. I couldn't even recall the last time.

We continued talking out on the street, as we walked up Madison. Although I was enjoying myself, I didn't want to follow her all the way to the museum, so I told her that I had to attend a "little cocktail thing" on Sutton Place in about twenty minutes. We stopped at the corner and she asked to borrow my pen and pad. "Since you're going to be in the city awhile, I'll leave you my name and number. Maybe we can get together again. I'd really like to. I mean, really." I was delighted, flattered, and I thanked her, but of course made no offer to give her my number. "'Jennifer Sweeney,'" I said, reading her note. "That's a very nice name." It also seemed to suit her. She asked me mine. "Peter," I answered, "Peter Chilton." "Very English," she said, "quite classy. So, Peter, don't forget to call." We shook hands and I watched her walk away. She turned suddenly and said, "Oh, and if a man answers, don't worry. He's not a boyfriend or a husband or anything, just my roommate. And he likes boys."

I must admit that Jennifer popped into my mind over the next several days. Not only her face and legs and breasts, but Jennifer herself, the way she talked, her expressions, her little gestures, the whole girl. I liked the way I had been with her, easy, relaxed, somewhat resembling a regular person. Now when I'd be reading my architectural books, my mind would sometimes drift from the page and I'd think of my Georgian house by the Thames and then see myself and Jennifer leaning against the terrace embankment under the tall trees in the golden morning light.

One night when I waited for a thunderstorm to pass so I could escape from my hotel, which was starting to remind me again of a funeral home, I took out my pad, went over to my French poof phone, and actually dialed her number. I got her machine, her voice sharp and clear and full of energy. The beep sounded, but I hung up. Was I mad? Calling to make a date as Peter Chilton? Who in hell was I kidding? There was no future in this. Especially not for someone who didn't even exist.

CHAPTER 7

I WAS SOUND ASLEEP when the phone rang. I didn't know where I was for a moment. With sunlight pouring into the room and the smell of flowers so strongly in the air I thought I might be in the country in my Georgian house, with my Georgian windows open to my fabulous garden. I looked over at the alarm clock, which I had forgotten to set, and saw that it was after nine. I had overslept. The phone kept ringing. "Damnit," I mumbled.

"Mr. King?" the voice said. I cursed violently in my mind and then continued to do so aloud. "You have the wrong friggin' number," I shouted, and slammed down the receiver. I'd never been one for cursing, had never been that type at all, but here I was in New York cursing almost daily like an uneducated, moronic slob. It was this city. It was being home. It was them.

I dressed quickly and hurried up to Seventh Avenue and my favorite public phone. "We have a job for you," the voice on the other end said, "a quick job." It wasn't the same man I'd spoken with before. This one had a gravel voice. He sounded harder, colder, more like a real boss, Mr. Big Onion himself. "A job?" I said. I didn't understand at first. Maybe I didn't want to understand. He asked me for the number on my phone, said he'd call me back in about a minute or so.

It then dawned upon me what was happening here. They can't do this, I thought. I won't let them do this. I had already planned my day. I was going to look for books on Nash and Robert Adam, another name that kept popping up in my studies. Then I'd spend some time at the Met, maybe go over to this other museum uptown called the Cooper-Hewitt, which sometimes had architectural exhibitions. Then, figuring that I'd best keep out of Central Park for a while, I'd end the day in Carl Schurz Park by the East River, where I could read a bit by the water and get a bit of a badly needed breeze.

The phone rang. It was him again. But now he sounded like he was talking outside somewhere. I could hear a lot of air and traffic in the background. "Like I said, we have a quick job for you."

"I thought I was on vacation."

"It just ended."

You son of a bitch. You phony bastards. "This was all planned, wasn't it?" I said angrily, unable to control myself. "You made me think I was here on vacation while all the time you had a job in mind."

"Hey, who the fuck do you think you're talking to with that tone? Do you know who I am?"

I reluctantly apologized. But I really didn't know who he was. And at this point I didn't much care.

"You think we have money to burn, son? Finance a transatlantic vacation for some British-American creep—American-British, whatever the fuck you are—just to do a little job over here? You're fuckin' dreaming. You just happen to be at the right place at the right time. Lucky fuckin' you. That's all. A man came into the city yesterday.

Out of the blue. No one expected him. No one really wanted him. But now that he's here, we may as well take care of the scumbag. He's about four blocks away from you. At the Hilton on Sixth. That's why you got the job. Because you happen to be four blocks away. You're available and already in place. So don't think you're so fuckin' important."

I reluctantly apologized again—and I mean reluctantly. The goddamn nerve of these people. Interrupting my holiday, once again ruining my mood, for a lousy job anybody else could do.

He gave me the phony name "the scumbag" was using and a brief description. "We don't know how long he'll be here. So this has to be done soon. I'm talking today, tomorrow, soon. Get it done and get it done fast. And then you can go right back to your creepy little vacation." Before he hung up he told me, ordered me, to call back as soon as I had completed the job.

I don't know what came over me then. My face started to burn, then the rest of my body. "They want a fast job," I said to myself and to anybody walking by at the moment, "then I'll give them a fast job. They're not going to screw up my day. No, sir. No way."

I thought fast. Maybe the fastest I'd ever thought in my life. I put it all together in a matter of minutes, standing there on Seventh Avenue at the tail end of rush hour.

I called Information, got the number of the Hilton, called the hotel, asked if "Joseph Kelso"—the scumbag's alias—was staying there, said I was supposed to meet him but was running late, got his room number, asked to be connected. "Yeah, hello," the scumbag answered.

"Mr. King?"

"Who?"

"Is this Mr. King?"

"No, you got the wrong number." He hung up.

I walked quickly down Sixth, taking extra-long steps, probably looking like one of those Nazi soldiers. I stopped at another phone booth along the way, called the scumbag again. "Mr. Sweeney?"

"Who?"

"Jack Sweeney?"

"What is this? You got the wrong number." He hung up.

I'd been in the hotel a couple of times in the past, to meet with some high-powered out-of-town hoods who needed a sensitive job done. The place hadn't changed as far as I could see. The outside—hundreds of dead gray windows, rising into the sky—looked just as ugly as before, if not worse. I used to think, though, that the inside was ritzy, as my old man stupidly termed any place that wasn't a total dump. Now I considered it fake-ritzy, sort of expensively cheap. If John Nash ever saw all this, I thought as I moved swiftly through the lobby, he'd drop dead a second time. I bought a paper in the little newspaper-souvenir shop. I needed a good-sized paper and *The New York Times* was perfect. I then found a row of phones, and for the last time I called the scumbag.

"How the hell are you, Harry?" I said when the scumbag answered.

"Who do you want?" he asked.

"Hey, quit kiddin', Harry, it's Lou."

"What the hell are you talking about? Jesus Christ. You got the wrong number." He slammed down the receiver.

I was glad to see that security in this place was as lousy as I remembered it. Hundreds of guests, visitors, strangers—you just couldn't keep up with all the human traffic. So you gave up trying. That's what happens when you build a hotel that's as big as an office complex. I went to the bank of elevators and waited for a car to the thirtieth floor. I'd forgotten that they had little television sets embedded in each car, in case you were a total idiot and needed to be entertained for the brief ride up or down. There was some confessional chat show on, and a fat pig, who needed two chairs to hold her, was crying fat tears and complaining that nobody appreciated her inner beauty. Lots of luck, I thought.

Two teens, probably brother and sister, got off with me on my floor. They looked West Coast or southern—blond, healthy, brainless. I waited for them to get ahead of me and disappear down the hall.

I searched for the scumbag's room, found it. I stood by the door. Checked the hall to my left. No one. To my right: a cleaning woman with her cart at the very end of the corridor. Just taking some stuff off the cart, about to enter an empty room. I removed my gun. Put it under the folded newspaper. Removed the silencer from my inside jacket pocket. Attached it while checking the layout again. Still no one to my left. Back to her on my right. She was inside the room now. The corridor was clear. I knocked on the scumbag's door.

"Yeah, who is it?"

"I'm checking the phone lines. We're getting complaints about crossed lines, wrong numbers . . ."

"Hold it a minute."

The corridor to the left was still clear. The same for the right. The door opened. He was tall, thin, with a pencil-thin mustache, just as described. Looked somewhat like a rodent. Yeah, a great big skinny rat with a mustache. I shot him in the head dead center. Blood splattered the sun-filled window behind him. He fell back, making a funny little sound. He hit the carpet. He was gone, finished. But I put two more in his chest. Removed the silencer, pocketed it. Returned my gun to the holster. Gently shut the door. Strolled to the elevator, reading my paper. Rode down to the lobby. A tennis match was on in this car. "What an amazing shot!" the announcer shouted. "Don't count François out of this match yet! Now you know why they call him the Comeback Kid!" "Go suck on a racket, you jerk," I said to him under my breath. This crudity was unlike me. But I suppose I had to release my tension. Two women standing next to me backed away.

"How's that for fast?" I said aloud as I hit the street. "Maybe now I can get back to more important things."

I crossed the street and walked up Sixth Avenue. I stopped at a phone booth just a block from the Hilton and called in as requested.

"Yeah?"

"It's Peter. The job is done."

"Come again?" It was the same tough, angry slob as before.

"The job is done."

"What are you talking about?"

"The mustache."

"Done? You gotta be kiddin'. I was just talking to you—what, about twenty minutes ago?"

"I'm telling you that it's done. I just got back. You wanted it quick, so this was quick."

"Let me get this straight. After we talked, you just went over there and did the job? Just like that?"

"Yeah. Did I do something wrong?"

"You mean, you just went over there—without even casing the place, staking it out?"

"Yeah. I know the place a bit. I was there a few years ago."

"A few years?"

"Yeah."

"Where did he go down?"

"In his room. No one saw a thing. It was completely clean."

"And he's gone?"

"Three times over."

"Shit. I don't believe it. I don't fuckin' believe it."

"It's true."

"Shit. I mean, this is one for Guinness. Unbelievable."

"They should find him soon. They're cleaning the rooms."

"You did this while they were cleaning the rooms?"

"I picked my moment."

"Fuckin' unbelievable."

"And now, if you people don't mind, I'd like to get back to my vacation, without any more interruptions."

"You're all right, Peter, you know that? A little nervy, but all right. I take back that 'creep' remark. You may be a creep, but you're a very talented creep."

"Thanks loads. Can I go now?"

"Sure, sure. Enjoy yourself. The money, as usual, will go into your London account. But please do me a big favor."

"Yes?"

"I understand you're planning to visit your hometown."

"Maybe."

"Why don't you do it now? Get out of the city for a while. You never know with this little job today. There might be some backlash."

"If it was such a little job, why would there be any backlash?"

"Come on, son. I don't have to explain this to you. You've been in the business long enough. You know when we do something like this that we're bound to offend somebody. So you'll take your little trip?"

"I'll consider it."

"Don't consider it. Do it. You understand? Am I talking English here?"

"I understand."

"It's impossible," I said as I hung up. "It's goddamn impossible. These people won't leave me alone. They just won't leave me alone. No matter where I am. They're always there. If I went to the bloody North Pole, they'd phone up. They'd find a way. I know it. Mr. King? Mr. King? Drop dead, Mr. King! You son of a bitch!" I must have looked quite a sight blowing up like a mental patient as I made my way up Sixth Avenue. I was definitely out of control. "Some vacation," I continued. "Some holiday. Damn stupid job! Idiots, slobs, the whole goddamn bunch of them!" Some people on the street probably took me for a fellow worker, an executive of some sort who had finally cracked. I upset them, touched them because they could identify with me and my problems. Or so they thought. But the truth is that a man in my profession can experience crummy working conditions too. He can get fed up with bosses just like anybody else. When you come down to it, all of us, in whatever line of business, have to work with or report to some bastard.

Instead of going back to my hotel, I turned on Fifty-seventh Street and went directly to Rizzoli. I had this urge to be with books, to buy them, take them home, wrap myself up in them. It's remarkable the calming effect they had. Once in the art and architecture section, the nutcase who had been terrorizing Sixth Avenue became normal, became, in fact, a quiet, harmless book fancier, a brain that needed to be fed. I found a book on John Nash, fairly fat with a lot of pictures. Great photos, especially of all the Nash terraces in Regent's Park. I'd definitely buy that volume. I found a book on Robert Adam, an oversize paperback with his elaborate designs for ceilings, cornices, fireplaces, whatever. I'd buy that one too. There was a book on Sir John Soane and his elegant, weird museum, which was in Lincoln's Inn Fields and which I'd never visited, pretty much because I'd never known it was there. This book was also a must.

When I finished with architecture, I went over to art, carrying my collection with me. I found the Constable book I had looked at before and decided to take it too. My old friend, the architectural nerd, recognized me, and I thanked him for recommending the show at the Frick, and I showed him the Turner postcard and we compared notes. The guy was a bit much. You couldn't shut him up once you got him started. But at least he took me away from everything that was happening. It was only at the register, as the cashier rang up my pile of books and loaded them into a double shopping bag, that I thought how very odd it was to be doing book shopping after having just put a bullet in some scumbag's brain.

My suite was centrally air-conditioned, but you could tell it was getting hot as hell outside. The afternoon sun seemed to be melting away the white curtains. According to the weather reports, the temperature might hit ninety-six. It was a good time to head for the hills. But I lay sprawled on my posh little sofa awhile longer, staring at the Turner postcard. It was a summer scene and I wondered how hot it had been that day in another century on Mortlake Terrace. And I thought of those people dressed to the hilt in their elaborate costume-like clothes and wondered how they had dealt with the heat. I definitely would investigate Mortlake itself when I got back to London. I hoped the slobs would allow me to return soon. As I studied the picture up close—and I mean having it practically against my nose—I noticed something that bothered me a bit. That wonderful small mansion didn't seem to be pure Georgian. No. It might very well be a mixture of Georgian and something else. Maybe what they called Regency. I wasn't completely sure. I wasn't completely sure what Regency was. But I convinced myself that if the house was, indeed, a kind of bastard, I could accept it. I had to be broad-minded if I wanted to expand my horizons. Yes, I could accept it. I had to learn to love other styles. After all, I thought, variety is an important part of one's education.

It was the early afternoon of that same day and I was in my hotel room preparing for this ridiculous trip. I had a hard time deciding which books to take along. But since I planned to rent a car rather than ride the train up, I pretty much could take them all if I so desired. I decided to take them all. I stuffed them into a duffel bag. The damn thing weighed a ton. I laughed to myself. Have library, will travel.

I filled a small canvas suitcase with a couple of shirts, some underwear, that kind of thing, just enough for a short visit. A few days was all I planned. A few days would be more than enough. I remembered that old joke—First Prize: one week in Melton; Second Prize: two weeks in Melton. I wondered why I was doing this to myself. Of all the places I could travel to, why was I going to a shabby little town that had nothing to offer but bad memories? I hated this place. It was the last place on earth I wanted to be. But maybe that was a big part of the reason. I'd now be a visitor, a tourist, someone just passing through. I could experience the dump and be thankful that I didn't live there. I could pity, even look down on, the miserable souls who did. In fact, this was a dream I'd had in my youth: after I escaped from Melton and was long gone, I'd return to it someday as a free man just so I could leave it again any time I damn well pleased.

CHAPTER 8

I PULLED INTO THE FLAMINGO MOTEL, about a half mile outside of Melton, just off the main road. The place had been there since I was a kid and had probably gone through several owners. But the famous flamingo statue had survived. It stood, as always, in the center of a circular flower bed in front of the cabins. I don't know what the bird was made of—plaster, baked clay, some such stuff—but it now looked weather-beaten, chipped, gnawed, and semi-filthy. Although it was supposed to be all pink, white underpainting showed through and the bird seemed spotted and diseased. It made you wonder, stupidly, how much longer it could balance itself on one leg. Why in hell a tropical bird was serving as the mascot of a motel in upstate New York was beyond me. I checked in and went to my room. It struck me immediately: the place was a dump. I found this particularly funny because when I was a kid I wondered what it would be like to stay at the Flamingo. I thought it might be romantic in a way. But I suppose what really appealed to me was the fact that if you were staying at the motel you were only a visitor to town, a tourist, with complete freedom to leave.

The cheap wood paneling reminded me of the sub-boss's seedy pub office in Whitechapel. Luckily, there was nothing much in the room in the way of decoration. The most noticeable item was hanging above the bed: a big, rotten painting of the nearby Hudson River. It was an autumn scene and the artist—a no-talent, or a drunk, or both—had gone crazy with color. The autumn leaves and their reflections were supposed to be beautiful but were, in fact, too loud and sloppy and made you feel a bit sick. The picture reminded me more of a nauseous stomach than anything else. I finally took it off the wall and slid it under the bed. It was an offense to any lover of fine painting.

I could have walked into town but since I didn't want to be noticed I decided to drive in and keep to my car. But as I rode along the main road—trees to the right of me, trees to the left—I realized that to stay hidden would defeat my purpose. If people didn't see me arrive, then my leaving wouldn't have any effect. In other words, how could I turn my back on them, when they hadn't even seen my front?

As I approached the Main Street intersection I began growing anxious. Wouldn't it be funny if I ran into my mother in town? Yeah, downright hilarious. But I knew that her shopping day was always Friday. It had been that way since I was a kid. And today was a Thursday. Then again, maybe she wasn't even alive. I passed my old public school and beyond that a large, grassy park where kids used to gather and play. Both these places instantly brought up bad memories. They flashed through my mind as the school and park flew by, a snippet here, a snippet there. But enough to make me angry and hesitant about entering the town itself. As far as ideas went, maybe this one, of returning home, was the worst I'd ever had.

I noticed a few kids walking just outside the park and a few running across the road up ahead. They were black, and that surprised me because in my day—which wasn't that long ago—blacks were rare in Melton. The truth is that the townspeople wanted no part of them. The truth is that they wanted all of those "city niggers"—as lovable old Dad called them—to remain down in New York City, where they belonged.

I turned left at the intersection and moved slowly down the central part of Main Street, which begins at the top of a big hill and ends at the bottom, followed by the train station and the river. Christ, I said, as I scanned the blocks. This was Main Street all right, the Main Street I'd walked along hundreds of times in the past. But it was almost completely different. New stores had replaced old. Buildings I'd known so well had been either renovated or torn down. Yes, the town definitely had a new modern look, what with its big panes of glass and cold sort of neatness. But it also had a new cheap quality, as if it had been rebuilt in haste and on a low budget, thrown together in a few weeks with flimsy, junky materials.

A bit shaken, to say the least, I turned off Main into Kimberly to look for a parking spot. My fear of being recognized had passed. The people on the street seemed quite foreign. Far more mixed than they'd ever been before. Blacks. Some Hispanics. Younger people. Poorer people. I had to take in this scene gradually, do a little exploring. Maybe it looked bad only from a car.

But, no. It looked just as bad on foot. The new stores and buildings already seemed slightly run-down. The new people seemed run-down as well. Tired, somewhat sad, going glumly about their business. Very few of the places I'd known were left, and even those places had changed. The bar at the corner of Monroe and Main was still there, but instead of Flaherty's it was now called Mike's Castle Bar, and instead of a white stucco front it was now done up in a cheap stone facing, sort of King Arthur on welfare. Frank's Market was still a market, but renamed Big Boy's, and had huge windows from almost top to bottom, which seemed sort of pointless since these great sheets of glass were entirely covered with signs announcing sale items. The bank on the corner of Connor and Main looked pretty much the same, though the big clock jutting out from it read on one side eight-twenty instead of two-thirty and on the other read nothing at all, because the hands were missing. The bank too was under new ownership—Dollar Savings had been taken over by some damn thing called New York Upstate Trust.

I looked around for the Ascot, the local movie house where I had seen a lot of make-believe killing as a kid, but it was completely gone, marquee and all. A kind of all-in-one store called Duane's Smart Shopper, selling everything from mouthwash to mops, filled the Ascot's space. The small four-story office building between Connor and Lang had been torn down. It had housed, among others, a real-estate broker, two lawyers, a doctor, and a dentist—my dentist: fat, jolly Doctor Becker, whose pot stomach always got in the way of his dental chair or vice versa. A dead modern three-story production, made of brown-tinted glass and black steel beams, stood in its place. Big gold letters, running across the street-level window, read COMPTON HEALTH GROUP, INC.

I walked about, in a bit of a daze, crossing and recrossing Main Street, trying to get a grip on it all. I recognized no one, and no one recognized me. Though a few people did turn to give me a look, probably because I was dressed too well. Unbelievable, I thought. I'm away from here for some eight or nine years and I come back to find another town with a whole new cast of characters. And I had to laugh when I considered its appearance. They had managed to take an old dump and turn it into a new dump. Christ.

The heat wasn't as bad up here as in the city. At least you could feel a breeze coming up from the river. But the sun was still threatening and I had to cool off somewhere. So I stopped in at the new bank, which was air-conditioned. I looked around, vaguely hoping that I might see someone I knew, like Mr. Harris, an officer of the former bank. My father used to refer to him as his banker. What a joke. The old man blew most of the little money he managed to save on guns, bullets, and other hunting equipment. I suppose I was standing too long by the desks in the corner, because one of the bank assistants called over to me.

"Can I help you, sir?" He was fairly young and either a light-skinned black or a dark-skinned Puerto Rican.

"No, thanks," I said, then changed my mind and walked over to his desk. "Yes, as a matter of fact, you can." I was about to do my Sir Peter routine but realized that it was totally inappropriate. Downright stupid, really. "I was wondering if Mr. Harris still works here. I think his first name was Arthur. Or Arnold."

"Sorry, sir, I don't know that name. When did he work here?"

"When this bank was a Dollar Savings."

"Oh, but that was years ago." He made it all sound like ancient history, which would make me some kind of an old bugger. "As far as I know," he continued, "a lot of those people were transferred to other banks or else retired."

"I see."

"Are you from around here, sir?"

"I used to be. Yeah, it seems a long time ago. But could I ask you—what in hell happened to this place?"

"Happened?"

"Yeah. The town has changed. It looks completely different. This isn't the place I remember."

"You know, I hear that same thing from some of the old-timers. I suppose it was a beautiful town back then."

"Not really. Just different."

"Oh, but I get the impression that it was very pretty, very quaint."

"It depends on your definition of 'quaint.' But like I said, what happened?"

"Well, I'm no expert on that. I've only been here myself about two years. But from what I understand, everything started to change about six years ago when the big drug company moved away from town."

"You mean Evans?" The old man had worked at that factory half his life. A big-shot foreman at the loading dock. He unloaded some of his anger there. But not enough.

"Yes. And when Evans closed, a lot of people were out of work. Apparently that company kept this town going.

So people moved away, property values dropped, new people moved in. The town changed."

"I see."

"I suppose you miss the old place."

"I wouldn't go that far. And, incidentally, I'm not that old."

"Oh, I can see that. It was just an expression."

"That's all right, son," I joked. "But I have to admit, I'm a little surprised by all of this. I'll be honest with you. I never had much use for this town. And when I got a chance to travel and see a lot of the great cities around the world, this place began to seem even crummier than it actually was. No offense, you understand."

"None taken, sir."

"But the thing is, I did spend a lot of time here. All of my youth, when you come down to it. And now it looks pretty much like it's gone. It's almost as if it was never here."

"I can understand that."

"It's as if someone shot it and killed it."

"Yes, I suppose it must be a little sad."

"What's really sad is that I wasn't here to see it die."

He just stared at me, puzzled. "I think you've lost me, sir," he finally said.

I paused by a Burger King along the way. This also was new. New and junky. Sal's Pizza used to occupy the spot. Sal's had been old and junky. But at least the place had sold good, natural food. Yes, Sal Donadio. I remembered the name. I remembered his son Anthony, probably would never forget that little wop prick. We had a fight once when we were kids. In that park by the school. It began as fooling around. I saw him talking to another kid and thought I'd surprise him by coming up behind him and grabbing his arms. A usual jerky kid thing to do. I must have been about fourteen. Well, the little bastard took this as some kind of an attack. He turned and applied a bear hug to me. Hey, Tony, I said, what are you doing? I was only kiddin'. But he kept on applying pressure and forcing me off balance. I grabbed his greasy wop hair and tried to pull him off. His friends yelled that I was fighting dirty, fighting like a girl.

But I didn't know what else to do. I wasn't used to fighting back then. My father hadn't taught me fighting. He hadn't taught me sports. He hadn't taught me anything but how to use a gun, shoot targets, and kill things. It was his theory that if you knew how to use a gun, you didn't have to know how to fight or worry about proving yourself at sports. Guns separate the men from the boys, he used to say. Why bother with all that other crap, when you can just get right down to it? It's all about power, he used to say, power and fear. I always get right down to it, he used to say, whether it's him or me, them or me. I get right down to it, and I always win. Because nobody else is willing to kill or willing to die.

I think his words crossed my mind when Donadio had me in that bear hug. Because although I didn't have a gun on me and couldn't get down to it, I recalled from somewhere that if you hit a man in the temples, using your bent index fingers like little hammers, you could possibly kill him. I stared at those deadly pressure points on Donadio's head as he crushed himself against me, as a group of kids gathered around us and urged us on. I was tempted to strike. But I held back. I was afraid. I thought I might actually kill him and was afraid. He forced me down to the grass, kicked me hard in the legs a couple of times and once in the chest, and walked away. The crowd cheered him and made fun of me, who was almost twice his size.

Strange how just seeing a Burger King can send your mind in weird directions. But I kept thinking about Donadio as I approached my car, and the old anger continued to build. I almost felt like searching for the bastard right now, tracking him down as a fully grown man, and taking him out after all these years. It'd be regarded as one of those "senseless" crimes they're always reporting, a murder with no apparent motive. I could hear myself finally confessing: Well, you see, I killed him because he got me in a bear hug when we were kids.

I started up the car and decided to drive down some of the side streets, take a little tour of the heart of Melton. I recognized quite a number of the sad little houses, though many of them had new paint jobs or new siding, and a few had enclosed porches that I didn't remember and extensions that hadn't existed in my time.

I'd finally settled with Donadio, though. Not thoroughly, but enough. In fact, I suppose I had him to thank for making a man of me, for paving the way for my future profession.

It happened some months later. I'd taken a while to come up with a plan and a while to convince myself to use it. But when I was ready I began tracking him each day after school, following him to the park where he met his friends, or to the family pizza parlor, or to his house with its little homemade wop shrine in the backyard.

It was an autumn afternoon, I remember, and he was alone and walking along the main road, which was just how and where I wanted him. I crossed the road and came up on his side.

"Hey, whataya know," he said, "it's Muhammad Ali."

That's when I pulled out the .32 from under my jacket. It was from my father's collection, which he kept in the garage. Good old Pop had already taught me how to use a handgun.

"What's that," said Donadio, a bit startled, "a cap gun?"

"No," I said, "it's a thirty-two and it's real. You see the bullets in the cylinder? They're real too. And if you don't do what I tell you, I'm going to shoot you right now."

At first Donadio tried to laugh it off, but you could see that he was beginning to shiver like a coward. I had him. I had him good, and he knew it. So I ordered him into the wooded area on the side of the road. "Okay, okay," he kept saying. "Don't do anything."

When we were deep enough in, I ordered him to stand against a tree. I remember that there was a blanket of red and gold leaves on the ground and clusters of the same sort of leaves in the trees. Some of them floated down on us.

"Let's be friends," he said. "I didn't want to hurt you. I didn't mean it. Hey, come on." He was pathetic. He had boasted for weeks about how he had beaten me up, beaten up that "big creep," and now he claimed he had meant me no harm. He was shaking fully and trying to hold back tears. "I didn't mean it," he kept saying.

I held the gun firmly. With my other hand I reached into my jacket pocket and removed the Red Delicious apple I'd taken from our fruit bowl in the kitchen. "Put it on your head," I ordered.

"What—what do you mean?" he cried.

"You remember the story of William Tell? Remember that story? We're going to play William Tell. Now do what I say, you prick."

He had trouble keeping the apple steady since he was shaking so much. It kept falling off his head. "Please," he cried. "Please. I'm sorry. I apologize. Let's make up."

"If you can't keep it on your head, you'll have to put it in your jacket. And that might make a mess."

He finally steadied the apple. I don't know how he managed it, because he was crying like a baby and was practically collapsed against the tree. I backed off and took aim.

"Don't," he cried. "Don't!"

"I'm a great shot," I told him. "You didn't know that, did you? Nobody does. But I can hit anything."

"Don't do it!" he cried. And that's when he wet his pants.

"You're real tough, Donadio," I said. "A real tough guy."

I fired and blew the apple to pieces. The bullet didn't even scrape his head. As he lay on the ground exhausted and weeping, I stood over him. "You're going to tell everybody how tough I am. How I challenged you and beat you up after school. If you see me near you in school or anywhere else, you're going to run away. And if I hear you make fun of me again or call me a creep or a faggot, I'll kill you for sure. You understand? Tony? Tony? Answer me. Do you understand?"

The groveling little worm cried, "Yes."

Before I let this poor, pint-sized excuse for a bully run away, I warned him not to squeal on me. "You're dead if you do," I said. But even if he did make a fuss, nobody would believe him. The story would sound too crazy. In school and outside of school, I was considered a very quiet boy, shy, a bit withdrawn, well-behaved, harmless. But, nonetheless, I decided to take no chances. I cleaned up the scene of the crime. Already, at this young age, I had the instincts of a professional. I gathered what apple fragments I could find, crushed them into the ground, and covered them with earth and leaves. I located the bullet in the tree trunk and pried it out with a penknife. To obliterate the bullet hole I cut out initials in the bark and surrounded them with a crudely carved heart. So much for evidence.

I don't know if Donadio ever reported me to anyone official, but no one ever approached me. My William Tell routine apparently did the trick. From that time on he kept his distance. And I noticed a change in other schoolmates as well. It was a nice change. Many of them used to keep away from me because they regarded me as a bit strange. Now they kept away because they were afraid.

In one day I had become my father's son. I felt bad about that part of it. And I was determined never to fully resemble him. He had taught me all too well how to stay above others, how to be independent. He had become not only my teacher but also my best friend. He was already close to fifty when I was born, so my best friend was actually a pretty old man. Old and bitter. What in hell kind of best friend was that? Yes, he had taught me independence all right. He was an expert on independence. But what he didn't quite figure on was that I'd eventually grow independent of him as well.

I was suddenly feeling quite lousy. I had the urge to get the hell out of town right then, to go somewhere else, anywhere else. Yes, I thought, why do this to myself?

I turned the car around and began heading in the direction of the Flamingo. But if I did leave here I had no idea where to go. I didn't want to travel aimlessly. I didn't want to run.

So when I reached Main Street I turned right instead of left, drove down to the river, and tried to find that little grassy rise overlooking the train station and the water where they had placed some park benches God knows how many years ago.

The spot was still there. But two of the three benches looked like they had been through a tornado or else had been repeatedly attacked by vandals. The narrow green planks that formed the seats and backs were cracked and smashed in, and the stone bases were cracked and crumbling. I sat on the bench that had managed to survive. Part of its back was missing and its seat was lopsided, but the damn thing was still usable if comfort wasn't your main concern.

I had taken several books with me in the car. I selected *Life in the Georgian City* for my bench reading. I tried to get into the chapter on "work and play," which began with a description of the way different sections of early nineteenth-century London operated on different timetables, but I couldn't seem to concentrate. The late afternoon sunlight sparkled on the river. I watched a cabin cruiser slowly cut through the golden patches of water. I followed a train as it pulled into the station and then glided away. Followed some returning commuters as they headed for cars parked by the station. And then followed the cars as they drove off for home.

The sun was blinding me and I put on my sunglasses. And although there was a river breeze, I began to sweat as I sat in the direct sunlight. I checked the entire area around me, behind me. Houses were high up on the hill and buried in trees. The road by the station was quite far away. The immediate area was completely deserted. So I removed my jacket. And there I was, sitting on an old bench on an old patch of land in my old town in my two-hundred-and-fifteen-dollar shirt, with my gun and holster fully exposed. I should have felt relaxed, free. But my old home, somewhere up there behind me in that forest of green, began to weigh down on my brain.

The next day curiosity got the better of me. And something else as well. For some reason, I had to find someone who used to know me. I was puzzled by this need. It was not about finding an old acquaintance so I could, so to speak, spit in his face and walk away. No, it was about something else, something more.

I didn't quite know what to do. Every plan seemed stupid, pointless. I'd go into all the buildings and stores on Main Street and search for who? People who used to ignore me when I was a kid? I'd ring the doorbells of neighbors, but what good would that do? After all, most of them used to pray that my angry, sarcastic father and his oddball son would move away.

Few people, I realized, had known me well. Very few. And even fewer than that had liked me. Then I thought: My mother used to know me. My mother used to know me pretty well. And once upon a time she even used to like me a bit. Besides, I thought, I can find out whether the old bird is dead or alive.

The house—my house—was at the end of a dead-end street. Beyond the dead end the land took a dip and what you had was an empty lot that had been overrun by weeds and shrubs and untamed, mongrel trees. It looked something like a miniature jungle, and as a kid I had imagined all sorts of weird creatures and bugs living inside.

The jungle was still there, wild as ever. When I saw it in the distance from my car, I thought of what a good place it would be to dump a body. I don't know why this popped into my head. I'd certainly come a long way from innocent-kid thinking.

The house was set back from the street. My heart was beating in my stomach as I slowly approached it and as it slowly came into view, appearing through the trees to its side. I was expecting to see the old gray clapboards. But what I found were phony red bricks. Christ. The dreary old wreck had been completely redone. But while the house looked newer and more solid, it also looked completely artificial—an annoying, obvious fake, like a lousy hairpiece. There was a woman on the little porch, watering some hanging plants, but it wasn't my mother. She was young and tan-skinned.

I parked the car in a space on the other side of the street and crossed over to her, this stranger making herself at home in my house. I noticed a baby sleeping in a little crib on the porch.

"Excuse me," I said, climbing the three steps—they used to be wood but now were concrete, "is the elderly lady who lives here around?"

"I'm sorry," she said pleasantly, "but what lady do you mean?" I gave her name. "Oh," she said, "she doesn't live here anymore. We bought the house from her about five years ago. Are you a friend?"

I said that I used to live in the neighborhood long ago, was just passing through and thought I'd look her up. "Do you know where she is now?" I asked.

"She moved to Miami, to live with her sister. I forget her name."

"Peggy?"

"Yes, I think that's it. I guess you knew her pretty well."

"She was friendly with my mother. We used to live over on Paul, by the church. She was a big churchgoer. That's how she got to know my mother. Through the church."

"She was a nice, quiet lady. Me and my husband got to know her a little when we were discussing the house. I don't think she had an easy life. Her husband must have been a real louse."

"Did she say that?"

"No, I heard it from one of the neighbors. The woman who used to live next door. Mrs. Barnes." Good old Gladys Barnes. She hated my guts, for some reason—maybe because she hated my father's. It was guilt by association. "Yeah, Mrs. Barnes said that the husband was sarcastic as hell, went around angry all the time, carried guns, even shot them off in the backyard sometimes."

"I never really knew him. But I think he was an amateur hunter or something."

"More like a professional nut, from what I hear. And then there was the son. Did you know him?"

"No. Bad news, huh?"

"Very. A creep. I think he broke the old lady's heart. Apparently he and the father had a big blowup one day. They fired shots or something. At least that's the story. Anyway, the son left town and never even gave his mother his address. He came back once, for his father's funeral. Then he disappeared and she never heard from him again. He never called her, wrote her, nothing. To this day she doesn't know where he is. Doesn't even know if he's dead or alive. Imagine doing something like that to your own mother, to a nice old lady like that."

I shook my head. "And Mrs. Barnes told you all of this?"

"Mrs. Barnes. And the old lady herself. I'm telling you, she left heartbroken. Lost her husband, lost her son. I mean, that's too much."

"And what happened to chatty Mrs. Barnes?"

"She moved to Maine or New Hampshire or one of those places. A lot of the people who used to live around here moved away."

"Because of Evans closing?"

"That. And because we started moving in. They'll talk to us, like Mrs. Barnes. But they don't want to live with us. They're afraid of us."

"Who's us?"

"All of us: Hispanics. Blacks. People of color."

I thanked her for the information.

"Would you like the old lady's address in Miami? We still send Christmas cards to each other. She might like to hear from you."

"No, not really. Like I said, she was more my mother's friend."

"Maybe she'd like to hear from your mother."

"My mother is dead."

"Oh, I'm sorry," she said.

I thanked her again. "Good luck with your baby," I said crazily. And then crazily added, like some baby authority: "And treat him well. Kids need that."

I just sat in my car for a while and stared at the house, trying to picture it the way it used to be. The bricks faded, and dull gray wood took their place. The whole house turned older and grayer and crummier the more I concentrated on it. I looked up at what used to be my room on the second floor. The new pink curtains disappeared and a white shade took shape.

I began to think of how I had lived in that little room all those years. Of how I'd been trapped in that room, that house, all those years. And at their mercy, at his mercy, the psycho hunter, all those years. The hanging plants that decorated the porch now reminded me of my mother's. She'd hung them in pretty much the same spots. She loved those plants. She paid more attention to them than she did to me. She was certainly more excited by them. If too many leaves turned yellow all at once, she'd get depressed, as if she hadn't given proper attention to her child and the kid had become terminal as a result. If new leaves appeared, she'd beam with happiness, as if she had been rewarded for her good mothering. Yes, in her own quiet way, the woman was a bloody lunatic. But she had one hell of a green thumb. Her hanging plants were turning into bushes. Maybe they would have turned into trees if I hadn't critically wounded them one day.

It was a Saturday afternoon, I remember. And my mother had gone to the city to visit her sister. I was home with Wild Bill and as we were having lunch in the kitchen he started to get on my case about the insurance company. I had just started there a week or so before.

"What a job," he said, talking to his franks and beans as if they were a third party. "What a place to end up. A clerk. A clerk at some two-bit company. A college-educated kid and he ends up as a clerk with a lousy salary. And he has to drive way over to another town to work this lousy job. The gas alone is half his wages." Suddenly he spoke to me directly. "And I'm sure, I'll bet on it, that they promised you the world, told you how this stinking little job was going to lead to something better. Right? Right? Of course. I know what I'm talking about. But do you know what a clerk's job leads to? I'll tell you. It leads to another clerk's job, and another one after that. I mean, it stands to reason. Have you ever heard of any executive who started as a goddamn clerk in his own goddamn company? Of course not. I mean, what kind of job is that for a young man? It's not a man's job at all. Typing, filing. That's a girl's job for Christ's sake. And it's certainly no job for someone with a college education."

I finally got a word in and reminded him that I had never finished college.

"And whose fault was that?" he asked.

"I didn't fit in there," I said. "I was just as smart as any of them—smarter even—but I didn't fit in."

"Fit in?! You weren't there to fit in. You were there to get a degree. I'm telling you, the trouble with you is that you still don't have your old man's guts. After all I taught you, all the training, you still let people bother you, walk all over you. I didn't get where I am today by running away, I'll tell you that."

"Where are you?" I said, my anger clearly showing through for maybe the first time since he'd started pushing me years and years ago.

"Where am I? Are you joking? I'm a boss, that's where I am. I'm an executive."

"An executive?" I said, laughing. "Is that what you are? I thought you yelled at men to pick up boxes. You began by picking up boxes yourself. Then after ten years of picking up boxes they promoted you so you could yell at other men picking up boxes. That's where you are. You and your boxes!"

I was about to explode completely so I left the table. That's when he exploded. "Come back here!" he yelled. "You ungrateful little coward! Who in friggin' hell do you think you are? To talk to me like that? You little bastard!"

"Drop dead!" I yelled back. I was already heading for the front door.

"Ahhhhhhh," he screamed in response to my "Drop dead." It was a scream they must have heard all through the neighborhood. The man had gone completely mental.

I was crossing our lawn when he fired the shots. They hit the ground close to my feet.

"Don't move another inch," he cried.

I turned and there he was on the porch with a rifle aimed at me.

I stood stiffly, facing him head on, giving him a perfect, easy target. "Go ahead," I said. "Shoot. Do it. Put a few in me. I don't care anymore. I'm going nowhere anyway. You said so yourself. Finish it. What are you waiting for? I'm perfectly lined up. Go on, Dad. Do it. Get it over with. Pull the trigger. Get right down to it, like you always say."

His hands started to shake and then his arms and then his whole damn body. He lowered the rifle and leaned against the porch. He looked like he was about to have a nervous breakdown. But he'd get no sympathy from me. Instead I walked straight to the garage and from the gun cabinet removed my own .45, which I had been secretly practicing with for the past year. I came out and aimed the gun directly at him.

"I knew you couldn't do it," I said. "You can kill animals. But that's all. And do you know why? Because rabbits and squirrels don't carry guns. That's why. When you come down to it, you can't do it, can you? Can you? But I can do it. I've been wanting to do it for years."

I started firing. I could have easily put a bullet in him, but I shot around him instead. He cringed and held his arms over his face, like the damn baby that he was. And then I aimed at Mom's precious hanging plants. They were hanging by ropes. Three in a row. I aimed for the top of those ropes, where they were attached to the porch. "This is with a handgun, Pop," I announced, "just a lousy handgun." I blasted away, hitting, severing each of the ropes. The clay pots with their stupid overloaded vines fell fast, one hitting the railing of the porch and cracking apart, the other two hitting the lawn and cracking apart. They looked terrifically pathetic cracked apart, the plants lying dead in their own dirt. "Beat that, you son of a bitch," I yelled.

Just then Mrs. Barnes shouted down from her bedroom window next door. "I'm calling the police! You people are crazy! Plain crazy!"

I shouted up to her. "You're lucky I just ran out of bullets, you ugly old bitch!" And with that I stuck my gun in my belt, got in my junky used car, drove out of town, and never saw my father again—at least not alive.

I returned some days later to pick up my clothes and stuff, and then about a year later I briefly visited the funeral parlor on Main Street to see the old bastard laid out. "I won," I whispered to his clammy, rubber face.

I was suddenly feeling slightly sick to my stomach. I started the motor, pulled away, and drove off fast. This whole trip had been a mistake. I couldn't understand anymore what I had wanted to prove. As I sped down the tree-lined streets, not even bothering to slow down at stop signs, I thought I passed Mrs. Wallace, a vague friend of my mother's, carrying home a bag of groceries. She had been quiet like my mother. She was a widow and raised a nerdy son. And when these two weird, quiet women got together they always talked in whispers. I couldn't say whether Mrs. Wallace liked me or not. If I was at home when she visited, she'd give me a quick, friendly hello and then ignore me, as if I were a pet or some such thing you could acknowledge and then forget. I was almost tempted to slow down and turn the car around just to satisfy my curiosity. But what would I say to the woman if she was Mrs. Wallace? What in hell was the point?

I had to get out of this place. It was doing strange things to my mind. I prided myself on thinking straight. And I wasn't thinking straight up here. Not at all.

I returned to the Flamingo, packed my clothes and books, and checked out. I started to head north, passing the Main Street intersection and continuing on along the main road. But as I drove on I began to have second thoughts. I had had quite enough of this area, of the suburbs, of all this small-town crap. Because I just knew that the next town would remind me of Melton and the town after that and so on.

I turned the car around and headed back south, for New York. I came to my old school again, but this time I stopped the car right in front of the place. It was closed for the summer, quite empty and dead, a kind of overblown mausoleum of education. It looked very much the same as I remembered it, except that they had sandblasted the facade so that it appeared more white now than gray. There was something I had to do. I didn't know why exactly, what sense it made, but I had to do it. Like I said, I wasn't thinking straight.

Remaining in the car, I drew my gun, took aim, and shot to pieces a few of the ground-floor windows. The sound of the shattering glass, of destruction, made me feel really good. "Go to hell," I said. I was almost happy for the moment. Some kids playing in the nearby park heard the noise and started running in my direction. I sped off.

In my rearview mirror I watched Melton grow smaller and smaller and then become just a green blotch. All that torture, I thought, for all those years. All the years of feeling rotten, all the craziness of the old man, the killing of helpless things, the tension each day, the stupid drama, and there isn't even a record of it. It's all gone. What had been the point of it? I wondered. If it was all going to vanish someday what had been the point of its existing in the first place? The only true record of it all was lodged in my brain. The only life it had anymore was in me. But with a little effort I could forget it. Yes, with a little effort I could kill it. After all, I was good at doing that. I was a master.

It was dark as I drove down the West Side Highway. To my left were row after row of buildings, an endless silhouette. They were all lit up, their windows glowing like yellow jewels. To my right the gray-black river trembled very slightly and reflected, way in the distance, the twinkling lights of the Jersey waterfront. I could have been floating in a dream. I felt soft, transparent, as if I had faded to nothing. I was here, yet not here at all.

I came to my senses by the time I reached West Fifty-seventh Street. I decided to check into a motor inn off Tenth Avenue. Nobody would expect to find me there. What the Firm didn't know wouldn't hurt them.

So for the next several days I remained on the West Side, sort of incognito. I visited the Lincoln Center area, which had become overcrowded with big ugly "luxury" apartment buildings. But I found a new Barnes & Noble bookshop there, with a pretty good architecture section. I even found a book on Regency style, which I thought I should investigate before saying for sure that I didn't care for it at all. And I stopped in to see a movie in the area. It was a gangster picture, the kind I used to love as a kid. But now these things tended to look really phony to me. Especially this one. Two guys trade about fifty bullets and don't even change their gun clips once. Neat trick, I thought. One guy hits another over the head with a board, but instead of cracking apart his skull he cracks apart the board. Give me a break, I thought.

When I figured enough time had passed for me to have been away upstate, I returned to my posh hotel and reported in. And I quickly got back into my regular routine, reading, taking notes, visiting the library. I definitely did not like Regency design, I discovered. And I thought a lot about London, couldn't wait to get back, in fact. I carefully planned my itinerary for visiting Georgian buildings. I added to my already long list. Not only houses in the city but those in the counties. I'd be traveling all over England, could keep myself busy for months, possibly years.

I was very excited when the "Mr. King" call finally came. September, after all, was just a few days away. I could already feel London in me as I dialed.

"We're sending you out," said the slob with the gravel voice. "Tonight."

"Good," I said, "I sort of miss London, to tell you the truth."

"London? Who said anything about London? We're sending you to Barcelona."

"Barcelona? What's in Barcelona?"

"A big job. Maybe the biggest you'll ever have. Major, son. Major."

"But you can't. Not now. I have other things to do."

"Are you pulling my leg or what? You do what we tell you to do. Are you fuckin' kiddin'?"

"I have buildings to look at. I have to be in London. The buildings are in London." I realize now that I was beginning to noticeably crack here. This might have been the start of it all.

"Look at buildings? What buildings? What the fuck are you talking about?"

I did have sense enough not to explain. "Can't you send someone else?" I asked. "I haven't been home in months."

"I thought New York was your home?"

"Not anymore. Look, do me the favor. There must be somebody else you can get."

"You're the one, son. We need a super marksman for this job and you're elected. Nobody else. Just you. You're the only one who can pull this off. And it's gotta be done. I can't stress that enough. We're counting on you. We're even praying for you. This is the biggest job of your career."

"But—"

"Start packin', son. We'll pick you up at three."

They can't, I kept saying to myself. They can't. They don't know what they're dealing with. They can't. They just can't.

But after all was said and done, the fact of the matter was that they could. They could. And I was on my way again.

Part III

CHAPTER 9

I LOOKED OUT AT THE MEDITERRANEAN. I was high above the city, in the hills. Barcelona was spread out below in a haze. You could hardly tell where the city ended and the Mediterranean began. You couldn't quite penetrate the glare. But that grayish band stretching across the horizon, sparkling silver here and there, was the Mediterranean all right. How odd, I thought. Just the other day I was in Melton and here I am in Spain, in Barcelona, looking out at the Mediterranean. People were going about their lives in Melton right now. They were trapped in that small, sad town, and here I was, a Melton native, looking out at the Mediterranean. The more you thought about it, the odder it seemed. Just two days ago I had been another person in another world. Who was that person? And who is this person here now?

Not only was I looking out at the Mediterranean, but I was looking out at it from the weirdest park I'd ever been in. And sitting on the weirdest and longest bench I'd ever sat on. It was a ceramic-mosaic sort of thing, made of what looked like thousands of pieces of cracked, colored plates that had been sloppily glued together to form little designs. The whole bench curved round, twisting in and out, like an enormous snake. It served as a kind of border for the flat but curvy-edged roof of what resembled a

Greek or Roman temple, only one built by Spaniards. The snake on the roof.

The entire area was called Güell Park. It could have been a village out of some fairy tale. A crazy, overdone fairy tale. The houses were fantastic, decorated with tiles and topped by thin, twisted spires. They were curvy, lopsided, as if they had been designed by a child who couldn't as yet draw a straight line. And they looked sweet, like candy. In fact, they made you think of gingerbread houses.

It was a very distracting place to conduct business, to say the least. But it also was a place for tourists. And that was how my Barcelona contact and I must have come across. Sitting there on the cracked snake bench with a map of the city spread out on our laps and photos resting beside us, we must have looked like two tourists planning their itinerary. We probably appeared quite innocent.

The contact was a small, slight, educated man named Isaac. He was friendly and told me his name. Most contacts don't. I thought it was a peculiar name for someone Spanish.

"I'm not Spanish, my friend," he explained. "I'm Catalan. There is a difference. You will learn all about it if you stay here long enough. I was named after Isaac Albéniz, the great Catalan composer. He lived right here in Barcelona. My mother was a piano teacher and named me after one of her favorite composers. You know Albéniz?" I told him that I wasn't much for music. "That is sad," he said. "In our business we need a little beauty." I wondered what a man like this was doing in our business. His life had probably taken a wrong turn somewhere. These things happen.

We finally got down to the job. I listened to him as he talked, indicated areas on the map, showed me various photos. I even made comments, asked him questions. And yet I felt somewhat distant from this entire business. It didn't seem quite real. And above all, it didn't seem to have much to do with me.

"This is the street," he said, pointing with a ballpoint pen to the map of Barcelona. "Ausiàs March. It is quite near the Plaça de Catalunya. In fact, it is not so very far from your hotel. You are up here, correct, on the Rambla de Catalunya. No, not very far at all. Ausiàs March is a quiet street with some very lovely old houses. The house where we are expecting our man is here." He indicated an inked-in red dot on the map. "And this is a picture of it." He reached down on the bench for his little deck of photos. The house reminded me of the kind you see in Paris, a sort of small mansion. "Interesting door," I said, for some reason. The front door was made of very thick reddish wood, which was decorated with a swirling carved design. "Somewhat floral," I observed. "A bit much, but quite nice."

My comments seemed to surprise Isaac, but he remained gentlemanly and helpful. "The door? Oh, yes, the door. You will see much of that in Barcelona. Art Nouveau. Modernisme. Very popular here many years ago."

"I'm a Georgian man myself. But this stuff has its place, I suppose. I wouldn't have thought so. But it works."

"Well, in any case, that is the door our man will be entering. Or, should I say, will not be entering because you will have to dispose of him before he does. And here is where you will be set up." He pointed to another dot on the map. It was across the street and quite a bit up from the target. "Roughly this house here. We have secured a flat on the top floor—facing the street, of course."

"That looks about a half block from the target. Couldn't you get something a little closer? More across the way?"

"They tried. But this is the closest they could get. What they did was send some of our men to canvass the street. The men had false identifications and said they were from the police. They told each concierge that there had been several burglaries on the block and that they were checking on which tenants were home and which were still on holiday. They said that they were particularly concerned about the unoccupied apartments because those, of course, were the most likely to be robbed. Our men discovered that many of the tenants who were still away would be returning soon. But there were a few who would be gone longer. One of those tenants, a doctor, has a flat facing the street. So this is the place they chose. This place here."

I was curious about how they had secured that particular flat.

"It was a matter of bargaining, you might say. The men returned to the doctor's building, but this time told the concierge who they really were. They said that they would pay him a very handsome sum if he would allow them to use the flat whenever they needed."

"And if he refused?" As if I had to ask.

"Well, that would not be so pleasant. The man came to understand this quickly. So he chose the money. It was a wise choice."

"It was the only choice."

"Yes, this is quite true. But he could have resisted. He could have been difficult."

"He could have been dead."

"Well, yes, this was most possible. But he decided to stay alive and also earn quite a lot of money. I believe he is very happy about his good fortune. You will see for yourself. You will meet him tomorrow. They thought you should get to know the place. Check for problems. Check your line of fire. The area in general. You understand this, of course. A man with your experience. These are not things I have to tell you."

"Do you have the keys to the place?"

"Yes, of course. Let me give them to you." And he handed me a set of gold keys.

"Fine," I said, "but I don't have to meet him."

"What?"

"The concierge. You said that I will meet him tomorrow. But I don't want to meet him. I don't want to see him. And I don't want him to see me."

"But he is on our side now. He is our friend now."

"He's not my friend. Keep him away from me. Make this very clear to him. If I show up, I want him out of sight. He doesn't ever see me. He doesn't ever know who I am. That's the way I operate. Understood?"

"Yes, my friend. Whatever you say. He does not see you."

It's a funny thing about habits. About self-preservation. About being a complete professional. I felt so far away from this business, yet I reacted as always to possible danger. My concern was almost laughable when I think about it now.

I asked to see the photos of the building again. I couldn't quite get over that door. "I'm looking forward to seeing this in person."

Isaac seemed puzzled by my comment. "Is the door a problem for you in some way?"

"No. No problem. It's just very unusual. Quite well made, from what I can see. What do you think the flowers are? The ones here and here? They look like lilies to me. What would you say?"

"This is important to you, uh?"

"It's interesting. I sort of like it. I'm surprised. I didn't think I'd care for this sort of thing at all."

"Good. I am happy for you. Good."

"What was that French word you used before, to describe this style?"

"You mean Art Nouveau?"

"Yes, that's it. What is it exactly? I think I've come across the term somewhere before. In my reading."

"I am no expert, you understand. But I suppose one might say it was very decorative. Many curving lines. References to nature. Elaborate. Fantastic. Very popular at the turn of the century. But, how foolish of me. I do not have to describe it. We are surrounded by it right here in this park. You might say this is Art Nouveau—Gaudí style."

"What style?"

"Gaudí. The great Catalan architect. The master of Barcelona. You do not know Gaudí?"

I didn't. So he told me about the man and this park—Gaudí's park—and about his famous Barcelona buildings and his great, unfinished church, the Sagrada Família, the weird spires of which Isaac tried to locate through the haze in the city below. And then he went on to mention other architects of the city—men with such names as Montaner and Puig—and talk about Jujol, who had collaborated with Gaudí to design the very bench we were sitting on. I took out my pad and pen and jotted down the information and, of course, got the spelling of the names. The man was incredible. A sort of scholar in his own right. And so unlike the typical Firm slob that it was hard to think of him as a criminal at all.

Isaac then stopped himself. "You know, my friend, I do not mind doing this. I love my city and I know it well. And I enjoy talking about it. But maybe we are straying too far from the business at hand."

"I know all about the business at hand. I don't know about Barcelona or its buildings."

"Let me point out that there is a time and a place for everything."

"Maybe not as much time as we think."

Poor Isaac. I was taking advantage of his good nature. "I have to stress the importance of this job," he said, trying to sound official. "Our man is to attend a meeting at this house. He must not get to that meeting. If he does, it will create a very great problem for us. We know he will be arriving in a week or so, but we do not know as yet the exact day. And we do not know where he is coming from. All we know is that he will be at this house in the afternoon. We believe that the time is four o'clock. As we see it, this will be the only opportunity to stop him. He will, of course, be arriving by car. Well guarded. They will probably send a few cars in advance. And when he does arrive and leaves his car, you may have only one good shot. You see, from the car to the door—the door you like so much—is only a few seconds. That is why we needed a marksman. That is why we needed you. You have a history of never missing."

"This sounds big. What is it? Something political?"

"This we cannot discuss. You know the rules. But you are correct in one respect. It is big. Very big. And we are depending upon you and your skill."

I should have felt flattered. But I felt nothing. Nothing at all. "And how do I get away?" I asked, still acting like the professional.

"That, I am happy to say, works out well for us. There is a rear door to the building, leading to a courtyard and to the rear doors of other buildings. Here is a rough map of the courtyard." He placed the drawing over the city map we'd been looking at. "Here is your building, the building you leave. And here is the building you go to. On the far right. We will make certain that the rear door is open. Go through that door and it will take you to this street here, where our car will meet you. You will be carrying your rifle in a suitcase that you will find in the flat. You will then meet up with another car, a taxi, which will take you to your hotel. You will pick up your luggage, pay your bill, and return to the taxi. All quite natural, quite leisurely. The taxi will then take you to the airport. And a plane will take you home."

It all sounded so simple, so easy, even a bit boring. The plan was meant for me, yet I listened to it as you might listen to a little story someone had made up and was reading aloud. Isaac waited for my opinion. "Very good," I finally said. "I like it. Fine."

He seemed pleased. "What sort of rifle would you prefer?" he asked. "We can get whatever you want. It will be in the flat tomorrow."

"Anything will do. I can use anything."

He suddenly did not seem pleased. "Anything? But this an important job. A difficult target. Perhaps you should use something special. Yes, I believe that something special would be correct."

It was almost as if he were nudging me to give the right answer. I had to think back. It was a struggle. I really didn't feel like thinking about this matter. But I reluctantly reviewed the guns I had known.

"Well," I said at last, "I'll need something long-range."

"Ah, well, yes."

"There was a Sako I used once. I think I might even have used it here, some years ago. I don't remember the model number. But it was a .308, held ten rounds, had an adjustable trigger and butt plate. Terrific accuracy."

"Sako," said Isaac, "made in Finland, I believe."

"Yeah, some foreign place."

"Yes, I know it. You have very good taste. A very fine rifle, very expensive. We will have it for you."

"Good. Thanks."

"And you may need a bipod for support."

"Never use them."

"But this may be a very difficult shot. You will need to be steady."

"I'm always steady. No, I don't like guns that are fixed in position. What if you have to move quickly? What if the target isn't where you planned?"

"But you can detach them quickly."

"Not quickly enough. No. No bipod or tripod or any pod. Trust me." I was amazed by how fast I'd called up all of this nonsense. And I managed to sound so sincere as well.

"And the scope?" he asked. "Anything special?"

"The standard one with that gun. Did you say there's a Gaudí building near where I'm staying?"

"A Gaudí building?"

"Some house near my hotel?"

"Oh, yes. But excuse me, I thought we were discussing the job."

"We were. But now we're discussing this."

"Maybe we should finish discussing the job."

Isaac was beginning to get on my nerves. "I thought we were finished."

"I had to ask you what time you would like the concierge to be at the building tomorrow."

God, but this business was so relentless. "Oh, twelve o'clock, one."

"Shall we say twelve?"

"Fine," I said abruptly, "—now where is that building?"

He told me that there were actually two Gaudí buildings within several blocks of my hotel. And, better still, they were two of his most famous. The Casa Milà and the Casa Batlló. They were both on the Gràcia, which runs parallel to the Rambla de Catalunya and is only a block away. I was really rather excited about seeing them. I never thought this trip would take such a turn. Spanish architecture? Who would have thought I'd ever get interested in that? Several years ago when I was in Barcelona for the first time, I hadn't even noticed the city much. Or if I had, I'd probably thought of it as looking a little like Paris and then immediately filed it away in the back of my brain. Then again, my entire stay lasted less than two days and I had other things on my mind, like killing four men. And, of course, I had no scholarly interests back then. None at all.

I was glad about this unexpected turn. On the plane over, I'd felt so frustrated and disappointed about not returning to London that I'd asked the stewardess for several drinks. I wanted to drown my sorrows, as they say. I wondered what in hell I was going to do with myself in Barcelona. Even though I was arriving as Peter Chilton, I couldn't see much point in continuing the full act. After all, neither he nor I knew Spanish, and even if I found some English-speaking Spaniards, would they be able to tell the difference between an English accent and an American? The drinks wore off by the time we landed, but I was still floating on air as I rode a cab into the city. I don't know if it was jet lag or what, but I felt weak and helpless, as if my poor body was being shipped around from place to place and I couldn't do anything to prevent it. My brain wanted to be elsewhere, but here it was, being carted off with my body to Barcelona. Where next? I wondered. Africa?

"Let me know how you find it," said Isaac.

"Find what?"

"The flat tomorrow. The view. The rifle. Everything. If there are any problems, we should know immediately so that we can correct them."

We were walking down the park's main stairway. It was made of more cracked tile and looked like something out of one of those stupid, elaborate movie epics—many stairs leading down from a great temple. A series of fountains with plants divided the staircase in two. As I stepped down the stairs I had climbed earlier, I looked again at the fountain area and its decoration—at the muscular, multicolored ceramic dragon clinging to a pool of water. And farther down at the large ceramic shield with the ceramic serpent's head coming out of its center. "Fantastic, uh?" said Isaac. "Crazy," I answered. This Gaudí character definitely had a thing for snakes, serpents, and assorted reptiles. And he was, of course, a total nut for tiles.

We were moving toward the entrance to the park when Isaac asked me how I felt.

"I'll be honest," I said, "I'm used to clean design. Georgian is clean. Elegant and clean. You can't get much more clean or elegant. Now this stuff here is overdone. Like that door in the photo. But it's so overdone and weird it becomes sort of interesting. And believe me, no one is more surprised than me that I find it interesting."

"What I meant, my friend, was the job. How do you feel about the job?"

"The job?" I said. "The job is a job."

"But you feel confident?"

"Wouldn't you feel confident if you never miss?"

Just as we were about to exit the park, Isaac reached

into the plastic shopping bag he'd been carrying, removed a plastic bag from some tourist shop, and handed it to me.

I peeked inside. It contained a holster, gun, and silencer.

"I hope there will be no need for this," he said.

"Thanks," I told him.

I decided to stay behind and explore the park more thoroughly. After all, this was a tourist haunt and I was, among other things, a tourist.

"So you will call tomorrow, yes?" said Isaac as we shook hands.

"Yes," I said, a bit annoyed by his persistence. "You can count on it."

"It is good to see your attitude," he said as he moved away.

"What attitude is that?"

"You are so relaxed," he said. "One can tell that you are a professional. You do not seem to have much concern."

For the next hour or so I walked about the park, climbing from one level to the next as the park and its weird structures rose up into the hills. I went inside the temple I had been sitting on top of earlier. I walked around its thick columns, which filled its interior like stone trees. I looked up at its elaborate rolling ceiling, decorated here and there with huge ceramic disks that resembled suns. I climbed some crooked stone steps and walked into a kind of arcade dug out of a hill. The inside wall was curved, a bit like a Tube station, and the area was shadowy and dead quiet, like in a monastery. Yes, everything in this crazy park made you think of other places, other things. Maybe it had been purposely designed to drive you a little mad.

I took it in stride, though. I was too tired to do otherwise. Tired and soft. That floating feeling was with me again. My feet weren't quite connecting with the ground. My muscles and joints had gone all buttery. I moved ahead, the ground advanced before me, different things came into view, yet I didn't know what was driving me on. I wasn't really in control of myself anymore.

I floated back down through the park and back to the exit and finally into a cab that took me back to the hotel. It's jet lag, I thought. Combined with the Barcelona heat and humidity—the stalled air, heavy, dead. Yes, that's what it is, I thought. But, then again, I was a traveling man, travel was part of the business, and I couldn't remember suffering this way before.

My room was on the top floor and overlooked the Rambla de Catalunya. I had a better view than most of the other guests because my room led out to a little roof that had been railed and partitioned off to make a kind of terrace. Leaning over the railing, I could look right down on the street below. There was a kind of traffic island in the middle of the Catalunya, with trees and benches, where people would gather at night. Across the street were the same sort of elegant old buildings that lined my side—mostly flats, I assumed, and maybe a few offices. The biggest attraction was a wide old mansion with high windows that served as a school for little Catalans. Their cries had awakened me early in the morning. Half asleep, I had gotten up, gone out onto the terrace, identified the noisemakers, and staggered back to bed again.

I floated onto the terrace now. I stood against the railing for support, as if I was too weak to hold myself up. I looked out at the rooftops, faded somewhat in the haze—gray, red, and white boxes, various sizes, uneven heights, all just piled together. I could make out a bit of the Montjuïc, the big park by the sea that the bellhop had pointed out when he'd first escorted me to my room. It rose up like a displaced mountain in the Mediterranean, an odd giant mass of earth just beyond the heart of the city.

I sat down on one of the white plastic wire chairs that were kept on the terrace for relaxing. All I needed, I convinced myself, was a brief rest and I'd be as good as new. Then I'd go seek out those two Gaudí buildings. The sun had a hard time penetrating the haze, but enough of it got through to bother me. With a great effort I rose up from my chair and slid it over to the area by the window, which was shaded by a striped awning. There in the shadow I sat and stared out at the city. I might have been asleep, for all I knew. Asleep with my eyes open. I obviously had calmed down since leaving New York—which had brought out the worst in me. But now I was so calm I could hardly move.

I'm in Spain, I thought again for some reason. It struck me as sort of amazing. I tried to call up Chilton but he was nowhere to be found. That tortured madman from New York was also gone—and good riddance to him. The hit man was still here, but only vaguely alive. I removed the Turner postcard from my jacket pocket and held it close to my face. I still liked it; it still moved me. I wondered if I would ever see Mortlake Terrace in person. A chill suddenly went through me. I didn't know why.

I must have dozed off about then. When I opened my eyes, I saw from my watch that an hour and a half had passed. It was already mid-afternoon. I was more than a bit surprised. I had never fallen asleep in a chair before. An uncomfortable chair, at that. I had never been so exhausted. In fact, I'd always prided myself on my stamina. I felt stiff so I moved my arms and legs back and forth, but I remained in my chair. I couldn't quite bring myself to stand. I'll get up soon, I thought. I'll go down to the street, find those Gaudí buildings. Any minute now.

But I continued to sit. Maybe my problem was that I'd always felt the need to be doing something. Here I was, doing absolutely nothing and getting pleasure out of it. Why deny myself? Who was to say that I had to do anything more?

I closed my eyes again. I thought about my Georgian house. The one in the country, in Derbyshire, Sussex, wherever. The one in the city, in Bloomsbury, Belgravia, Regent's Park. It all seemed like a distant dream now. Maybe I had to be back in London for the Georgian house to seem more real, more possible, more white.

Another half hour went by. I remembered an elegant pastry and coffee shop I'd passed in a cab that morning on my way to Güell Park. It was only about a block and a half away, up on the Catalunya. I decided to make that my goal. I struggled up from the chair. My legs were half asleep and I had to walk a little in place to get the blood properly flowing again.

I felt like I had a hangover as I stumbled over to the elevator and rode down, clinging to the elevator wall. The fresh air will do me good, I thought stupidly—"stupidly" because I then realized that I'd been in the "fresh air" on the terrace. Yes, I'd been outside all the while. I'd been outside even when I'd been inside. I'd been outside most of the day.

I returned with a cup of espresso and a small box of homemade cookies. As I said, I'm not one for sweets. But I thought a little sugar right about now might give me some needed life. There was a small, square wrought-iron table with a glass top standing in the corner of the terrace. I pulled it over to my chair and put down the cookies and coffee.

When you haven't had cookies in a long time—particularly rich cookies coated with chocolate and filled with jelly—they can taste disgustingly sweet. That's how one of these tasted. I nearly spit it out. It was so richly sickening. But the slight nausea it produced woke me up a bit. And a few sips of the very strong espresso, which was thick as mud and almost as revolting, woke me up even more.

I decided to give those Gaudí buildings another try. Taking along the map the Firm had provided, I went out into the street and tracked down the houses. It seemed hotter in the street than it had on my terrace—felt, in fact, a little like a steam bath—but I pressed on, determined to continue my studies.

The Casa Batlló was closer to my hotel so I visited it first. Drunken, with ceramics, capped by a kind of lopsided helmet and decorated on one side with a spire and cross, the building looked like something from Güell

Park, only on a larger scale. The broken tiles, which had a bluish tinge, gave the facade a kind of peppery appearance, as if it were coated with clinging confetti. The balconies were really weird, like nothing I'd ever seen before. They could have been made of bone and resembled huge masks. And they gave the impression that the house was staring at you. Insane and overdone as the house was, I rather liked the whole bloody mess. Not to live in, you understand. Not like the Georgian house. But as a thing in itself. As a kind of work of art—wacky Catalan art, Gaudí art.

I walked several blocks back up the Gràcia until I came to the Casa Milà. You couldn't really miss the damn thing. There it was, occupying the whole corner, looking like some big, fat off-white seven-layer cake that was melting in the heat. John Nash would have taken ill on the spot. I myself thought of the stuff displayed in that mental hospital the old man had taken me to, particularly the crazy works of clay. Yes, that's what this could have been—a building modeled after a clay house slapped together and sloppily molded by a nutcase.

And yet I liked this place too. It was different. And I was definitely learning to appreciate things that were different, that had a kind of character all their own, that were downright strange. A few tourists were hanging about the area, snapping pictures of the house or posing in front of it to be snapped. I kept stepping back, wanting to get a good view of it as a whole. When I was far enough away—about a quarter of a block—I could see the roof with its huge, bloated chimneys that looked like swirls of whipped cream and also like giant creatures, creepy guardians of the place.

Rather than return to the hotel I decided to look for a bookshop. I felt the need for information. Something on Gaudí. Possibly a guidebook to Barcelona buildings. I could, of course, pursue my British studies, but Georgian architecture did seem a bit beside the point in this ornate city.

I returned to my room with several books I'd picked up in a so-called drugstore, just a block or so away from my hotel. It was similar to the kind of places they have in Paris—a loud, crowded space filled with a variety of shops, something like a one-floor mall. I found a good, thorough guidebook to the city, a small but chunky and scholarly paperback on Gaudí, and, best of all, a long, narrow handbook on Barcelona architecture with small black-and-white photos of each of the buildings, along with brief descriptions that told you what special features to look for. I was very happy as I left the place, cutting through a modest afternoon crowd. With these books I felt in control again, like I had a handle on this foreign city. I also felt again that I had a kind of goal, a kind of purpose. Passing a little souvenir shop, I noticed some local freaks just hanging out, a collection of poofs with teased and dyed hair. Christ, I thought. British poofs were bad enough, but poofs speaking Spanish with a lisp were bloody ridiculous. Then again, maybe I had to exercise a little tolerance, like I had done with Spanish architecture.

Maybe that was the mark of a true intellectual—someone who could accept the weird.

I sat down again on the terrace chair and was about to dip into my new books when I glanced over at the little table. The sight made me jump. The sight made my skin crawl. Because there, attacking the box of cookies, which I'd stupidly left open, was an army of ants. Hundreds of them, coating the cookies like sprinkles. "What in hell—" I said as I stood up and stared down in disgust. I then noticed that these tiny bastards were coming out of a small grated square drain in the floor of the terrace. They traveled from that drain, up one leg of the table, to the cookie box. They were still advancing, as far as I could tell. The yellowish cookies were getting blacker by the minute. Christ, I said. This was a five-star hotel, for God's sake. But what it really was was a bloody five-star ant farm. The hotel looked so neat and tidy, yet it had this crap going on in its walls and floors. It was like some marks I had known. Fine on the outside, yet rotten within.

I went down to the front desk to complain and to ask for someone to clean up the mess and stomp the ants. "Excuse me, sir, but what did you say they were?" The desk man was an ultra-cool Catalan who acted like he was doing you a big favor by just responding. "Ants," I said angrily. He shook his head. He seemed like an educated sort so I found it hard to believe that this English word meant absolutely nothing to him. "Ants," I said again, "insects, bugs. You know, you usually have them at a picnic. They're always looking for food." "Pick-neck?" he said, puzzled. "Christ." I was about to pull out my gun. I was almost convinced that this dumb routine was an act designed to make a complaining foreigner—me—look stupid. I asked him for paper and a pencil. This request he seemed to understand perfectly.

As best I could, I drew a picture of an ant. Actually, it came out better than expected. I held it up before me as if I were admiring a work of art. I was rather proud of myself. I didn't realize that I had such talent. "Ant," I finally said to him, poking at the bug picture. "Oh," he said, his face lighting up, and then he came out with some word—in Spanish, Catalan, whatever in hell he was speaking—the word, I assumed, for "ants." "Right," I agreed. "Ants. They're all over my terrace. They destroyed my cookies." "That is very strange," he said. "No guest has ever complained of such a thing." "You have an ant problem, my friend." "We will see," he said. "Don't see. Just get an exterminator." "A what, sir?" "Exterminato. A bug killer. A hit man with a can." "What? What are these words?" "You and your ants are disturbing my peace. You see, I was winding down. I was floating. I was nowhere. I was half dead. And then those little bastards ruined everything."

CHAPTER 10

THAT NIGHT, still in a soft, weakened state, I thought I'd save what little strength I had by staying in for supper and eating in the hotel dining room. I'd order something non-Spanish and non-oily, like an ordinary steak with white rice and sliced tomatoes. But then I began thinking of those food-loving ants. I imagined the little buggers scaling the kitchen counters and feasting on any food left unattended. The thought sickened me enough to dine out. I went to a neighborhood café that seemed popular with tourists. There were some healthy Scandinavian types about, along with a number of chunky Germans. I don't like Germans, chunky or otherwise. I think of them as giant tubes of knockwurst, which I hate. And aside from the fact that they bombed my adopted city during the war, I don't care for their manner, their pushiness. They remind me too much of my old man. I took a table as far away from them as possible. But at one point one of them passed my table on his way to the loo. He gave me an odd, German look. I gave him a brief Nazi salute. I think he was thinking of coming at me, he and his German pot belly, but my jacket was open and apparently he saw my gun and decided to tolerate the insult.

I was chewing something resembling a steak—it was charbroiled, black, and could have been horse for all I knew—when I heard some guitar music playing over the speaker system. Spanish music to put the tourists in the mood. I'm not one for music, for sentimental rot, but I had to admit that I was taken by this melody. It had a certain beauty to it. It made me think, for some reason, of traveling through the Spanish countryside and coming to a Spanish village, even though I'd never been to either the Spanish countryside or a Spanish village. When it ended, another little piece came on, very rapid, tense, and catchy. It made me think of, among other things, hurrying after a mark through the streets of Barcelona. My enjoyment surprised me. And I found myself calling over the waiter to question him about these two pieces. I even gave him my trusty pad and pen and asked him to write down the titles and the composers. He went away for a while and then returned with the information. The first piece was called "Recuerdos de la Alhambra" and was by Francisco Tárrega. The second was written by—of all people—Isaac's namesake, Isaac Albéniz, and was titled "Asturias." The waiter had even written down the name of the cassette. New assignment, I thought: track down the tape and buy a Walkman to play it.

The flat on Ausiàs March was filled with potted palms, old photographs and pictures, big bulky cabinets and chests and other furniture from another age. You could imagine the owner returning home dressed in a black cloak and top hat and holding a walking stick. Yes, the place certainly had a lot of old-world charm and, in fact, resembled a museum. I didn't mind its Victorian look at all. It was sort of quaint and cozy. And I liked the high ceilings. I admired the tile work in the very spacious foyer. I thought the paintings old-fashioned but generally pretty tasteful. There were quite a lot of old drawings hanging about, portraits mainly, done in what looked like charcoal. The people in them seemed nineteenth century—the women done up in lacy, frilly things; the men, with beards or long mustaches, wearing vests and topcoats. These drawings, I thought, weren't half bad and went very nicely with the musty rooms.

The living room, which was where I'd be shooting from, was huge, with two sets of long, curtained French windows decorated with red velvet drapes. They faced the street and became large hazy rectangles of yellow when the sun struck that side of the building. The potted palms were bigger here than in the other rooms, standing by the windows like trees and sucking in any available sunlight. And taking over one front corner of the room was a grand piano with a dozen or so framed photos resting on top. The rifle—modern, deadly—looked weirdly out of place here. They'd left it lying on the sofa, just lying out there in the open for anyone to see. Years ago I would have been very impressed by such a sleek, classy piece of equipment, a mere rifle costing a few grand. But now I just went over to it, picked it up briefly, felt its weight just for the hell of it, and put it back down, as you might do with some item in a store you're curious about but have absolutely no intention of buying.

There was an upholstered chair with a high back in a shadowy far corner of the room. I went over to it, sat down, and simply relaxed. I again took out my Turner postcard and gave it a good, hard look. And then I took out my pad and reviewed my list of Georgian houses to be visited. You see, I didn't want to lose sight of London, of England, but I felt that it was happening, against my will. I didn't know why, but another one of those chills ran through me.

I must have sat there for God knows how long. I don't know how I managed it. The room was stuffy and hot. The windows were still closed, because no one was supposed to be at home. I didn't bother to open them. My energy had failed again.

I preferred, of course, an orderly Georgian room to this heavy, somewhat overdone interior. But while I was here I thought I'd make the best of it and enjoy thinking about the past, even if it wasn't a Georgian past. When in Rome, as they say, and all that nonsense.

I'm in Spain, I reminded myself again. In Barcelona. I'm sitting in a room in a flat in a building on a street in Barcelona. I could almost hear those Spanish melodies. But I couldn't quite remember them. I tried humming them, tried putting little bits together, but I kept getting cockeyed music. I realized that these pieces were more complicated than I'd thought. I was determined to find that tape today, just as soon as I finished with this damn fool business.

So I got up at last and went over to the window on the right side of the room, the window closest to the target area. I pulled one curtain aside and looked up the street, pressing my cheek against the glass. I could just about see the door of the target building. It was at a bad angle. A bit too severe, a bit too sharp. Which meant that to make a successful shot you would have to extend a good part of the barrel out the window. You couldn't just shoot from inside the room. Of course, the more visible you and the gun were, the more dangerous the job became. This one was shaping up as very lousy—a potential disaster.

I picked up the rifle and took it over to the window. I wanted to see what the target looked like when viewed through the scope. That would be the real test. I wrapped and tied the curtains around the drapes and pulled open the set of windows. I slowly extended the barrel out the window and put my eye to the scope. The crosshairs bounced and jerked about the general target area—the scope picking out some wrought-iron balconies, some stone, some shutters—until I found the target door and remained fixed on it. Oddly enough, throughout this whole routine I wasn't concerned about being seen by tenants in the houses across the street. It was as if I were conducting a kind of scientific experiment and anyone was welcome to observe. Yes, I was running through this job for the sake of research.

I could see only parts of the door—a bit of reddish wood here, a bit there—because a tree in front of the target building badly obscured the view. I tried shifting the rifle, tried shifting my body as well—leaning, bending, crouching—to find a wide enough gap between the leaves, but I had no real luck. Jesus, I thought, they don't need a marksman here, they need a bloody magician. I hoped that someone would enter the building right then as a kind of test. In that way I'd be able to see how much of an actual body was visible between the leaves. But no one entered or left.

I tried imagining a car pulling up to the building. If it didn't pull up directly to the door, then the mark would be exposed when leaving the car. But why would anyone do that? When you pull up to an entrance, you pull up as near as possible. Then again, another car might be parked at the curb, in which case you'd have to double park to let your passenger off. The mark would really be exposed then, appearing from way out in the street. But from what I could tell parking wasn't allowed directly in front of the building. So we were pretty much back where we started. Either you'd have to take him out through the leaves as he made for the door or else you might go for a quick head shot just as he emerged from the car and his skull rose briefly above the roof.

This job was a real challenge, I concluded as I closed the windows, put the curtains back in order, and returned the rifle to the sofa. But I had tackled worse jobs in my career. This one was difficult but not impossible. Employ a first-class marksman and hope for the best. Considering the blocked view, you might not be able to pick out the target; to be on the safe side, you'd have to take out everyone making for the door. You might be shooting blindly and you might end up with a bit of a slaughter fest, but in all the mayhem you'd probably hit your man.

I came up with one idea that might reduce the risk somewhat. It just popped into my head as I was preparing to leave the flat. If some leaves could be removed from that damn tree—say around midpoint—the shooter would have a somewhat cleaner view. Maybe they could get someone to do a little pruning in the dead of night. Yes, it was a peculiar idea. No question about it. And a suddenly leafless tree might arouse some suspicion. But the more I considered this idea, the more oddly brilliant it seemed.

I felt that I had done my job and done it well. All the thinking and figuring had drained me. My tolerance for this business was definitely decreasing. For me a little work now went a very long way.

Once outside, I walked up the block to the target building. I crossed the street and approached that incredible door. It was even more impressive in person. The photos hadn't quite done it justice. And, of course, I hadn't been able to see much of it through the scope. Standing right before it, the door—a double door, really—appeared huge, massive, as if ten-foot people were expected to pass through it. The wood was so thick it looked like it weighed hundreds of pounds. The elegant carving, the swirling, curving lines, cut so deep that crevices and shadows were created. I was glad to see that I'd been right about the design: on each door was a giant lily. The flowers bent over to touch each other. I nodded my head in approval. This was one damn good, ornate piece of work. I wouldn't want it on my house, of course, but here on this building, in Barcelona, it was completely appropriate—and pretty spectacular besides.

I went over to the stupid tree that had ruined my view. Yes, it held too many damn leaves. They were all over the place. I backed up a little, toward the door, pretending that I was the target. Through the leaves I tried to find the window I had just left, tried to trace the line of fire. As expected, I could only vaguely see the window. I kept my eye on what little of it I could see and I moved toward the door and then away, trying to determine the spot where the mark would be the most vulnerable. I moved slowly across this small area of sidewalk, stepping back and forth repeatedly and looking up through those damn leaves. But I couldn't find any really clear line. One or two spots were slightly better than the others, but all of them were pretty lousy. That tree, I said to myself, has got to go. As I was testing these spots, weirdly stepping back and forth, some gentleman walked by and looked at me as if I was totally insane. It's funny, though. Because once again I was going through my paces like a scientist, a researcher engaged in a public project. "Just a little experiment," I said to him. But he didn't know what in hell I was saying, and moreover, he didn't care.

I found a street phone and rang up Isaac. He quickly rang me back. I had a question or two for him and needed answers now.

"So," he asked before I could get a word in, "how did you find it?"

"Find what?"

"The job, of course, the setup."

"Terrific flat. Not quite my cup of tea, but it has its charm, no question about that. I'll tell you, I could probably learn to live with it. I assume the owner, this doctor, is very well off?"

"Oh, yes, I believe he is a man of considerable wealth. From a very wealthy family. But what I—"

"What kind of doctor is he?"

"I believe the concierge said he treated infants."

"A baby doctor, huh?"

"Yes, that is my understanding. But I—"

"I'm definitely in the wrong profession. You know, my mother wanted me to be a doctor once upon a time."

"Oh yes?"

"Yes. I think that's why she always took me along with her to visit dying relatives in hospitals. I think she wanted me to get used to such places, to sick people, to death. She succeeded in a way, when you come to think of it." And then I laughed a little.

"What I—" said Isaac.

"Yeah, she wanted me to be a doctor. Or a priest. I guess she hoped I'd save people, one way or another. And I suppose I have saved people. I've saved them from living." And I again laughed.

"Yes," said Isaac, "this is all very interesting, but what I wanted to know is how the job looks to you. That is my concern."

"The job. Well, I've seen a lot better, and I've seen a lot worse. This one's a bit tricky. But it can be done."

"*Tricky*, you say. In what way tricky?"

I went on to explain. Again, I didn't feel like I was directly involved in this business. I was merely reporting test results. A researcher noting the good news and the bad. More an observer than anything else. Yes, I was feeling removed. I was feeling quite peculiar. I concluded with my tree plan. For a while there was silence on the line as he took it all in.

"You are joking, of course?" he finally said. "I mean, it is very amusing. And I enjoy good humor, a fine jest. But, you know, my friend, this is, as I said, a very serious job. Very serious."

"Let's say I'm not exactly joking. Let's say that crazy as it sounds, this may be a way of making the situation easier. Maybe the only way."

"Cutting leaves from a tree? Who has ever heard of such a thing? I have been in this business for many years, my friend, and I have never heard of such a thing. Have you ever heard of such a thing? Have you ever done such a thing?"

"No. But maybe that's because I never thought of doing such a thing. The way I see it, it's just a matter of several branches. Let's say you hire some kids, some vandals to run by and pull off a few branches. A kid thing, you know?"

"I do not see this happening on Ausiàs March. Besides, how are they to reach the branches, these children? Do you suggest they carry a ladder?"

"They climb up on each other's shoulders. Weren't you ever a kid, Isaac?"

He still couldn't accept the plan. "Consider what you are saying," he went on, "consider the reasoning. Suppose you had to dispose of someone in a flat in the distance, but a sign or a billboard interfered with the view. Would you tear down the billboard? I mean, my friend, let us be reasonable. There is a matter of discretion here, of not announcing to the world our intentions."

"All right, forget it."

"I must. If I ever mentioned this to them, they would not appreciate it."

I began to laugh again. I was having a regular high old time of it. "Maybe we should just cut down the whole bloody tree," I said, breaking myself up.

Isaac suddenly seemed relieved. "Yes, I knew it. I knew you were joking. I could not be certain, but I suspected as much. Very amusing. Very clever. You had me believing it. Very good. I forgot again that all of this is routine for you. So you jest. You are a very amusing man. I suppose I am not accustomed to this American sense of humor."

"British," I corrected him.

I allowed him his relief. Because, of course, I really wasn't joking.

"I wanted to ask you something," I said, getting down to more urgent matters. "That's pretty much why I called you from the street. I'm still in the area. I figured, why go back to my hotel if I'm only going to leave it again?"

"Yes, of course. What is it?"

"Would you know where around here I can buy a Walkman and a pre-recorded cassette? A music shop? Or an electronics shop? Or both?"

"This is the question?"

"Yeah."

"You are a very amusing man. This I thought was going to be an important question."

"It is important. I've had these guitar tunes in my head. But I can't quite remember them, can't get them right. You know how something like that can drive you a bit mad."

"Guitar tunes?"

"Yes. One of them, in fact, is by your friend Albéniz. It's called 'Asturias.'"

"'Asturias.' Yes, very famous."

There was a long pause. Either because he was thinking of a store or because I had upset his Catalan balance again.

"You are not far from the Plaça de Catalunya," he responded. "You might try El Corte Inglés. It is a very large department store."

"Yeah, I remember being in one when I was in Madrid. Thanks. I'll walk over there right now."

"Or, if you are willing to travel a little, there's Sony Mito on Balmes, quite a distance beyond your hotel. They have a very large selection of music and electronics."

"Sounds good. I might try them as well."

"Yes, you are an amazing man, Mr. Chilton. A man of surprises."

Before we bid our farewells, Isaac returned to business. Despite his intelligence, his pleasant manner, he seemed fairly devoted to this slob work. He asked about the rifle. I said that it was fine, a real gem. He suggested that I might test it somewhere, take some practice shots.

"It's perfect," I said, "trust me. I tried the trigger. Nice action. A beautiful feel to the thing. A beautiful machine."

"But you might want to adjust the scope."

"The alignment is perfect. Trust me."

"Of course. I am glad. I am glad you feel this way."

"I feel better than ever. Believe me."

"Good. You probably will not hear from us until early next week. We will know for sure then. So I would say in the meanwhile—well, go and enjoy Barcelona." I assured him that I would do just that, that I suddenly had many buildings to cover. "Pleasant wanderings," he said.

"Thanks again. And listen, Isaac," I joked, "don't forget about that stinking tree."

He let out a little chuckle. "Very amusing. Very."

CHAPTER 11

IN THE DAYS THAT FOLLOWED I wandered the streets of the city with my Walkman and earphones, my guitar cassette, and, above all, my architectural guidebook. Although I used to think that only morons walked about in public listening to Walkmans, I stuck the stupid plugs in my ears and had a Spanish guitar playing in my brain as I viewed the buildings described in my guide. I really do think it added to my pleasure, lulling me, tugging gently at the old heartstrings, and also making me feel at times that I was in a kind of movie about Barcelona architecture.

The book was absolutely stuffed with sights to visit, from the really ancient buildings in the Gothic Quarter, which looked like they belonged to some medieval town, to all the showy Modernista stuff on the Gràcia and elsewhere, to the new dead-ugly steel-glass productions that reminded you of dopey sci-fi sets and had gone up all over the city. Apparently the sci-fi architects had been let loose before the Olympics back in '92 so they could wreck parts of the city in time for the event and for the arrival of tourists from all over the damn world. The guide even included parks and other places where you could find outdoor artwork—all sorts of big eye-catching, eye-irritating junk thrown together by "international artists."

I decided that I wanted to see it all. The old, the new. The good, the bad. The buildings, the parks. Everything. Or nearly everything. I suddenly felt like a crazed tourist, a sight-hungry maniac who realizes that he has only several days left in a city and then will be gone, maybe forever. He's determined to take in as much as possible, even if he kills himself trying.

But besides this mad sense of tourist pressure, there was something else going on in me. Something a lot weirder and a lot harder to explain. I had the feeling—as I moved about the city, full of energy one hour, exhausted the next, vaguely up and then suddenly down—I had the feeling that time, in general, was running out.

I might have been a pensioner, some tired old bugger who was making one big push before the end. A pensioner? I thought, laughing at myself, at my confused brain. It's come to this? Not a hit man anymore. Or a delivery boy for a collection of slobs. Or an angry, cursing New Yorker who hates his city. Not a pathetic weakling who allowed his loony father to wreck him. Or a schoolboy weirdo. Or a snobby, filthy-rich Englishman with artsy tastes. Not an expert on Georgian houses. Or an unbelievably deadly marksman. No. None of these people. A pensioner had replaced them all. Was this hilarious or wasn't it? A pensioner. A retired something, with who knows how many months, days ahead of him.

That's how I felt. There was no explaining it. At least, not to my satisfaction. You could say that I admired the freedom of a pensioner. He has no job anymore, no real responsibilities, maybe no real ties at all. He's alone, forgotten. He doesn't matter. So he can do whatever he wants—go tourist crazy in Barcelona, for example—or do nothing, if that's his wish. Yes, you could say all of this, but I'm not sure that it would explain much. Something was happening to me, something was going very wrong. Thoughts weren't connecting right. Maybe a screw, as they say, had come loose. But strange though I felt, tired as I was, I still had the urge to visit buildings and places, to check off sight after sight in my guidebook. My body seemed shot, but my sick brain was still active, and it kept me going. It kept on wanting more.

Funny, I thought as I walked along the Gràcia to the Casa Albert Lleó i Morera while "Recuerdos de la Alhamba" strummed in my head, in London I felt English, in Paris I felt English, in New York I felt both English and American, depending on my mood. But here I don't feel like much of anything. I feel, in fact, like nothing, no one.

I stood back far enough so I could take in the whole building, get the full effect. Another Tárrega piece came on in my head, something called "Capricho árabe." By pure coincidence, this pleasant melody—a sort of exotic little number—seemed to go well with the building I was viewing. According to my guidebook it dated back to 1906 and was designed by Lluís Domènech i Montaner, one of the city's great architects. It looked like something out of one of those old, corny Arabian Nights movies I used to see on TV. Particularly the top, which had Arab-like pinnacles and turrets and what was described in the guide as a "cupola." This domed production reminded me of the kind of thing you see on top of a wedding cake, with a dumb miniature statue of a bride and groom.

In the sunlight the building had a pinkish white glow. The whole jagged, elaborate design stood out against the light blue sky. My Walkman kept playing the guitar music. I kept standing there on the Gràcia, staring, listening, in a kind of Barcelona trance. A strange thought entered my brain, pushing aside for a minute another Spanish tune. If I faded away right here, I thought, vanished on the Gràcia—dropped dead, in other words—it wouldn't be so bad. I'd go out while pretty much doing what I wanted.

I suddenly stopped myself, stopped this old-bugger thinking. Christ, but I was taking this pensioner notion too seriously. Rather than ending, I had to think of beginning, starting from zero, starting fresh. That's the way I had to think. But as I strolled along to my next building—the Casa Fuster, another Montaner creation on the Gràcia—I couldn't help but wonder, old-bugger-like, where all of my energy would come from.

I approached the Fuster. It was less of a production than the Arabian wedding cake. The guide said that it recalled a Venetian mansion. I myself couldn't say. I had never been to Venice. I was supposed to go there on a job once, but the mark ended up in Rome instead. So that's where I ended up, tracking him to a building on the Via Merulana. I shot him in the back as he climbed the stairs to the second floor. He tumbled down like a comedian doing slapstick. Jesus, I thought, that seems like thirty years ago. Jesus, I also thought, what memories I have. Other people remember girlfriends and great dates, promotions, terrific vacations, first love, and all that crap. I remember dead bodies in cities around the world.

The cassette reversed again. I was just letting the same tape run on. Old Albéniz was back. "Asturias" again. My eyes strayed from the mansion for a few moments. I considered the people walking by me. Catalans. Tourists. A steady stream. The people kept advancing, then moving off. A few of them gave me a quick nothing glance, the way you do with strangers. No one knew me. And I knew no one. I wondered if any one of them even bothered to wonder who I was, what I did, where I came from.

At night in my room or outside under the terrace light or down in another nearby café—this one, the Roig i Roig, had a quite decent steak—I'd study both my architectural guide and my city guide and plan my itinerary for the next day. When I'd tire of them, I'd crack open my Georgian books. I'd been feeling guilty about abandoning them and my country, so it was good getting to know them again. It was like returning to old mates.

I think those dark, old-bugger thoughts were beginning to pass. Or at least they weren't taking full shape so often. My energy was coming back. It wasn't that tired sort of pensioner energy I'd been feeling lately. No, it was different. It was fresh. It was even a little wild. I couldn't stop it. I had this urge to fill each day, cram it to the brim. I was incredibly restless; suddenly, for no good reason, alive again.

I've always been a fairly sound sleeper. Once I hit the pillow I'm out. But now I'd lie awake forever, struggling to fall asleep. I couldn't get my brain to rest. Couldn't get the damn thing to stop running. And when I'd finally get to sleep, I'd manage a stretch of only an hour or less. Sometimes I'd go through the old toss-and-turn routine with no success, curse the whole business, angrily get up in the middle of the night, select a book, bring it back to bed, and then read until my eyes collapsed.

That method would usually work. One morning I woke to a sunlit room and felt a terrible pressure on my chest. I thought for a minute I might be having a heart attack. But then I realized that I had fallen asleep with my two-ton Constable book lying open on top of me. I raised my head and stared at the double-page color picture and thought for a minute that I had gone semi-blind during the night because the painting was all out of focus. What in hell? I said, panicking a bit. But then I remembered that the picture was a blowup of a section of *The Leaping Horse* and that's the way these so-called details looked—fuzzy, smudgy, sloppy. I didn't know what in hell they were supposed to prove—other than that Constable's stuff appeared great from far away but was a real mess up close.

I don't dream much. I have no patience for dreams. When they crop up, I destroy them before they get too far. I have a way of instructing my brain to simply erase the stupid little show immediately. My brain listens. But during these restless Barcelona nights it was so active, so independent, that I couldn't interrupt and ruin the dreams. It was like a telly you couldn't shut off.

The dreams were fortunately short. Quick flashes. Brief nutcase images. Ridiculous combinations. In one dream I was back home in my tiny Melton room. I don't know if I was still a kid here. Because I never see myself in dreams. I'm like a camera. I see only others. Well, I'm in my room when the door flies open and there's the old man with a dozen or so bullet holes in him. He's bleeding like a son of a bitch from between his eyes, from his chest, his legs. He staggers toward me. I've been shot by a fuckin' squirrel! he yells. Before I have a chance to find out what happens next, I find myself alone again in the room. The room is dark now. It's the middle of the night, I'm in bed, and I feel something crawling on my legs. I pull off the blankets and pull down my pajama pants. For some reason I'm able to see in the dark. And there on my naked legs are big black Catalan ants. I begin crushing the disgusting things with my hands. They're so fat they go *crunch* as I squash them against my skin. Suddenly I see more. They're all over my mattress. I can't keep up with the bastards. I crush one, and five more take its place. This battle—and that's what it becomes: an attack and counterattack—this battle is absolutely filthy, absolutely sickening. More ants appear. They're climbing through the open window. They're coming through the crack between the door and the floor. I begin to panic. I realize that I'm outnumbered. I realize that I can't possibly win. I realize that I'm finished.

I kept traveling the city, kept checking off the buildings in my guidebook. Despite the heat, despite my blazer, which added to the heat, I was unstoppable. It was like those last days in London—they seemed so long ago now, everything seemed so long ago now—when I couldn't stop walking. Yes, I was enjoying myself again, in much the same way, and didn't want the feeling to end. I knew deep down that I had to maintain my pace if I hoped to see everything before I'd be required to go off to do the job and then escape home. In other words, the day of the job would really mark my final day in Barcelona. And it wasn't so very far off now, damnit. But I was determined to file that thought in the back of my brain and regard each day as only one of many I had to look forward to. Yes, I was filling each day with new places, pictures, facts, just for the hell of it, just for the pleasure.

I visited Gaudí's colossally weird Sagrada Família church. Hawksmoor, for one, would have spit on it. This Gaudí character was either very brilliant or completely nuts. The very long brownish gray spires looked like the kind of formations you might see rising up from the floor of some ridiculously enormous cavern. Even before you reached the church, you could see these damn things from blocks away, invading an ordinary neighborhood and turning it into something fantastic and mental. It was as if aliens had purchased property here and started building this temple to their alien god. Anyway, the thing was still under construction after more than a century and no one could really say when it would be finished. Old Gaudí knew that the church wouldn't be completed in his lifetime. I liked that idea, for some reason—of starting something you know you'll never finish. The starting itself is the important thing. It doesn't really matter whether you finish or not. As it turned out, Gaudí died before he had a chance to croak naturally—hit by a streetcar. Yeah, you never know.

I took in a lot of buildings that day. One by Josep Puig i Cadafatch, done in red brick with big pointed towers, could have been a gigantic rectory or a religious academy of some sort but was actually an apartment house. And there was Josep Maria Jujol's Casa Planells, which had rounded balconies and reminded me of a control tower. I also visited Salvador Valeri i Pupurull's Casa Comalat, a 1911 building with two facades. Big, ornate windows on the front looked like the rear of an old wooden sailing ship, the place where the captain had his quarters, and the back facade, made up of large, connecting bay-like windows, appeared more Japanese than Spanish.

Mixing styles the way they did, these architects could give your brain a real workout. Their buildings always looked like something they were not.

And so it went over the next several days. I'd get an early start and visit buildings in the morning, take a short break for lunch, and then continue my house hunting in the afternoon. I couldn't seem to get enough of them. When I'd come upon an interesting house by pure accident and find that it wasn't covered in my guidebook, I'd curse the author for his laziness. Since my wanderings took me into different parts of the city, I'd consult my general Barcelona guidebook and seek out recommended sights in the area. Soon both guidebooks were filled with little check marks to indicate the buildings and places I had knocked off. All the checks made me feel good. I suppose I was experiencing what they call a deep sense of accomplishment.

But what began to bother me was how much more there was to see. Although I tried to forget about it, that upcoming job and the sudden departure were beginning to bear down on me.

Yet I couldn't be stopped by the thought of having to stop soon. One morning I made a special trip to the Montjuïc, the largest park in Barcelona. Spread over more than five hundred acres, it was a lot bigger than some towns I'd been in. There were a lot of museums throughout the park, but I particularly wanted to see the Museum of Catalan Art, which the guidebook made such a big deal about. So I saw it. What the book called "Catalan Romanesque" and praised to high heaven wasn't quite my cup of tea. Religious stuff with saints. But at least it wasn't hammy. And I sort of enjoyed the way the people had a cartoon look about them and I liked the strong colors. Later I traveled over to the Spanish Village, where they had re-created and thrown together parts of different cities and towns in Spain. It was all supposed to serve as a mini-tour of the country and its architecture, but I thought the whole place was kind of junky, designed more for undemanding tourists than for an architectural scholar like myself.

Monday morning arrived. Too soon. I was looking over my itinerary for the coming week. My schedule was jam-packed with sights and addresses, from one end of the city to the other. I wondered if I was being way too optimistic. I'd need more like several weeks to cover everything on my list. I hadn't even explored the Gothic Quarter yet, and that was supposed to be something of a medieval gold mine, the most historic section of Barcelona. There I had to see the famous old spiky cathedral and the famous old plaza, the Plaça del Rei, which looked so ancient, big, and bare that it seemed fake, like a set for a movie about knights, serfs, and that baloney. These two sights were absolute musts. I'd already inked in little stars next to their names in the guide. The phone rang. It was a Mr. King call from Isaac. Christ, I thought. Bloody Christ. I didn't feel like hurrying away from my room to get to an outside phone. After all, I was deep into my itinerary. So for the first time ever in my career I violated the phone rule. I called Isaac from my hotel room. I figured that with the door to the terrace open I'd probably sound like I was outside anyway.

"It will bc Wednesday at four-thirty," he said, sounding very serious and businesslike. "Not four o'clock as we thought, but four-thirty. Four-thirty exact. In two days. Wednesday. At thirty minutes past four o'clock. This is clear?"

"Hey, Isaac, lighten up. You're not talking to some nincompoop."

"What is this word, this 'poop'?"

"Nincompoop. You know—a jerk, an idiot."

"I am very sorry. I did not intend— But I have to be certain we understand each other."

"What's there not to understand? Wednesday. At four-thirty."

"Yes. Good. We suggest, of course, that you arrive a little early. Simply to be safe. In the event of any problems."

"You said it was four-thirty sharp. Well, is it four-thirty sharp or isn't it?" After all, I was working on a tight schedule as it was. I would now have to squeeze in this damn thing.

"Oh, yes, it is sharp. It is exact. We are most certain. But one never knows in our business, as you are aware. Things, they happen."

"So you're certain, but you're not certain?"

"You are somewhat confusing me. We are as certain as we can be. But, of course, he could arrive a little early, a little late."

"But a little late wouldn't matter. If I'm there early, I'm there. If he comes late, I'm still there."

"I do not think I am understanding you."

"Forget it. Wednesday at four-thirty."

"Yes. And if you could get to the flat earlier this would be good."

"Wednesday. Four-thirty. Anything else?"

"I assume everything is fine with you? You are enjoying Barcelona?"

"There's a hell of a lot to see. A hell of a lot."

"Oh, yes. Barcelona is wonderful. Very interesting, very educational."

We both said nothing for a while. For me, at least, there wasn't anything left to say.

Isaac finally spoke. "So, my friend, I suppose I will not see you again. I wish you the best of luck. It was a pleasure to do business with you. And very amusing. If you are ever in Barcelona again, but on holiday, we must have a drink, perhaps even meet for dinner."

I thanked him. He was a pleasant man. Too bad he worked for a collection of crude, pushy, boring, uneducated pricks.

Oddly enough, the call didn't faze me much. Or maybe I'd already made the decision to take the job in stride. Just because the Firm took it so seriously didn't mean that I had to. After all, we hardly shared the same interests. Our minds worked in very different ways. For example, did any of them care the least bit about Georgian houses or Barcelona buildings? Did any of them visit bookshops? Did any of them even crack open a bloody book?

I was determined to regard the job as something minor, a bit of a nuisance to deal with when the time came. I was too involved in my wanderings to give it much thought.

But I couldn't ignore the time limit so easily. I had little time left in the city. Two and a half days and that was it. I considered my list again. I still had to see Gaudí's Casa Vicens, his Casa Calvet, and his Palau Güell. I had to see Domènech i Montaner's Casa Lleó Morera and Casa Josep Thomas; Josep Vilaseca i Casanovas's Casa Joaquim Cabot; Puig i Cadafalch's Casarramona Yarn Factory and his Casa Macaya; the Plant House by Josep Fontserè i Mestre; the Baixeras School by Josep Goday i Casals; Antoni Gallissà i Soqué's Casa Manuel Llopis i Bofill. And that was only scratching the surface.

And, of course, there were still all the parks and plazas to be seen. And the crazy so-called outdoor sculpture by the so-called international artists.

And the museums, big and little, old and modern, and a few that were just downright strange, like the Museum of Footwear and the one—originally designed by old Montaner—that now had a gigantic tangle of steel wire resting on top. It's a good thing Montaner is in his grave, I thought, because seeing this piece of art crap, this giant Brillo Pad on his elegant house, would have crushed him. But I wanted to see the thing in person. A photo in a guidebook wasn't enough. I assumed I'd hate it, but I wanted to hate it in person. The same went for the other modern-art museums I'd avoided so far. I'd give them a try at least. I was willing to make the effort. Then I could hate them with some authority.

For the rest of that Monday, the day of the last Mr. King call, I roamed the Gothic Quarter, moving through the narrow streets and passageways, suddenly coming upon a quiet courtyard here, a quiet courtyard there, with stone steps and a balcony, centuries old. A place for some monk or maiden. Or for me. Because I appreciated the calm, the peace. You couldn't hear the city around you. You couldn't hear anything except your own footsteps. You could wrap yourself up in a place like this. That suited me just fine. Walk into a maze of medieval streets, enter an ancient courtyard, climb the steps to an ancient wooden door, enter an ancient room and settle down in that room, die overlooking that courtyard.

Tuesday was a mad day. They could have committed me on Tuesday. I took cab after cab, trying to cover as much as I could, racing from one sight to another. Although I tried to dismiss the feeling, the pressure was on. I kept checking off sights as I knocked them off. I rambled a bit down the Ramblas, an endless thoroughfare that runs from the Plaça de Catalunya to the sea. Sidewalk musicians, flower stalls, book stalls, bird stalls, fortune-tellers, religious nuts, artists—you name it and the Ramblas has it. I saw it all quickly, but at least I saw it. I checked off "Ramblas" on my list. I passed the big food market, the Boquería. I looked in briefly. Check. I walked to the Plaça Reial, noted the palm trees, gave the streetlamps designed by Gaudí a quick once-over. Check. I grabbed a cab down to the waterfront. Saw the famous Columbus Monument, with him on top pointing out to sea. Check. Took another cab back to the Montjuïc. The Miró Foundation was supposed to be a major attraction, though I didn't know who in hell Miró was. I looked at the place and its dopey kid art for a few minutes. I didn't get this kind of stuff. Not yet, at least. I should have known. Anyway: check. And then I took another cab to another sight, the Ciutadella Park and its museums.

Wednesday. More of the same. I decided to at last cover a bunch of buildings right on the Rambla de Catalunya. I'd been saving them for, as they say, a rainy day. But there hadn't been any rainy days. So it was now or never.

I then took a cab across half the city, going toward the hills, to visit for a minute the Plaça Sóller, which was supposed to have interesting sculptures by some famous modern Catalan artist, Corberó. They were "abstract" and probably lousy, but they were set in a lake and sounded odd enough to check out.

The park itself was peaceful, with pleasant trees and a step-like man-made waterfall, and I tried to calm down, but I couldn't get a complete grip on myself because time was running out and I had other places to cover. The lake sculptures weren't half bad for stuff that didn't look like anything. They were just oval and crescent shapes made of very thin sheets of pinkish white marble and they stuck up out of the water looking like shapes that didn't look like anything. I actually wanted to take in this nonsense a bit, try to see them as the islands and ships the guidebook described, but I had no time to pause and let my artistic mind stray. So I made my check, hurried out of the place, found another cab, and traveled way west to the next sight on my list, the Spanish Industrial Park.

As the cab moved down street after street—modern white houses gliding by, elegant old gray ones, trees, Catalans of all shapes and sizes—I felt a little dizzy. And I realized I was sweating. It was all the hurrying about, this madness. "Christ," I said to myself aloud, right there in the cab, "this is ridiculous. Bloody goddamn ridiculous."

There was nothing particularly industrial about the park. It was flat, with trees. According to the architectural guidebook the area had once been filled with textile mills, which apparently had been a very big deal. I finally found what I was looking for: tall, round towers overlooking a huge man-made lake. With observation platforms and spotlights, they could have been the guard towers of a prison. They'd looked strange in the guidebook and they looked even stranger in person. Why in hell would someone want to build something like this? I wondered.

There were long white steps leading down to the lake, which, again according to the guide, was the biggest artificial lake in Spain. A few people were sitting on the steps and staring out at the water and at a young couple in a rowboat moving slowly across it. I thought I might as well sit down too. The sun was blazing, and the drooping leaves of what seemed to be willow trees on the opposite bank were swaying slightly in a slight breeze, looking like strands of very long, thin light green hair, and I thought I could hear Catalan birds chirping in the distance, or maybe I was just imagining the sound to go along with the lazy, soft mid-afternoon mood. It was a restful time. My body was vaguely sleepy. My mind was fairly empty. It was a nice feeling. So I continued to sit and gaze out, covering my warm, droopy eyes with my sunglasses.

But another feeling came over me. And it was not so nice. I became conscious, for no particular reason, of the space around me. Of the people in the distance. And of this park—me sitting in this foreign park, with foreign people enjoying their leisure and living in those foreign houses beyond those foreign trees. I was a stranger. I was alone. I was alone in Barcelona. In Spain. I imagined myself from a distance, even from above. Small against all this white. In my blazer, a mere speck of dark blue.

I was someone, of course. A person. I was sitting here. I had a body. I was taking up room on the steps. But that didn't seem to amount to very much. Not very much at all. A lousy feeling took over my stomach. It seemed to come all at once. It was more than just an emptiness from not having lunch. It was a kind of nausea. And if I had allowed it to continue and worsen I might have vomited right there on the white steps. But I got control of it. I still had willpower. I couldn't be done in so easily. No, sir. Not me.

I quickly shifted my focus. I checked off the Parc de l'Espanya Industrial in my guidebook. And under that listing I also checked off the Baths of St. George, which was what this particular area was called, St. George being the patron saint of Catalonia. In fact, not far from me was an enormous abstract metal sculpture that was supposed to be St. George's dragon but looked like metal cutouts made by a giant kid. I avoided looking at the annoying thing.

After checking off this crappy sculpture, by someone named Nagel, I flipped through my book and noticed all the checks that weren't there. I needed more time in the city. No doubt about it.

This line of thinking reminded me to check my watch. It read four past four. "Shit," I said, which was unlike me. I had to leave. Grab a cab to Ausiàs March. Immediately. This was urgent. This was important.

I couldn't bring myself to hurry. I wasn't in a hurrying mood. I looked down at my watch again, followed the second hand as it advanced, waited as it completed a minute and the minute hand advanced. It was now exactly five minutes past four. It was getting late. Very late. I should be leaving. But I decided to stay awhile longer. Just a little while.

I haven't even been to the Tibidabo, I thought. It was way up in the mountains and the guidebook had color photos of the church of the Tibidabo and of an old single-engine red plane, the big attraction of the Tibadabo's little amusement park. The plane was attached to a sort of horizontal crane that carried it around over the edge of the mountain and then back again to the park, giving passengers a fake plane ride. I thought this unusual and stupid enough to check out.

When I looked at my watch again it read eight past four. I'd leave in a minute or so. I still had more than a full twenty minutes.

I followed another couple crossing the lake in a rowboat. I imagined for a while Jennifer and me.

My watch now read ten past four.

Somehow I snapped out of my mood, lifted my drowsy, half-dead body, and managed to hurry from the park. I then started to run—and I mean run—to a street, any street, to find a cab. I told the driver the address on Ausiàs March and told him to hurry. "*Vamos*" was something Spanish I'd heard in cowboy films as a kid, so I tried that. I told him "*Vamos*." I guess he got the idea—from my Spanish or English or maybe just from my gesturing like a damn fool—because he increased his speed.

Seventeen past four now. Wouldn't it be funny, I thought, if the mark's limo and my cab arrived on the street at the same time? Yeah, hilarious. My shirt felt wet and sticky. For the first time in a long time I was sweating like a pig. I opened the window more to get more of a warm breeze. "Ridiculous," I said aloud again. "This is bloody ridiculous. Just once I'd like to stay in a city and do nothing. Nothing except what I want to do. Just me."

I looked at my watch again. I could still just possibly make the job. But I knew what I had to do. Maybe I had known it all along. And I knew the consequences. "The hell with it," I said. "It's too late anyway." I told the cabbie I had changed my mind, to take me back to my hotel instead. And I told him again to *vamos*.

When I arrived the snotty desk clerk said that a "Mr. Isaac" had phoned earlier but had left no message. "When did he call?" "Four o'clock." "And there was no message? He said nothing?" "No. He asked where you were. I told him that you were out. He said, 'Good,' for some reason I did not understand." But I understood. They were checking up on their boy, making sure he had gone on his errand. These people were unbelievable, and they would never change.

As I rode the elevator to my floor I thought of the big black car pulling up at the building on Ausiàs March, bodyguards stepping out first and then the man himself, the mark, the major hit. And I thought of the baby doctor's empty apartment and the rifle remaining on the sofa, useless, harmless, with no one there to pick it up and make it come to life as a deadly weapon. And I thought of the big man approaching the impressive lily-carved door, that terrific Art Nouveau production, and remaining alive as it was opened for him. What I was imagining now was what was actually happening now—in short, nothing. Or at least nothing that involved me. I smiled stupidly. Now I'll really mean something to them. I've just been elected

Man of the Year, just gone to the top of their Most Wanted list. Congratulations, I thought, and then stopped smiling. You're now a corpse.

I packed quickly, if you can call it packing. It was more like throwing stuff into bags. I was careful, however, with my two-hundred-and-fifteen-dollar shirt, or as careful as I could be while racing the clock, as if I was trying to break the world's record for evacuating a hotel room. I folded the shirt semi-neatly and put it on top of the mound of crumpled clothes that rose up from my canvas suitcase—sort of the place of honor for a luxury garment. My collection of books—and it was quite a library—went into the other canvas bag. When I finally managed to zip it shut, the bag looked like it had a very bad case of swollen glands.

I headed to the elevator lopsided, the suitcase of books in my right hand weighing far more than the suitcase of clothes in my left. I must have looked wacky. I know that I felt wacky. Four-thirty was gone. The mark had survived. But I was a dead man.

I told the desk clerk that I was checking out and wanted to pay my bill. "You are checking out now?" he said, a bit surprised. "Right now," I said, "this minute." "Everything it is satisfactory? There is a problem perhaps?" "Yeah, I'm tired of all the ants. They were even in my bed." "But this is not possible," he said, highly insulted. The pompous ass had no sense of humor. "It's a joke." "Joke?" "My father died in London. I have to return home." "How very sad." "Yeah, heartbreaking. Now, look, could you make it quick. I have a plane to catch." While he processed my bill, I kept my eyes on the entrance and the street and kept my hand on my gun. I must have looked quite weird posing like Napoleon there by the front desk. But I half expected them to arrive at any second. Half expected a shoot-out in the lobby.

The clerk instructed the doorman to take my bags and he himself came outside to signal for a cab. My dead father story had obviously melted his cold Catalan heart. When the cab pulled up he instructed the driver to take me to the airport and to hurry—I knew this because he kindly translated what he had said. Maybe the guy wasn't such a jerk after all. He just had to warm up to me and vice versa. "Visit us again," he said as I sat back in the seat and at the same time looked about for an approaching car filled with assassins. "Not until you get rid of the ants," I said as the cab pulled away.

CHAPTER 12

I WAS GLAD the desk clerk thought I was going to the airport, because he'd tell them that when they came looking for me at the hotel. Of course, it was too late for the airport. They'd have it covered already. I'd never get out of the terminal alive. But although I knew how good they were, maybe they themselves didn't. Not finding me at the airport, they might think that I'd already caught a flight out. At least that's what I was hoping they'd assume. Or it might dawn upon them that I had changed my mind at the last minute and left the city by car or train. Then they'd issue a Firm alert at border crossings and in train stations across Spain.

So I decided, crazy as it may sound, to stay in Barcelona. I figured that this would be the last possibility on their list. After all, who would be stupid enough to take such a chance after blowing a major hit in the same city? I realized, of course, that I was probably finished no matter what I did, where I went. Deep down I think I had known a long while ago that I was never going to see London again.

But I needed some time to myself. Time spent completely alone for once in my life. Without having to tolerate mental abuse of any kind. I'd been taking orders, reporting in, ever since I was a kid. Somebody was always after me. Even back then there were bloody Mr. King calls of one sort or another. Now I just needed some time to myself. Some real, open time. Some time to take in a city thoroughly, to concentrate on it and nothing else. And to roam about knowing that there never would be anything else. I wanted that feeling. I wanted that relief. So many cities I'd visited on the job were blurs in my mind. I'd traveled all over Europe, but often it hadn't much mattered where I was. All the cities became one city. All the targets, one target, one head, one body. Yes, I needed time. But how much of it I'd get would depend on how successfully I could lie low and how determined they'd be.

"Airport," the driver said, more as a confirmation than a question. "No," I told him, "I changed my mind. Take me to the Gothic Quarter—the Barrio Gótico." I'd sort of picked up the lingo from the guidebook and I thought I'd finally try it out, though it was more Spanish than Catalan. "Barri Gòtic?" he said, very puzzled—like where in hell did I expect to catch a plane down there? "Yeah," I said, "*sí*. You can drop me off by the cathedral." The cabby shook his head and drove to and then down the Via Laietana.

My thinking was this: the Gothic Quarter was made up of dim, narrow, maze-like streets and passageways. Some of them were overcrowded with Catalans and tourists, particularly those just beyond the cathedral. I could easily get lost in this area. It was the perfect area to get lost in. Then again, this virtue could be a fault as well—with so many people about, you couldn't keep track of them, of all the activity, and you might pick up a tail without even realizing it. But I decided to take my chances. Now that I had thrown away my life, I needed to make it last a bit longer. Just a bit. I lugged my suitcases through the old streets until I found the kind of dumpy small hotel that I could disappear in. If you were rating it, the way they do in guidebooks—from budget to moderate to luxury—you'd have to create a new and lower category: moderate fleabag. The place was semi-crumbling atop a shop stuffed with religious items—cheap statues, crosses, rosaries, pictures, plates, even bloody salt and pepper shakers for all I knew, devoted to good old Jesus, his pals and relatives. My mother would have loved it.

My room was on the second floor—there were only four floors to the whole joint—and faced the street. I had specifically asked for such a view and the small, old Catalan bum at the desk, who knew only a little English, finally understood my request after I'd done a kind of moronic pantomime—pretending to open a window, look down, wave to people in the street below. I must have looked like an idiot.

The room was a tight little cell with a window and cracked, swollen walls. The window seemed too big for the room, but I was grateful for it. As far as I was concerned, the more you had of the window, the less you had of the rotten room. More window, less dump. The entire place probably looked a lot worse to me than it had to other poor souls who'd flopped here. After all, I was used to class places, to the best accommodations. Here you couldn't even figure out the color of the walls. It was either off-white or light gray or pale dirt. There was an enamel, once-white sink in the corner with a scratched, chipped mirror above it. But there was no toilet—that was outside the room, down the dim, short hallway. The sink had a permanently jagged green ring around the drain and when I lifted the chained rubber stopper from the hole a God-awful smell drifted up and out and quickly filled the room. It reminded you of the stink from a sewer and was powerful enough to make you sick. There was a beat-up chest of drawers to the right of the sink. I put my clothes inside and my books on top, arranging them in neat piles, with their spines facing me. The bed, with a mattress that sank badly in the middle, had seen better days. Like about fifty years ago.

I couldn't help but think of my little room back home in Melton. I'd come a long way since those days. I didn't even remotely resemble that weakling. That kid had been someone else. Not me. Not me now in any way. Look at all I'd done. All the tough bastards I'd disposed of on my own. And all the places I'd been. So isn't it odd, I thought, that I've ended up in the same sort of room I grew up in. In fact, the room at home, thanks to good old Mom, had been a lot cleaner. Like a small private room in a hospital or nuthouse. Yes, this turn of events was odd and rather funny, a bit of a sick joke on me.

Going through another stupid routine, I asked the old bum to do me a favor. If anyone came by to inquire about me, he was to say that he had never seen me before in his life. At first, he couldn't quite get my meaning, but when I gave him what amounted to around fifty pounds he suddenly seemed to grasp English. "And there's more where that came from," I said. "*Mucho*." Yeah, I was really getting the hang of Spanish. Again, he seemed to have no trouble understanding and he smiled wide, revealing his crooked, half-missing teeth. "Incidentally," I added, "my name, in case anybody asks, is Juan Casas." He smiled again, nodded his head, and winked. The old bastard.

For the next few days I kept to my room. I got back into my Georgian studies, though they didn't excite me as much as they used to. Maybe because the houses themselves seemed so far away now and impossible to actually reach. But I had to give the whole business a chance. After all, I reasoned, I've had a lot of other things on my mind lately. So I returned to those Georgian houses, and I stuck up one of my Mortlake postcards on the mirror, using an old but unused Band-Aid I'd found in the dresser. I also considered my Barcelona itinerary again: buildings, areas of interest yet to visit. And I got back to doing my daily exercises, which I'd let slip. And I killed a few Catalan bugs and spiders that surprised me on the sink and walls.

I got to thinking a lot in my foreign fleabag. About what I had just done. About how I had reached this strange, miserable point. Part of it was that I badly needed a change, a new profession. Badly. Very badly. That was pretty clear. But what change? What profession? I knew only this sort of work well, and I had a real talent for it. I seemed born for it. My entire early life seemed to lead to it. I had a genuine instinct, a true gift for this kind of killing. But maybe that was because I had never been led in any other direction. I might have discovered other gifts. Who could say? Considering my interests now, I might have the talent of a scholar or an architect or even an artist buried deep inside me. Yes, there might have been other professional possibilities. But nobody had encouraged me along those lines.

Everything, as I saw it, had come too late. The books, the Georgian house, all the buildings, the museums and the art, the need to fill my eyes and brain. A taste for style and fashion. The two-hundred-and-fifteen-dollar shirt. London. England. Someone like Jennifer. All too late.

Maybe I should have been grateful that I'd at least had these thoughts and experiences. A lot of people hadn't. They hadn't been so lucky. I'd really lived, to some extent. More so than I ever expected. And I'd seen the world. As far as the Georgian house was concerned and thoughts like it, perhaps the thoughts were enough, all I could have hoped for. They certainly had kept me going for a while. And they didn't seem to be quite dead yet.

Yes, I was reasoning here like an expert on the telly, one of those masters of human relations and the human mind, one of those bloody know-it-alls. And I got to thinking suddenly about what Jennifer had said. I got to thinking that most people spend a lot of time thinking about things they will never have, people they will never meet, jobs they will never get, places they will never see, people they will never become. It's all so damn frustrating, but, as I said, it keeps one going and maybe that's good enough. Thinking so much about the Georgian house was almost as good as having one. After all, I had lived in one—lived in many—in my brain. That was something. Wasn't it? Did I have to actually own one to be completely satisfied?

From my window I'd check on the street below several times a day. I'd be very careful not to expose too much of my head. I'd hug the wall, inch my way to the very edge of the window, and then sneak a quick look down. I'd check the right side of the street and then the left, but not at the same time; I'd be sure not to stand directly in front of the window.

But I saw no one suspicious, nothing unusual. Just a customer or two going into or coming out of the butcher shop across the narrow, shady street. The butcher chopping apart or pounding some carcass. I couldn't see him quite clearly, but I could make out his arm swinging up and down as he chopped or pounded. Once or twice I thought of myself as the piece of meat. My brain, needless to say, was going a little off during these days of watching and waiting. But what can you expect when you're tense much of the day and night? Once I thought I saw a big, chunky, threatening bloke standing in front of the so-called antiques shop—more like an enclosed trash heap a doorway past the butcher's. He seemed to be examining some of the junk mirrors displayed on the sidewalk. When he turned slightly, I noticed a handbag hanging from his arm and realized that the he was actually a she—a very fat Catalan woman dressed completely in threatening black.

I began to tire of the tension that I myself was creating. This was hardly the mood of relief I'd hoped for. Getting up in the middle of the night to hug a window and check on a dark, empty street was not my idea of carefree living. Even though I'd abandoned them, the bastards were still in my head. But there was no evidence of them except in my head. They were nowhere to be seen. Not on the street. Not in the old houses directly across the way. Not at the front desk. Nowhere. Their absence gave me confidence. Maybe I had managed to escape them, at least temporarily.

I began to go out a bit. At first I strayed just a block or two from the hotel. Then I went a little farther, increasing my distance each day. A few narrow blocks away I came upon a junky old shop selling cheap old clothes. There was a rack outside with a dozen or so moth-eaten men's jackets of various colors and materials. I spotted a blue semi-wool one that looked about my size, and I held it up against me. It seemed a close-enough match and was thick enough to cover my gun without showing a bulge. I noticed that one edge of the right pocket was torn a bit and flopping over, and parts of the jacket were so worn they shined, particularly when viewed from a certain angle and light hit them in the right way. Perfect. I also picked up a battered old beret, the kind of thing you see a lot of old Catalan men wearing. For pants, I decided to use what I already had back at the fleabag. The black slacks from my suit had gotten badly wrinkled in my suitcase when I'd crazily vacated the ant hotel, and there's nothing like a few wrinkles to make a garment look slobbish.

I wanted to achieve a down-and-out look. Conscious though I'd become of stylish apparel, this was not the time to make a fashion statement. To stay in a fleabag hotel and then exit wearing a blazer and a two-hundred-and-fifteen-dollar shirt was asking for attention and trouble. I had to dress down, much as I disliked taking on the appearance of a pathetic loser. While I was at it, I also let my beard grow so that I'd look even more like a hopeless bum. Sunglasses and a head of uncombed hair were the final touches. My own mother, as they say, wouldn't have recognized me. I hardly recognized me.

The Catalan tramp made his first big debut in the Plaça Reial, where I noticed a few other tramps and seeds. Maybe I'd overdone my outfit, because when I sat down at one of the outdoor cafés the waiter gave me a nasty look, as if a pile of garbage had just invaded his sacred territory, and he said something nasty in Catalan, taking me for a fellow countryman—a fellow countryman he wanted to throw out. "A glass of red wine," I said, and I flashed my loaded wallet at him. He was surprised by my English and my wallet and probably figured he had mistaken a foreign eccentric for a Catalan bum. He hurried off to get my wine, without offering an apology.

As I sipped, I surveyed the plaza. The whole layout, the arcades and all, reminded me a little of the Place des

Vosges in Paris and even more of the Plaza Mayor in Madrid, which I'd seen for a minute one day when tracking a rapidly moving mark through the old quarter.

My eyes traveled over to the Gaudí lampposts, which I had visited days before as a non-bum. They took in the palm trees, which still struck me as weirdly out of place. And they settled for a while on a man in a dark suit and sunglasses who was half sitting on the stone rim of the plaza's big fountain. He wasn't doing much of anything except smoking a cigarette and he wasn't even looking my way, but in my situation I couldn't ignore a possible hood. I glanced away every now and then, but I kept returning to him. I remembered from the guidebook that this plaza was supposed to be a hangout for pushers and assorted creeps and I hoped that this character was just one of the local vermin. As it turned out, the man was joined by another man in a suit. They shook hands and wandered off toward the Ramblas. He was nobody, I said to myself, smiling. I signaled my favorite waiter and ordered another wine, as if to celebrate.

When I was leaving the plaza, a middle-aged couple stopped me, held out a Barcelona map, and started chattering on in what sounded like regular Spanish. I finally gathered that they were Spanish tourists who had taken me for a native and wanted directions. I was very pleased by this case of mistaken identity. But I didn't know what in hell they were talking about so I pointed to my mouth and shook my head to indicate that I was a mute.

As the days passed and no one appeared anywhere, I began to really loosen up. Oh, I knew that they would find me eventually. They weren't brilliant. They weren't intellectuals. They weren't readers. But they were damn smart when it came to tracking down traitors. I knew all this. I knew my chances. I knew that I was surviving now on pure luck, that each day I remained alive was a kind of miracle. No, I didn't have any illusions. But when I woke up each morning and realized that I had made it through another day and that I had still another whole new one ahead of me, a completely free day, without even the possibility of a damn Mr. King phone call, I decided to take advantage of thc situation, enjoy myself no matter what.

Though I remained conscious of them as I moved about, I put that thought way back in my brain. I was alert, in other words, but I didn't allow that alertness to interfere with my pleasure. Since I had, as they say, eyes in the back of my head, I let those eyes go on their own merry way while I concentrated on other things, things resembling fun—artsy, architectural fun. "Fun" wasn't a notion I had known much in my life. But that's the way I now began to think of my renewed wanderings and studies. Yes, I saw myself as having a moderate blast.

I started to catch up with the buildings and sights I had missed the first time around—that is, when I was still a professional on call. Not only was I unemployed now, I realized, but I no longer had an occupation. I was finished with all that. I was moving about now, seeing the city now as a different person, someone without a career, in limbo, a sort of nobody, a pure fun-seeker.

Late one afternoon I walked over to Gaudí's Güell Palace, which was in my neighborhood, just across the Ramblas. The usual crazy Gaudí production. The outside of the building looked something like a big, fat organ, and the inside had an Arabic feel, with an incredible dome filled with holes. I imagined that mosques were like this, though I had never been in a mosque. Another day, continuing my Gaudí tour, I went by cab to the Casa Vicens, way up on the Gràcia. It took me a while to get a cab, since most were reluctant to stop for what appeared to be a filthy tramp. Anyway, the Vicens was interesting, though a little less elaborate than other Gaudí buildings. Arabic-Moorish stuff, with sharp angles and colorful ceramic designs. A building that looked like it belonged more in Morocco or in the desert or in some parched, hot, Arab place.

Since I had traveled so far I thought I might as well travel farther, so I ended up going to the Tibidabo—rode the funicular, saw the dopey plane ride, went to the top of the church. A bit of a disappointment, really, but at least I was able to finally check it off in my book. On still another day I took in Montaner's fantastic Palau de la Música Catalana, which the guidebook had noted as a must. Following the instructions in the book, I called in advance to get on a tour, and then showed up at the place late one afternoon, a culture-hungry American dressed crazily as a Catalan bum. The tour guide regarded me with caution.

The place was amazingly ornate, with stained glass all over, usually floral in design. Thick columns were covered with colored tiles arranged in fancy Arabic-like patterns. The concert hall—the main attraction—was overstuffed and incredible, with stone carvings of trees and composers and horses and an inverted stained-glass dome that served as a kind of chandelier. Even the back of the stage was ridiculously decorated, with a mural of musicians. But not your usual mural. Here the figures were half painted and half sculpted—painted below the waist, sculpted and three-dimensional above. It was as if the designer of the hall hadn't known when to stop, like a baker who keeps adding more and more crap to his cake.

The Palace of Catalan Music. Check.

At night, after a day of sightseeing and studying buildings and just plain wandering, I stayed hidden in my room. At least that's what I did at first. Because the streets that surrounded the hotel weren't safe for me after dark. They went dead at night. Only a soul or two moved along these streets, lit here and there by the ancient lamps that hung from houses. These shadowy people didn't seem to belong at all. I had forgotten about the threat up to a point, but I hadn't grown totally careless and stupid. Walking out into the night in this area was like asking to be killed.

I concentrated again on *Life in the Georgian City*, dipping into the chapter on servicing the house. For some reason, I got hooked on Georgian plumbing. There were good sections on water supply and drainage, and a particularly good and disgusting one on cesspools. I read about the "nightmen" whose crummy job it was to clean out Georgian house cesspools in the middle of the night and then carry buckets of revolting matter back to their carts for disposal. I realized that although Georgian houses were neat and orderly, Georgian people, what with their lousy plumbing and sanitary conditions, lived a bit like pigs. People always seem to ruin things, I thought. Here they were, dirtying my picture of the Georgian house. But my curiosity kept getting the better of me and I continued reading on, wanting to know more about these people and how they lived from day to day. This interest surprised me.

A thunderstorm hit one night and there was a drenching rain. The beat of the drops against the window reminded me of London and my flat and got me to thinking, stupidly, if I might in some way return. What if I let things cool off for a while and then tried to make my way back indirectly by boat? After all, Barcelona was a port city. I might sneak down to the docks, worm my way onto a freighter stopping in Algeciras or Lisbon, then grab a plane back to the U.K. Or I might get bold and simply take a boat stopping off at Southampton. The plan appealed to me. It gave me a little hope. The problem was that once I arrived in London I was as good as dead.

I went over to the mirror, peeled off the Turner postcard, brought it back to my bed, sprawled out, held up the picture to my face, and just stared at it. I eventually reached over for my Walkman resting on the broken-down night table and listened to Spanish guitar music while I continued to stare at the Turner. It was an odd sort of mix, putting me in two different places, two different countries, at the same time. But that was pretty much my state anyway so I was able to accept the confusion. I kept looking at the card. And a kind of longing came over me. A kind of sadness. I wanted to see Mortlake Terrace in person before I died.

CHAPTER 13

I SPOTTED THE FIRST ASSASSIN in the Plaça de Catalunya.

It was around two in the afternoon. I had gone up to Provença to check out Come In, which was supposed to be the largest English-language bookshop in the city, but I had gotten there just as they were closing for the midday break. This siesta business was one Spanish tradition I could do without. It seemed to put a halt to the day. A damn waste of time, as far as I was concerned. And for me at least, time was now too valuable to waste. Anyway, I returned downtown and ended up in the Catalunya, sitting on one of the chairs facing the huge circular plaza.

I was admiring all of the check marks in my two guidebooks when I noticed that a young Spanish-looking guy in a white suit and rose-tinted sunglasses, who had already passed by me twice, was walking by still again. He glanced down at me briefly, just as he had done before, pretending, just as before, that it was a purely idle glance.

What an amateur, I thought. Not only was he a bad actor, but he was ridiculously dressed for a tracking job. I shook my head and smiled. I loved that white suit. He might as well have been wearing neon lights.

My outfit and my beaten, derelict appearance had obviously thrown him and he was trying to determine if I was really the man he was after. Stupidly puzzled, not sure what to do, he finally sat down on one of the chairs just beyond the path that divided one line of chairs from the other. Again he glanced my way while pretending not to be glancing my way. This kid was hopeless.

I kept one eye on my book and the other on him. I half read the section in the city guide devoted to Barcelona history. He suddenly removed his fashionable sunglasses. I thought it might be nice to know a little about this place I was reluctantly living in, how it had come to be, how it had developed, like some baby, from absolutely nothing. He was now, I noticed, reading a small piece of paper he held in his hand. I put on my sunglasses so I could hide my eyes while watching him more directly. He was going through a rather odd routine—he'd look down at the paper, then over at me for a few seconds, then back down at the paper. It finally dawned upon me what this Catalan clown was doing. The piece of paper was probably a photo or sketch of me and he was consulting it while trying to figure out if I was the traitor in question. What a dope. I chuckled to myself.

Fool though he was, I had to take care of him before he could contact them about a possible sighting. I got up and walked from the plaza. I maintained a fairly slow pace, so that even a fool like him would have no problem keeping track of me. I even started limping a bit, like an old bugger, to confuse the kid still more. I must admit that even at this point I was vaguely hoping that I might be wrong about the guy, that he simply looked and acted suspiciously but was actually no one at all. I wanted to believe that I was still safe.

But as I limped on, I could sense him behind me. I could even hear him following. No question about it. This pathetic kid was one of them.

I moved along a street called Fontanella, which sounded like the name of a wop restaurant, and then into the Sant Pere. I made an abrupt and peculiar left on Girona, peculiar because having walked downtown, I was now heading back uptown again. The white suit followed.

Suddenly I found myself in a familiar part of town. I had hobbled onto the good old Ausiàs March, not far from the scene of the crime that had never happened.

This cat-and-mouse routine couldn't go on indefinitely. I had to make a decisive move soon. It wasn't a matter of simply shaking him. It was a matter of getting rid of the bastard for good.

He was keeping his distance. I figured he was about a quarter of a block away. He was probably even less sure now that he was tracking the right man. My limping routine had really gotten him nuts.

I was debating in my head about what to do next as I made a right into Carrer de Casp. Just past the corner a cab stopped and a man got out. A plan popped into my head out of nowhere. I had to act and act fast. Before the white suit turned the corner and could see what I was doing, I grabbed the cab. The driver looked at me, bum that I was, very suspiciously, so I immediately handed over enough money for a few miles. I told him, as best I could—speaking simple English, gesturing like a moron—to circle the block slowly. He finally understood and did what I said but obviously thought me a bit crazy. "Round?" he said in a kind of tortured English.

"Yeah," I said, "go around the block. All around. until we reach Casp again."

We eventually arrived back at the corner where I'd picked up the cab. I told the driver to go extra slow. And, sure enough, there on Casp was the kid in the white suit. As we crept by I watched him while he crazily searched for the old bum who had just vanished into thin air. What a jerk, I thought. He looked ridiculous and I wanted to laugh again. But I noticed that the kid had his right hand inside his jacket. This wasn't so funny. He was prepared to use his gun. He was ready to kill me.

I told the driver to go around the block again. "Round?" he said. "Around," I said. "Again?" "Again." He shook his head but began circling the block. When we reached Casp again, I could see the puzzled kid walking way down the block. It looked like he was about to turn the corner, make a right into Bailén. I instructed the driver to take that same turn very slowly. As we creeped to the corner, I sneakily removed my gun, lowered it to my lap, and attached the silencer. We were now inching along Bailén. The kid was about a quarter of the way down the block. He seemed to be checking out parked cars, but only halfheartedly. He knew that he'd blown it. He had lost his man.

I told the driver to stop, got out quietly, and waited for the cab to drive off. Holding my gun against my side, I hugged the buildings as I neared the kid's white back. I think that in those final few seconds he realized he was in big trouble. His body jerked a bit just before the bullets entered his back. He moaned in pain and hit the ground hard. His white jacket was already turning red. I kept right on moving as if I had nothing to do with this messy, over-dramatic character. As I walked, I removed and pocketed the silencer and returned my gun to my holster. I moved swiftly, but with a sort of casual, carefree air, down the empty block and away from the dead body sprawled out in the middle of the sidewalk.

That night and the next day I stayed close to my hotel. I was a bit shaken about having been spotted. But then again, I thought, it had to happen sooner or later. And, of course, I realized that by taking out one of their men I had given myself away, more or less announced that I was still in town. Unless they interpreted it as a revenge hit from a rival firm—which was unlikely.

But I couldn't keep worrying about them. That was no way to live. And I had a lot more of the city to cover. So I resumed my travels and studies, and even began going out in the evenings and returning through the dead streets at night. I continued to wear the old Catalan clothes, adding a beat-up raincoat to the ensemble, because the weather was getting a bit chilly.

I spotted the second assassin one night in a café off the Gràcia. I was sitting alone at a corner table, sipping a glass of red wine. I was acquiring a taste for the stuff, no doubt about that. I found it a pleasant way to relax in the evening, looked forward, in fact, to the little buzz it gave me. The place I had wandered into by pure chance was decorated with tiles and mirrors. The lower half of the walls was done up in tile, the upper half taken over by mirrors. You couldn't get away from yourself in this joint or, for that matter, from anyone else. Everywhere you turned you were faced with your reflection and theirs. You had to focus on your drink or a book or newspaper to get relief from all the eyes. I must have been feeling particularly carefree and adventurous that night, because this wasn't exactly the sort of place for a hunted man to be curling up in. Either carefree and adventurous or just plain drunk.

I couldn't decide if the man at a nearby table was big and husky or simply a fat slob. I suspected, though, that his plain, dark clothes—the black suit, the maroon turtleneck—were hiding a mass of blubber. I thought of that bodyguard in Lisbon. This man could have been his younger brother. And he looked just as mean and crude. That's what tipped me off, I think. The dumb, nasty look—a Firm look if ever there was one. And the way he was staring at me in the mirror every few minutes. Just to test him, I'd occasionally stare back. He'd immediately turn away.

I could be wrong, I thought. I wanted to be wrong. But I knew that my instincts were right. I just didn't want to go through this whole tense business again. It seemed too soon. Too damn soon. After all, I had disposed of the kid in the white suit only a few days before.

But I had to find out for certain. I tried to be philosophical. Any way you looked at it, the evening had been ruined. Even if he turned out to be just a harmless tub, he had interrupted my pleasant buzz, reminded me of them and my possible death. So I got up, put on my raincoat, and moved toward the door. As I cut around the tables, I glanced at the various mirrors. Sure enough, he had gotten up too. He looked even bigger and fatter now that he was on his feet. Somewhat like a wrestler. Haystacks Henry. Sam the Slob. Decked out in evening attire.

It was Saturday around ten o'clock, a crisp, clear, beautiful night, and the city was alive with people. I considered my situation and his options. He might want to avoid a crowd. But he might just as well want to take advantage of it and take me out on the street. I thought of what I would do if I were tracking me.

I decided to get back inside somewhere. There was a club up ahead, a big, splashy place outlined elaborately in neon. THE GIANT PEACH, the joint's sign read in English. Behind me I could feel pedestrians parting to make way for the turtlenecked tank on my tail.

I cut into the place. Music blasted me in the face. It was so loud it hurt. Disco crap. It sounded American. American disco crap. Old crap. The floor shook with it.

The joint was even larger than expected and neon was everywhere, thin pink and blue tubes lining the long, winding bar and mirror, the rim of the circular dance floor, lining the staircase leading to a balcony crazily resembling the running track of a gym, lining the railing of that balcony. Neon and darkness and music pounding your skull, reaching down into your guts. Who needs this? I thought. But now I had to immediately mingle, like it or not. And the best place to do that, to get lost fast, was on the crowded dance floor—crowded more with thirtyish and fortyish types than with kids. I couldn't dance, had never been tempted to learn. All those steps and gestures made you look like a complete fool. But I could see the Tank standing by the doorway and scanning the room so I had no choice but to plunge deep into the crowd and jerk myself around like a hopeless spastic. The music beating down from giant speakers was "YMCA," one of those golden oldies for faggots. So there I am, a mustached Catalan bum, his raincoat draped over his arm, gyrating to the beat with a bunch of Catalan yuppies in a candy-colored, semi-dark disco. Laser beams shot down from nowhere every few seconds to get you even more worked up. You could feel "YMCA" running all through you, entering your bones, your bloodstream. It was as if the place was trying to give you a music orgasm.

The Tank couldn't spot me. Which maybe wasn't so surprising, since I lost track of him several times even though I had the advantage of knowing the general direction he was in. The jerking bodies kept blocking my view, but still my eyes managed to catch up with him and follow him as he moved past the bar toward the illuminated staircase leading to the illuminated balcony. Obviously he thought he'd have a better chance of spotting me if he was above the crowd. Here again I had to think and act fast. I immediately weaved my way through the spastic couples, left the dance floor, and followed him as he climbed the stairs. He seemed exhausted when he reached the top and stopped to catch his breath. The fat slob was in sad shape. Needless to say, I didn't sympathize.

It was darker on the balcony than it was below and I could easily cling to the walls and vanish in the blackness. I'd expected the balcony to be just an observation ramp but it was more elaborate and spacious than that, with a block of carpeted steps that served as seats, something like bleachers for relaxing and drinking and enjoying a bird's-eye view of the dance floor. At first the Tank stayed by the railing, trying to find me in the scene below. He circled the track, pausing every so often to look down at a slightly different segment of the dance floor and bar. Repeatedly finding nobody, he took a seat high up in the bleachers, three steps from the top. I moved along the back wall until I was in line with him. Even from the back, in the near dark he looked huge, like a Buddha.

Only a few people were up here. Below him, to the right, was a couple having a heated discussion or just an out-and-out argument. And below him to the left, in a somewhat darker spot, was a couple pawing each other intensely. I already had my gun drawn, with silencer attached, and was hiding it under my draped coat. Another American song came on and began pounding the whole place senseless—some woman proudly yelling "I will survive." That's appropriate, I thought. The Tank started shaking his big fat head from side to side and snapping his fingers. He was really into the tune and he couldn't keep still. He seemed to have forgotten the main reason he was in the joint. Christ, I thought, this guy is worse than me.

I sat down on the top step, just one full step away from him, and slowly aimed my coat down at that stupidly active head. What else could I do? These damn people just wouldn't let me be. I fired once, hitting him directly in the brain, casually got up, and made my way to the aisle and the staircase. I watched him out of the corner of my eye. He slumped forward and then rolled down the steps, looking now like a boulder that had come loose. As I descended the neon-lit stairs, I wondered if the metal railing would be strong enough to break his roll or if he would crash through it, plunge to the dance floor, and crush a few dancers. Cries sounded from the balcony, only they were a little hard to hear because of the blaring music. The Tank's body hit the railing and remained there. I think I heard more Catalan cries as I casually exited the bar. Two down, I said to myself.

Maybe this is the end of it, I thought as I walked back to my hotel, the last of them. Because I figured that these sightings had been purely random. If they hadn't been, the Firm would have already cornered me at the fleabag. No, the Firm had simply put a lot of their people on the alert. The two dead men—the kid and the Tank—had probably come upon me by chance and then had followed through. Maybe they even thought they could score some points with their bosses if they took care of me alone. But they hadn't counted on the quality of the man they were up against. No one fools with me, I thought proudly. Or madly. Because here I was, challenging the Firm, declaring war on them. I was stupidly, fatally carried away with myself.

The bastards gave me no rest. Two days later, I returned to Come In, the bookshop on Provença. This time I made sure that I arrived before it closed for siesta. I bought two paperback books—one on Catalan art, the other on Montaner—was happy, and decided to stroll the streets for a while. I realized that in buying the books I was being optimistic. I was assuming I'd remain alive long enough to read them.

I headed downtown. As I was strolling like a carefree moron, I noticed that a small white car was vaguely keeping pace with me in the street. I thought nothing of it at first, but then I noticed that when I turned the corner it did so as well. Again, I had to know for certain. So when I reached the next corner, I stopped, as if I were unsure of the route I had taken and had to orient myself. Out of the corner of my eye I could see the car. Damnit, I said. Here we go again. And to make matters worse, it looked like there were two men in the car. Again like the other spotters, they probably weren't completely sure if I was their man, or else they would have already shot me to bits.

Since the turning-the-corner routine had worked so nicely for me before, I thought I'd use it again. I was coming up on another corner. The car was still following, though it was beginning to lag just a little behind now. I kept it in view, with those eyes I had in the back of my head. As I moved on I decided to put the two paperbacks I was carrying into the pockets of my raincoat. For what I was planning, I had to have both hands free. The Montaner fitted easily into my left side pocket. But I had trouble getting the somewhat chunky, extra-wide Catalan art book into my right. I tried bending the damn thing a little and forcing it into the pocket, but since this bum coat had seen better days, the pocket began to split. Christ, I said, like I don't have enough problems. Finally I located an inside pocket, which up until this point I never knew existed. The book fit perfectly, though it pressed annoyingly against my heart.

The sun was shining with incredible strength. These particular streets were lined with modern white buildings and they were all glowing now. The damn white car was glowing as well, and its windows were gleaming with miniature suns.

I suddenly noticed a change in the side window. It had just gone black. Which meant that they had opened the window so they could take a shot.

I had no choice now. I broke out into a run, rounded the corner in a flash, headed for a parked car, squatted down in front of it, removed my gun, quickly attached the silencer, and using the front fender for support aimed at the tires of the white car as it rolled in my direction. I shot out both front tires, the car slammed into a parked car on the other side of the street, I ran up behind the open window and fired into it repeatedly, aiming at what appeared to be heads. All of this, everything, seemed to happen in a few seconds. I was expecting to be hit somewhere, was prepared for the pain. But nothing touched me. There was no movement inside the car. I peeked in. Two bloody men were slumped over the front seat. I had managed to take out both of them.

There were, I now realized, a couple of people on the street. But since the shooting had happened so fast, they weren't sure what in hell was going on. As they recovered from the shock and started to cautiously approach the dead car, I walked back up the street, turned the corner, and hailed a cab. I told him to drive over to the Gràcia and then head downtown. I tried thinking positive thoughts. Maybe everyone would see this as a terrorist attack of some sort. Maybe the Firm wouldn't link it to me at all. But I knew that I'd been mad to start all of this.

Back in my room, I closed the shutters and rested on my bed. I imagined the Firm sending out dozens upon dozens of hunters into the streets of Barcelona to track down this madman and destroy him before he could do any more damage. I could see them coming from all directions, waves of them. The Slob Brigades.

I tried to understand what had possessed me to counterattack rather than simply and wisely sneak quietly away. But there was no understanding it. I was totally out of control. I had gone completely mental.

Late that night I asked the old man at the desk—his name, I finally learned, was Josep—if I could use his phone in the back room. I explained that I had to call New York and I gave him roughly twenty bucks to pay for the international call. He understood the money immediately.

It was roughly six-thirty in New York. I don't know what I intended to accomplish, but I hoped that Jennifer was at home and available. As I said, I was completely mental at this point.

The phone rang several times. Jennifer answered. She sounded very surprised. Pleasantly so. Said that she had given up any hope of hearing from me. I thought this a nice touch. I was immediately charmed again.

"I'm sorry I couldn't get back to you," I said. "My father took ill and I had to return home."

"You're calling from home?" She was very impressed.

"Yes. From Derbyshire."

"From Derbyshire, no less. Well, how nice of you. How sweet. I'm very flattered. But I hope your father isn't too seriously ill."

"I'm afraid he is. Heart disease. It could go either way. He might come out of it. He might not. But I'm prepared for the worst. To tell you the truth, I'm not sure that he wants to go on. I think he feels he's had enough."

"How old is he?"

"Close to seventy."

"But that's not terribly old these days."

"I think he feels very old, though. That's the thing. He hasn't been a very happy man."

"Oh?"

"Yes, he keeps saying how his life didn't turn out as expected. That he didn't turn out as expected."

"What did he expect?"

"God only knows. But whatever it was, it wasn't what he got."

"What does he do—did? I mean, his profession?"

"*Did*. He's been retired for years." I had to think quickly. But I was good at that, good at making up stories. "He was a businessman. An executive of sorts. Ran the family business in London. Got totally fed up with it. Finally sold the company and made quite a fortune."

"What was the business?"

"Pest control."

"You mean, like exterminators?"

"Yes. That's pretty much it."

"How weird. I mean, I don't think of that as a business for an English gentleman, a man who owns a country house."

"Well he couldn't just laze around Derbyshire all his life. And there are a lot of bugs in England. Somebody has to deal with them. And, quite frankly, it's a very profitable business."

"I'm sorry. It's just that I find it a little incongruous. A kind of aristocrat living in a Georgian house, or whatever, and heading an extermination company. It seems strange. Even on an executive level, an ownership level. Come on, Peter, you have to admit it's strange."

"Well, as I said, it's just something he got into. His father pushed him into it. He didn't have much choice. He intended to work at the business for a few years, make the old man happy, earn some good money, and then pull out. But somehow he got sucked in too deep. People came to rely on him. After a while, he was stuck. They got used to him. He got used to the job."

"What would he have done otherwise? Did he have some other profession in mind?"

"Who knows? He had an artistic side to him. Liked looking at paintings and all that. Even drew a bit. I remember a drawing he once did of an ant. It was first-rate."

"An ant? How strange."

"Yes. The old man might have been an artist if he'd put his mind to it. Who can say?"

She changed the subject by asking how I was. I told her

that my health could be somewhat better. "You know," I said, "I have the oddest feeling that something is wrong with me, seriously wrong."

"You're probably under a lot of stress because of your father. I'm sure that's all it is."

"I don't know. Maybe you're right. But I keep having this feeling. I keep wondering if I'm going to survive the year."

"That's ridiculous, Peter. You're young. And you look like you're in great shape. I'm sure it's just stress."

"Maybe you're right. But I have the oddest feeling that I don't have long to go, that my days are numbered."

"Trust me. Stress can do weird things. I can hear the tension in your voice. In fact, you don't sound like yourself."

"How so?"

"You seem to have lost some of your accent. You sound more American than British. It's weird."

"Maybe it's the connection." Jesus, I thought, I was out of practice. I hadn't done Peter Chilton in quite a while. "Or maybe," I tried to joke, "I was in New York far too long. It must have rubbed off on me." I quickly changed the subject to her, asked her how Beddoes was doing.

"Still dead. Still crazy. It's coming along." She laughed a bit. "What can I tell you? It's something to do."

We chatted some more. It was, when I think about it now, a pretty odd conversation. Then again, the whole thing between us was pretty odd, since most of it was based on lies. I wondered how she would have reacted had I been truthful. Who was I kidding? She would have been revolted.

I told her that someone in the house was calling and I had to go. "Well," I said, "I just wanted to say that it's been nice knowing you."

"Please, Peter, that sounds so final."

"You never know."

She predicted that my depression would pass, and then she asked for the Derbyshire number, said she would call to see how both my father and I were doing.

"Be right there!" I interrupted her, shouting to no one in Josep's dumpy back room. Some Georgian mansion, I thought. "Sorry, have to go," I said to her, "bye," and abruptly hung up. And that was that. That was Jennifer. Jennifer Sweeney.

I lay low for a few days but then started to travel the city still again. I was convinced that they didn't really know where I was. At least I'd feel that way for a while. Because then suddenly, for no special reason, I'd feel threatened again, sense them closing in, see an assassin in any stranger who looked vaguely suspicious. I realized that I had to get a grip on myself. This business with strangers could get out of hand. After all, for me Barcelona was a city of strangers.

The more I visited nice areas and shops and cafés, the less I liked being regarded as a bum. Yes, I began to grow self-conscious of my bum appearance, began to hate my bum clothes. I didn't appreciate the looks I got, the discourteous treatment, the you-don't-belong-here attitude. I wondered if the suspicious strangers I kept coming across were simply people who were somewhat disgusted by a bum and looked at him with contempt, distrust. I wasn't a target to them at all—I was just a bum.

I decided that I wasn't going to take it anymore. I still had several thousand dollars in traveler's checks—I had come prepared for this job, almost as if I'd expected trouble. Here I was, retired and loaded. Why live like a pauper? Because of them? To hide from them? To hell with them! I hadn't worked so hard and well to end up this way, to end up a bum. I remembered how people had regarded me as a kid. They'd looked at me oddly then. And they were looking at me with disrespect now. No, I wasn't going to stand for this. I was a world traveler. I had seen the best cities, stayed in some of the best hotels. I was a professional. Prematurely retired, but a professional just the same. I'd been, in fact, one of the great professionals in my field. Had they given trophies for my kind of work, I would have received enough to fill a bloody room.

It was Saturday, the end of a week. I had survived. I wanted to begin the next week completely fresh. And I mean completely. So I went down the list in my guidebook of the best hotels in Barcelona. A place on the Gràcia sounded just the thing. Relatively new, luxurious, with a host of rooms with terraces. The tourist season was over so I knew I'd have no problem in getting a room.

I gave myself a clean shave—my first since becoming the Catalan bum. And I shaved off the Spanish-looking mustache. I scrubbed my face well, combed my hair down neatly. And then I stood there in front of the cracked mirror admiring myself. Yes, I was beginning to look like the old me.

I put on my two-hundred-and-fifteen-dollar sports shirt, exchanged my wrinkled black pants for my wrinkle-free gray ones, and slipped on my blazer. Now that's more like it, I said to myself in the mirror. Now you look like somebody.

I packed the rest of my things and my collection of books. I gave the bum jacket, bum raincoat, and beret to Josep, who seemed to appreciate them. I paid my modest fleabag bill and threw in some more money for Josep—a kind of additional thanks for having kept his mouth shut. The old man had done more than all right by me, and he knew it. He smiled and shook my hand.

"And remember," I said in parting, "I was never here."

As I left the dump—good-bye and good riddance—I wondered what the old bugger had made of me. I'd checked in as a well-to-do man, then had suddenly turned into a bearded bum, then a mustached bum, and then, just as suddenly, had turned distinguished again.

I walked through the old streets feeling almost cheerful, like I was about to start still another life.

CHAPTER 14

There have been no signs of them at all. No more chance encounters in the streets. No more cars or white suits or fat bodyguards. No one. No activity. So I've been enjoying myself. The peace. The leisure. The return to a standard of living that suits me. A posh hotel. A room with a view. And it has been good strolling weather in Barcelona. There's been a definite nip in the air. I had to go over to El Corte Inglés to pick up an all-weather coat. It's dark green and I look quite nice in it. Maybe green is my color. And it's a solid, serviceable coat to travel around in and visit buildings and other sights. Has pockets that are wide and deep enough for guidebooks as well as most reasonably sized books.

I've been traveling around quite a bit, yes, quite a bit, and I have, as I said, been enjoying myself. Yet over the past few days I've sensed someone on my tail. Which is odd since I haven't really seen him. When I feel him nearby, I turn quickly in his direction. But he's never there. How he can disappear so quickly is beyond me. Unless, of course, he was never there to begin with. But I have a sixth sense about these things, and I know someone is out there. Late one afternoon I was visiting an art gallery on Petrixol in the old quarter. It's called Sala Parés and is supposed to be the oldest gallery in the city. I was looking at the paintings of a man long gone named Rusiñol. He was a friend, I learned, of good old Albéniz. And his work wasn't half bad at all. Anyway, there I was, roaming about the gallery, when I turned slightly and saw a shadowy figure—him or what could have been him—standing outside by the window. I turned more, looked harder, but he was gone. I went out in the street to check—hand on gun, of course—but he was nowhere to be seen. Whoever he is, he's a real pro. And he's apparently biding his time. I don't know why. Unless he's afraid to make a move, afraid he might meet his match. Who knows?

Every now and then I do think of leaving the city, making a run for it. I think again of my boat plan and heading for the docks. But these thoughts pass. I still haven't seen the city to my complete satisfaction. I'm relatively free and relatively happy and at real peace for the first time in my bloody life. When I choose to feel threatened, I can easily summon up the feeling. When I sense my shadow, I can take him seriously or dismiss him. What I'm saying, I suppose, is that I can pretty much do or feel what I like.

I still think of the Georgian house. And of all the houses yet to see in London. And I think of how I might have been a scholar of some sort, a man of learning. Or of how I might have been an artist of some sort. I've been trying my hand at drawing. I do a damn good ant. I've been practicing on paper napkins in cafés. The other day I even bought a sketchbook. Yes, I might very well have been an artist. The trouble is, though, you can only be one person at a time. And for some reason the person you settled on first a long time ago is damn hard to get rid of. He stays with you. He won't leave. It's not only your fault. Other people helped you settle on him. Then they got used to him and couldn't, wouldn't, accept anyone else.

But I try not to think much of the past anymore. And I don't think much about the future. In my situation, it's best to think only of the present, the here and now, today. Thinking that way you sort of become no one, as if you're waiting to be born or are already dead. It's a weird feeling, but not half bad.

Yesterday I felt his presence very strongly. I ignored it as best I could. In the morning I went back up to the English bookshop. I bought a book on Barcelona history and another one called *The Catalans*. I also bought little Catalan and Spanish phrase books, figuring it was about time I fitted in a little better.

In the afternoon I strolled along the Ramblas. It was a crystal-clear and cool Saturday and the avenue was packed with people. I sensed him as I walked along. Go to hell, I said to him in my mind. How dare you ruin my day? Just then, just in the midst of my anger, I spotted a flower stall. I gently nudged my way through the mob over to the mass of flowers on display.

I selected a white carnation, paid the vendor, and asked him for a pin. I pinned the carnation proudly, spitefully, to my lapel and smiled.

I am thirty-three years old. My next birthday is in the spring, on April 3. My father's name was Carl. My mother's name was Ruth.

My name is John Cole.

ACKNOWLEDGMENT

A huge thanks to Noah Lukeman for his unwavering commitment to this novel and for his support for all my work throughout the years.